Sue Walker is a television journalist. She started out in her native Edinburgh, eventually moving to London to work in BBC TV's News and Current Affairs Department. For the past fifteen years, Sue has concentrated on documentaries specializing in crime investigative work and miscarriages of justice, mainly for Channel 4. Sue now lives on the Sussex Coast.

The Dead Pool is her third novel, following The Reunion and The Reckoning

visit the author's website at:
www.sue-walker.com

THE DEAD POOL

Kirstin Rutherford's return to Edinburgh after two years away is tinged with sadness: five months ago, her father-in-law Jamie drowned in a deep pool in the Water of Leith, known locally as The Cauldron. And no one is sure whether it was a tragic accident or something more sinister . . . One person who may know is the enigmatic Morag Ramsay, for her boyfriend and his secret lover were murdered at The Cauldron just months before Jamie's drowning. Kirstin befriends her, convinced that she holds the key to Jamie's death, but her brittle and unpredictable manner makes her less than a reliable witness. Kirstin begins to suspect everyone's motives, including those who died. Who can she trust? And, more importantly, who should she fear . . .?

SUE WALKER

THE DEAD POOL

Complete and Unabridged

CHARNWOOD
Leicester

First published in Great Britain in 2007 by
Michael Joseph
Penguin Books Limited, London

First Charnwood Edition
published 2008
by arrangement with
Penguin Books Limited
a division of
the Penguin Group UK, London

The moral right of the author has been asserted

This is a work of fiction, and all the characters and events described are entirely the product of the author's imagination. Any resemblance to persons living or dead is coincidental.

British Library CIP Data

Walker, Sue, 1960 –
The dead pool.—Large print ed.—
Charnwood library series
1. Drowning—Scotland—Edinburgh—Fiction
2. Detective and mystery stories
3. Large type books
I. Title
823.9'2 [F]

ISBN 978–1–84782–237–6

Published by
F. A. Thorpe (Publishing)
Anstey, Leicestershire
Set by Words & Graphics Ltd.
Anstey, Leicestershire
Printed and bound in Great Britain by
T. J. International Ltd., Padstow, Cornwall

This book is printed on acid-free paper

For Tom and Finn

Acknowledgements

As ever, I owe enormous thanks to my editor, Beverley Cousins, and to my agent, Teresa Chris. Their hard work and support have been invaluable.

1

She had crossed the bridge now. She was in the wood. It was so quiet. Except for the weir, giving out its soft, summer shushing noise. Trickling down from the Cauldron, on its way to the sea.

'Find us if you can!'

The shout sounded miles away. Too echoey to make out. How long did she count for? A whole hundred?

And again. A different noise.

'Hey! You're not scaring me, you know. I'm going to catch you in about ten seconds flat. Ten . . . nine . . . eight . . . seven . . .'

A cough like a retching this time. Someone had been drinking even more than her.

'Six . . . five . . . four . . . three . . .'

What was that?

'Two . . . one . . . got y — '

The vivid colour broke through her dazed senses first. No! They had stolen her sarong to lie on, the vermilion floral pattern screaming out through the dark foliage. They must have heard her, but they hadn't bothered to cover their nakedness.

'You bastards!'

Not a movement. But that noise again. And more vermilion. From his mouth this time. Dripping on to her face . . .

'Get up! Wake up! Now!'

'Morag Ramsay! Get up! Wake up! Now!'

'Why is th — '

The lock was being turned. The cell door banged open.

'Get dressed, Ramsay. They're letting you out.'

She hated making the journey along the walkways and stairs, even though this time she was on her way out.

She waited for the chorus to start. Sure enough.

'*Witch! Witch! Witch! Bitch Witch! Bitch Witch! Witch! Witch! Witch! Cauldron Killer! Cauldron Killer!*'

The rhythmic chant from the all-female chorus — oddly melodic thanks to one or two fine voices in the throng — made the nausea wrench at her gut as she passed into the public area, the part of the prison they had tried, and failed, to make look normal. At least it was soundproofed from the hell that lay within. But still, in her head, she heard it. Knew she would always hear it. In sleep, on waking, in night terrors. In nightmares. *The* nightmare.

'*Witch! Bitch Witch! Cauldron Killer!*'

The Return

1

Four months later

How Well Do You Know Edinburgh's River?

Why Not Enjoy a Guided Walk Along the Water of Leith?

Whether you were born and bred here, or you are a tourist from another part of the world, all should sample the delights of the Water of Leith, the river that winds through Edinburgh. From its source in the Pentland Hills, the river meanders through some of the most beautiful parts of the city, ending its 35km journey down at the port of Leith, where its waters pour into the Firth of Forth.

And you can share that journey with one of the great authorities on the Water of Leith, Jamie Munro. A former lawyer and well-known face in the Scottish courts, Jamie has owned a riverside house for more than thirty years. He has spent his retirement getting to know our river intimately, and Jamie now heads up our team of volunteers who patrol the Water of Leith and offer guided walks.

Kirstin Rutherford folded the bright green A5 flyer, put it back in her pocket, and knelt down

5

to tend the rose bush she'd planted a few minutes earlier.

'Christ, Jamie. What the hell happened to you?'

She lost her balance as the tears started, and had to grasp on to the edge of the headstone, its shiny grey marbled surface reflecting the sun's piercing rays into her eyes.

JAMES ROSS MUNRO
Born 24 March 1936
Died 11 February 2007
Devoted husband to JEAN
Loving father to Ross
'I AM HAPPY NOW WITH MY JEANNIE'

Kirstin eased herself back up on to her feet, offering a last caress to the smooth headstone as she turned to its neighbour.

JEAN MARGARET MUNRO NÉE KEIR
Born 20 December 1941
Died 2 March 2004
Beloved wife to JAMIE
Devoted mother to Ross
'TAKEN TOO SOON BUT WITH US ALWAYS'

She nodded, a sob catching in her throat.

'Kirstin?'

She scrabbled in her bag to find sunglasses before turning round. She was damned if she'd let him see her crying.

'Kirstin? I thought we were meeting at the cemetery gates? I've been waiting back there for ages.'

6

At last she turned to face him, already bristling at his familiar peevish tone. Her outward composure was back, but she was keeping the sunglasses on for protection. From Ross, and from the searing day. She almost burst out laughing. Ross was doing exactly the same.

His sunglasses were locked firmly in place. He looked overheated, even in shirtsleeves, his suit jacket slung too casually over his shoulder. She could sense he was nervous, as well he should be. She felt his scrutiny and ignored it. Yes, she looked in better shape than he did.

He cleared his throat. 'Well?'

A one-word demand that hauled her back through years of happiness, semi-happiness and, finally, misery. Well, she wasn't married to him any more. Didn't have to explain herself to him. Quite the reverse. She turned away again and made some unnecessary rearrangements to the newly planted rose bush, her trowel pinging out sharp notes as it hit the stony ground.

'Why didn't you tell me earlier, Ross? Your father would have wanted me to see him buried, you know that.' She continued her over-vigorous pummelling of the earth. She'd kill the damn bush if she didn't watch out.

His feet shifted behind her and the nervous clearing of the throat was back. 'Oh, God! Not this again. We've been through it all on the phone. I had trouble tracking down your address. I told you. All I knew was that you'd been abroad and were, or *might* be, living in Devon now. You've changed your mobile, so what could I have done?'

7

She dropped the trowel and stood up, tugging off her sunglasses. 'Donald Ferguson has always kept in touch with me. At least a card at Christmas. You knew that.' She paused, willing herself to cleanse the mixture of grief and anger from her voice. She *had* to keep control, hold vulnerability at bay, or he'd have the better of her. 'You know, I wasn't going to do this on the phone. But I will now. Donald told me that you expressly asked him *not* to get in touch with me about your father's death. That you'd make arrangements for me to come to the funeral. Lying to your father's best friend! Unbelievable!'

She halted again, the fury and grief making her legs shake. 'I can't believe I'm here, tending Jamie's grave, five months too late, and . . . and not even the chance to say goodbye. That was a nasty thing to do to me, Ross. The lowest of the low, no matter *what* you've got against me. I simply *cannot* believe it. That he's dead. That you didn't tell me.'

A silent sob caught in her throat. She bent down to pick up her trowel and bag, praying that he hadn't noticed the tears starting again.

'That's not fair, Kirstin. It wasn't like that. I've had a lot to cope with, what wi — '

In one swift movement she stood up again, turned round and brushed past him, ignoring his outstretched hand.

'Where are you going? I thought we could have lunch or something. I want to explain.'

She stopped halfway down the dusty path, her tone still icy. 'I don't think so. Tell me, Ross.' She knew she sounded demanding, needling even, but didn't care. She wanted some answers. 'How did your father die? Donald said it happened down at the Cauldron, of all places.'

Ross nodded. 'That's right. Though why the hell he was down there when the river was in full spate, God only knows. We'd had a right downpour. He shouldn't have been anywhere near the place in those conditions. His body was found nearby. At the weir. Drowned.'

Kirstin shook her head. The anger was still simmering, but she wouldn't give in to it. Not yet. *Keep control. Don't let him win.* She took a deep breath, struggling to keep her voice low and even. 'But why would he be down there in such bad weather? Your father knew the river better than anyone.'

Ross stepped towards her, frowning. 'No one knows. But the inquiry looked at two possibilities. Either it was a pure accident, the result of poor judgement. Or . . . what happened was, as they put it, *intentional*.'

Kirstin stared back at him in disbelief. He looked away from her. 'The fact is, life had been hard for Dad once Mum had gone.'

'Suicide? *Rubbish!* Jamie cared about life. Even after your mother went. And I don't recall him ever suffering from poor judgement. It's no answer, Ross. When I last saw Jamie, he was a vibrant and energetic old man. Now we're being asked to believe that he was either incapable of making important decisions or was a suicidal old codger. You're not trying to tell me that he underwent a complete personality change in less than eighteen months?'

9

She stared at Ross, waiting for an answer. He shuffled his feet on the gravel, clearly uncomfortable. As a peace offering, he removed his own sunglasses.

His eyes looked tired. 'Actually, that's pretty much what *did* happen. It's complicated. It wasn't just Mum's death or Dad having had trouble adjusting to retirement. His river work got out of hand. It took over his life. There was a falling-out with some people. Then something happened that chan — ' He stopped abruptly to let out a long, dramatic sigh. 'But here isn't the place for all this. It's too complicated. Dad *was* different and I just didn't notice in time. I . . . I don't know . . . I hadn't been seeing much of him. I'd had a lot on this past year. Appearing in court practically every day and . . . ' He gave up. The excuses clearly weren't working on her.

'You mean you'd not been paying him enough attention. Situation normal.' Kirstin frowned her disapproval at him. 'Well, I'm going to give your father some attention now.' She'd just about reached the end of her tolerance. Once more, Ross had succeeded in pressing all the right buttons to irritate her. She should never have agreed to meet him here. 'You know, I don't believe that your father could have changed that much. And if he did, I want to know why. What the hell is wrong with you, Ross? Didn't you ask any questions about his death? I'd like to think he had an accident, since it would be infinitely preferable to thinking he was so distressed that he threw himself into the Water of Leith. And, if I'm wrong and your father *did* take his own life,

10

then I, at least, would like to know *why*.'

She paused to shake her head again at Ross, who was clearly dumbstruck by the ferocity of her outburst. But she wasn't finished with him yet. 'I don't care if it sounds clichéd, but Jamie was like a father to me. The one I never really had. He mentored me in work, introduced me to you, cared for, *loved* me like his own. I can think of nothing more important to his memory than to find out *exactly* what happened to him. So you'd better get used to me being around again.'

At last Ross found his tongue. 'What do you mean?'

She turned on her heel and threw her answer back on the hot breeze.

'I *mean*, some cold, bureaucratic inquiry might not care much about what happened to one old man no one knew the first thing about. And it seems *you're* not that curious either. Well, I am. And I'm not leaving Edinburgh until I find out how and why your father died.'

2

They'd been settled for a few minutes and still Kirstin couldn't get comfortable. The nineteenth hole of Donald Ferguson's golf club seemed designed to prevent any form of relaxation, with clubhouse chairs forcing the sitter bolt upright. Maybe that was why Donald looked so fit, posture erect, movement sprightly. Or maybe it was the result of his formative years having been spent in the army, along with Jamie. Eventually both men had wanted to do other things with their lives, and they had left the service but remained firm friends. In his mid-seventies, Donald was a bit older than Jamie would have been, but absolutely on the ball, mentally as well as physically. He was offering her his customary open smile as he poured them each a cup of tea.

'You look so well, Kirstin dear. You back to stay up here for good, then?'

'No. Just here for a while. At my old flat in town.' Kirstin paused, deciding against repeating her dramatic promise to Ross that she would stay until she'd discovered what happened to Jamie. She glanced out of the window that overlooked the first tee. It wasn't quite that golden hour before sunset but at least the day had lost most of its blistering heat. She felt relieved to be here. The first telephone conversation with Donald after Jamie's death had been awkward. He had clearly assumed that she deliberately stayed away

12

from Jamie's funeral, and she'd had to work hard to convince him that Ross had told her nothing about the arrangements. She looked across at Donald, nodding her thanks for the tea. Finally, she leant forward.

'Look, Donald. I don't have to tell you how fond I was of Jamie and . . . how much it hurt to not see him any more. Ross was . . . well, he wanted me to cut all family ties. It just became too awkward.'

He smiled weakly at her. 'I know, and Jamie understood. But you kept in touch with me. I enjoyed your few lines on a postcard from time to time. And maybe that was almost as good as being in touch with Jamie, eh? We would talk about you a lot, you know.'

She returned his smile. 'That's a comfort of sorts. But . . . I don't know . . . if only we could change the past. If I hadn't let Ross bully me . . . ' She shook her head, momentarily lost for words.

'You can't change the past, Kirstin. But I want to say this. It's been an unsavoury business. Ross's behaviour, I mean. Even if there had been bad blood between you, that was no excuse. Jamie cared deeply about you. Ross knew that. He's been unfair to you. And to his father. *And* he's misled me. I shall be having words with Ross about this.'

She nodded her agreement. 'Fair enough. You'll not be surprised to hear that I've already done so. But let's not dwell on Ross's shortcomings just now. I want to know what happened. At the Cauldron, for goodness' sake!

13

It's such a beautiful, peaceful place.'

'Yes, it is that, my dear. Lovely.' Unhurried, Donald took a sip of his tea and pushed the cup to one side, a bony forefinger tracing a pattern on the wooden tabletop. 'Right, well let's start from the beginning. You'll remember that after Jean died he knew he needed something to pull him through. And he found it in the river work. He gave it his all. Made a big impression. His boss, a young chap called Glen Laidlaw, really took to him. You should go and see Glen, you know. Within two years he'd made Jamie head volunteer. But you'd gone by then, hadn't you?'

She felt the familiar sensation of guilt that had been growing daily since she'd first heard about Jamie's death. 'Yes, I missed all that excitement. He must have been so proud.'

'He was. Jamie went at the job with gusto. Took no prisoners. Had it in for those who sullied his river. He hated polluters, people leaving rubbish or folk disturbing the wildlife. Did you know, even when he was close to retirement, that the last two years or so before he left the firm, and for a while afterwards, he was becoming interested in environmental law? He did some pro bono work for a couple of small wildlife charities that were trying to stop a building development on the east coast.'

'No, I had no idea. I knew he did a couple of evenings a month at an advice centre, handling debt queries, helping small businesses from going under.' Kirstin smiled to herself. 'Jamie was always very generous with his expertise. But I didn't know about the environmental work.'

Donald gave a single satisfied nod. 'No, he liked to keep that sort of thing to himself. His firm wouldn't have looked kindly on that, since many of their clients were construction firms and property developers. He'd have made quite a few enemies if what he was doing had got out. I know for a fact he didn't tell Ross. He felt Ross would never have approved of something like that. And anyway, it would have put Ross in an impossible position at work. By the way, did you know Ross has been made a partner at his dad's old firm?' Again, Donald gave a single confirmatory nod. 'Yes, Jamie gave quiet, informal help to those who needed it against the big and powerful. I think he had become increasingly depressed about his main legal work at the firm and his other interests. You know what a decent man he was. He said that if he'd had his career again, he would have spent it working for the underdog.'

The comment drew Kirstin back in time and she had to stop herself from giving in to the tears that threatened to overwhelm her. 'Yes, a few years ago, when I was thinking of trying to qualify beyond a paralegal to become a proper solicitor, he urged me to follow my passions, my conscience. He said that, in his day, he just fell into property and commercial law. It provided well for him and his family but I'm not sure it brought him much professional happiness.'

Donald returned her smile. 'That's right. So, his keenness to be involved with the river association was no surprise to me. He really threw himself into the new job. I saw him go

15

berserk when he caught some youngsters firing an air gun at the mallards and their brood last year. Also, when things get a bit dry, there's always a risk of fire. Especially in a hot summer like last year. Setting fires is strictly forbidden and that's what first got Jamie tangled up with one particular group of river users. 'That shower', as he liked to call them. I think what really got his goat was that they weren't children, or even teenagers.'

Kirstin raised an eyebrow. 'Who were this lot?'

Donald leant back. 'They were all a fair age, in their thirties, had good jobs, well off by all accounts, and had homes in the area.' He began counting off his fingers one by one. 'First of all, there was . . . Alistair, 'Ally' as he was called, and then Iona Sutherland. She and this Ally were brother and sister. He's a financier, or some such, and she was some sort of artist and gallery owner. Then Fraser Coulter. He was a bit of a ruffian and a vulgarian, Jamie said. A builder-cum-property developer. Lots of money. Was in business with the Sutherland lad. Then there was Bonnie Campbell, a New Agey type. Did massage and meditation, that sort of thing. She runs a homeopathy clinic. I think Sutherland was also financing that. And then there was Craig Irvine and his girlfriend, Morag. Irvine was a scientist. Clever, doing well in the world of pharmaceuticals, and Morag worked for a big headhunting firm. So they were far from being a bunch of useless nobodies.'

'But why did Jamie get himself involved with these people?'

'For the simple reason that he couldn't ignore them or their behaviour. I said to Jamie at the time, it was as if they were all going through their second flush of youth. Behaving in unruly ways. Wine bottles all over the place, camp fires into the evening, abusive language and . . . well, lots more besides. Like I said, I think they were trying to grab the last of their youthful freedom before settling down. It's not an unknown phenomenon.' Donald shrugged. 'Anyway, Jamie was appalled. Said if Ross had behaved like that, and he was near enough the same age as this lot, then he'd disown his son. Though Ross, as y — '

She didn't want to get back on to the subject of Ross, and cut across the old man's thoughts. 'But couldn't Jamie have just got the police to have a word, if these people's behaviour was that bad?'

The old man slid the teapot away from him. 'Well, that was just it. Apart from setting fires, and the police would want actual proof of that, it was suggested that Jamie relax about the other things. The police were, shall we say, not going to get too exercised over the antics of a few overgrown adolescents. Jamie took the whole matter to the committee that oversees the care of the river, its conservation, the volunteers, all that. The offenders were sent letters on several occasions, but they just went on doing what they pleased. I told him they'd grow out of it, but Jamie had the bit between his teeth. He was livid and got worse the more they ignored his admonishments. I think baiting Jamie became a sort of game for some of them.' Donald gave a

17

pitying shake of his head. 'And, to be frank, it became a bit of an obsession with him.'

Kirstin frowned. 'In what way, an obsession?'

'Oh . . . you know, doing regular patrols day and night. Just to keep an eye on things. But, in reality, it was far beyond the call of duty. He kept a sort of record, or 'surveillance logs' as he liked to call them, of the entire goings on, all of it charted in various notebooks that he'd type up on his computer. And, as if that wasn't enough, he would fire off emails for posting on the river association's website. Quite the . . . what do they call them? . . . yes, quite the 'silver surfer', our Jamie. Incredible really. He was an old dog who certainly could learn new tricks. And that's what kept him going. He thought of little else until . . . until the Cauldron killings.'

'Cauldron killings?'

'You mean, you don't know? Didn't Ross tell you?'

She shook her head. 'I only saw him for a short while today. What on earth are the Cauldron killings?'

Donald sighed. 'Well, brace yourself. I wouldn't have dreamt of telling you about this in our occasional postcards. I assumed Ross would have filled you in as soon as he saw you. But never mind.' He paused to take a long breath, obviously readying himself for an unpleasant task. 'I don't think anyone will ever know exactly what went on, but one day last summer — Sunday the thirteenth of August, to be precise — they were down at the Cauldron and weir area having an all-day party. Jamie had got wind of it and was all fired up. Morag Ramsay had told him about it. She'd asked him to turn a blind eye, just for once. Mainly because, after that, the friends were all going their separate ways for the rest of the summer. Jamie had no intention of letting them get away with it, but he was thwarted. When it came to it, he couldn't get down there on patrol that day. His hip was playing up. Nor could he get any other volunteer, or his boss, Glen, to attend. Maybe it was just as well. Those deaths left a terrible mark on the community and on Jamie.'

Kirstin leant forward. 'In what way?'

'Well, human nature being what it is, everybody was absolutely horrified *and*, simultaneously, captivated by the terrible killings. I don't particularly want to go into every distressing detail.' He paused to gulp greedily at his tea, as if knocking back hard liquor. 'There had been a lot of drinking, drug-taking and other horsing around throughout the day. Eventually the group decided to play some sort of hide and seek game with Morag Ramsay as the seeker. She found them. The bodies. To put it bluntly, Craig Irvine and Iona Sutherland had been battered to death while having sexual intercourse. It happened in the wooded area on the other side of the Cauldron. They were naked and he was sprawled on top of her. It was very bloody, apparently. Catastrophic head injuries.'

Kirstin felt suddenly chilled. '*My God!*'

'Quite. It was awful.' Donald looked away towards the window, clearly uncomfortable with what he'd had to report. 'And Jamie felt terrible.

19

Guilty about all the trouble and arguments, now some of those same folk were dead. And then they arrested Morag.'

Kirstin leant back, trying to force down some of the now cold tea, struggling to wipe from her face the horror at what she'd just heard.

Donald was looking directly at her again. 'Jamie took an active — morbid, even — interest in Morag's case. Visited her in prison. Offered to help out on the legal side of things. Used to say she was the only one of that shower who had any substance to her. Morag had apparently helped him by talking about Jean and his loss. I think he felt he owed her. And, of course, he believed her to be wrongly accused and Jamie couldn't abide injustice of any sort. And to add to it all, she tried to commit suicide when on remand. Apparently she made some sort of garrotte from her clothing, attached it to the sink in her cell, and tried to strangle herself. Jamie was appalled by that and swore to help her if he could.'

'That sounds like Jamie.' Kirstin smiled. 'And what's this Morag like? Have you met her?'

Donald gave a quick nod of the head. 'Only briefly. Said hello to her once or twice when I was out on the river with Jamie. She seemed a bit stand-offish to me. Not that forthcoming. To be honest, I was quite surprised that they had clicked. And I know Ross was suspicious of her motives in befriending his father. He thought she might be manipulating Jamie, getting him to look less sternly on her group in order to gain some gratitude from them. I'm not sure I'd go that far. But anyway, Jamie was adamant. He liked her.

Described her as a 'lost soul'. Unhappy, depressed but trying to hide it. I know he thought her boyfriend, Craig, was leading her a merry dance. And that she didn't fit in with the others perhaps? And I think he saw something of himself in her. Like him, she could be a bit sharp-tongued, appear cold and snooty. You know how Jamie could get if he was upset or outraged by something. So, that was it. They got on. It was only last year that he started regularly doing the patrol that takes in the Cauldron. That's when the trouble began. Before that he'd been on perfectly civil terms with the group, as far as I know.'

Donald looked tired now. The conversation, and perhaps the memories it had brought up, seemed to have visibly drained him. 'I'm an old man now, Kirstin. At that age when people, the police and suchlike, don't take me too seriously. However, I knew Jamie very well. We saw each other through most of life's ups and downs, joys and sadnesses, and I'm ninety-nine per cent certain of one thing. Jamie would not take his own life. There would have to have been some unimaginably appalling reason for him to do something like that. It must have been an accident. And yet, he knew every inch of that stretch of river. 'It's a living thing,' he used to say.'

Kirstin shifted in her seat, feeling chilled to the bone. 'So, what do you think happened that night? I could only get the bare bones out of Ross.'

Donald paused, a look of hopeless despair on

his tired face. 'I really don't know, even though I went to the inquiry. It's all supposition. It looks as if he went out that evening, sometime after nine. I know that because I spoke to him on the telephone shortly before to arrange a game of golf. Is that the action of a suicidal man? I ask you. I told the inquiry this but . . . '

He stopped to brush a hand over his thinning hair. 'All I know is that he was found the following morning. His body was caught on the weir. In those conditions — heavy rainfall, flooding — it would be expected to go over, but his clothing had snagged on broken tree branches for some poor dog-walker to find. The so-called forensic experts reckoned that he'd fallen or let himself be swept into the Cauldron just after the entrance to the footbridge. It's a bad spot in high water. They thought he'd been pulled under by the current and then hit his head on some of the stones and rocks that pepper the Cauldron's bed. They surmised that he was unconscious by the time he reached the weir. I pray to God that's true.' He slumped forward, head drooping, in a pose of utter hopelessness.

Kirstin reached across the table to take his hand. 'Donald, I'm sorry, so sorry.'

He gave hers a gentle squeeze in return. 'Something's amiss. Jamie was different in the weeks before it happened. Obsessive, secretive. I should have paid more attention. I thought he might have been going through another stage of grieving over Jean. But, when I think about it now, there was something else bothering him. I don't know if anything untoward had occurred. But if anyone or anything caused us to lose Jamie before his time, I think we should know, don't you?'

Slowly, he got to his feet and wandered over to the window. He stood with his ramrod straight back towards her, a stance which in other circumstances he would have considered uncommonly rude. But she knew he was thinking about more important matters than social etiquette. Still with his back to her, he stared unseeingly towards the golf course, his voice a quivering whisper.

'Frankly, Kirstin, I've not had a proper night's sleep since he went. The thought of him out there, in a place he loved, where he felt happy and secure, suddenly finding himself struggling against the waters, helpless, in terror. It's left me worried, very worried.' He turned to face her, eyes pleading, body rigid. 'And, if truth be known, a bit frightened.'

3

The sun would be setting soon, but Kirstin knew she had time before dark. She paused at the Roseburn Cliff entrance to the river path. She was always amazed at how, within moments of leaving this bustling area of shops, flats and a main road, she could be down on the walkway and enjoying the quiet, riverside bliss. As if she were in the middle of the countryside. From here she could make it to the Cauldron in a few minutes if she hurried. Kirstin breathed in the evening air gratefully, glad to be free of the stuffy golf club atmosphere. There were still a handful of dog-walkers, joggers and evening strollers about.

The last time she'd been along here had been with Jamie, on a crisp autumn day, so unlike now. After her divorce from Ross and well after Jean had gone. Jamie had enjoyed showing her his latest enthusiasm. His voice had held an almost childish excitement . . . *'This river work is going to save me from old age and despair. I find it so hard to manage without Jeannie but all this beauty around me, and showing it to others, will help. It's got to.'*

And had it? Jamie was certainly rejuvenated and enlivened that day, reaching out to her with an intimacy she now missed. He'd shared an acute insight into his son and had been brutally honest as they'd strolled along the riverbank.

'I didn't want to raise anything like this with you when you were married, but I always thought Ross wasn't good enough for you. That may seem wrong coming from his father, but . . . '

He'd looked directly at her then. Seeking permission to go on?

'But I think he's far more driven than I ever was or, rather, driven by the wrong things. Ambition can be a fine quality if it's kept separate from ruthlessness and selfishness. But too often it turns into a callous, self-seeking crusade. Not good. I've always hoped he'd mellow with time . . . '

The strain of doomed hope in his voice seemed to oscillate round her head as she walked the last few yards to the Cauldron. At this point she had a choice. Turn left over the wooden footbridge and up the steps to the art gallery high above. Or follow the river as it turned right towards the weir. Tonight, like every summer evening, the waters moved sluggishly under the footbridge, coming almost to a complete halt at the Cauldron.

A shiver suddenly took hold of her. The temperature had dropped. The sun's rays were hitting the top of the hill above but wouldn't make it any further down into the river valley tonight. She sat by the pool's edge, keeping both the glassy smooth surface of the Cauldron and the gently flowing waters of the nearby weir in sight. But disturbing images of what Donald told her had happened here ate into any momentary enjoyment of her surroundings.

What the hell had Jamie been doing here? In February. In the pouring rain. In a flood. It was madness. Both Ross and Donald had said that Jamie had been different in the weeks before it happened. Obsessive, secretive. Certainly, once interested in something, Jamie would become utterly captivated by it, trying to convert others to his latest passion. The river work had been the most recent, and final, example. Still, she'd always thought that to reach his age and still be enthused by the world was a quality to be treasured. However, there was a fine line between passionate enthusiasm and obsession . . .

And what of this secretiveness that Donald had remarked on? That was something completely new to her. Jamie had always seemed open, never one to hide his feelings. Yes, he could have a sharp tongue. She'd seen him tick off junior members of staff from time to time. And he could be a formidable complainer, especially when it came to the quality of service in restaurants or shops. Jamie had been an old curmudgeon on occasions, though always with reason. But secretive? No. What you saw was what you got with Jamie. In fact, that very notion was a bit of a badge of honour for him . . . *'I'm a plain speaker who believes in straight dealings, Kirstin.'*

And speaking of secretiveness, she'd not been aware of this at the time. But now, thinking over the encounter with Donald, it came home to her. Donald had seemed hesitant, reluctant at times. Perhaps wanting to say more about Jamie? But then pulling back. Or had she imagined it? He was obviously still very upset at the death of his lifelong friend. And maybe feeling, albeit without reason, a bit guilty. Could he, should he have done more?

She closed her eyes, trying to picture this summer idyll as it must have been a mere five months ago. Radically changed. Unwelcoming, uninviting — savage, even. Savage to Jamie. But strangely, her thoughts kept drifting further back. To last summer. Two young people . . . partying with their friends by the river . . . laughing . . . enjoying life . . . falling for the aphrodisiac beauty of their surroundings . . .

The screech of a wild creature roused her. An owl venturing out early perhaps? She opened her eyes and the light seemed to have all but gone, leaving the Cauldron in gloom. The last golden tints had disappeared from the top of the hill above. Time to go. As she headed away from the burbling weir, she quickened her pace and cast a last glance behind her at the now black waters of the Cauldron and the wooded bank opposite. The image she'd been seeing behind her closed eyelids returned. She could almost make them out over there. Two bodies . . . suntanned and naked . . . clinging to each other in hot desire . . . writhing in shared passion . . .

The creature's screech interrupted her thoughts for a second time. Looking away from the river, her pace turned into a jog. But the worst part of the image remained stubbornly with her. Two lovers forever entwined.

In a bludgeoned, bloody mass.

4

Kirstin tried to suppress a yawn as she approached the house. Sleep had not come easily after the previous evening's visit to the Cauldron. She'd spent a fevered night tossing and turning; images of Jamie, the Cauldron, bloodied corpses, infusing what little slumber she had found.

Two minutes later, she'd reached her destination. It was a lovely house. And unusual. Detached, brilliant white, art deco style, with the front garden wild and untended but a true riot of summer colour. Kirstin pressed the bell once. No answer. She smiled to herself, gently shaking her head at a familiar feeling. It was odd. Sometimes when you visited a house, knocked on the door, rang the bell but got no answer, you knew, just *knew*, there was someone in. Kirstin tried the bell again and stepped back, craning her neck as she strained to look upwards. Nothing. Curtains drawn and blinds down, on upper and ground floors. She'd already had a look at the side gate. Stout, secure, firmly locked. The whole place shouted 'stay away'. Hardly surprising. If she'd been Morag Ramsay, she too would have lived in a fortress.

She moved towards the front door and bent down to the letter box. It didn't have much give and she flinched as the flap pinched her fingers. 'Hello! Morag Ramsay! Hello! Please, my name is Kirstin Rutherford. I'm Jamie Munro's daughter-in-law! Can we talk?' She took a breath, wondering at her present-tense use of 'daughter-in-law'.

She bent to call one last time and then she heard it. The flip-flop sound of sandalled feet on a wooden floor. She stepped back again, suddenly nervous. There was a cacophony of clickings and clankings as multiple locks were released and then the door opened halfway. The woman *was* wearing sandals, brown leather ones, and a cool linen shirt with trousers, and, oddly for what looked to be a darkened house, wrap-around sports sunglasses. The eccentricity added a glamorous, almost retro touch, as she had her hair piled up high on top of her head. She might have walked out of a Hollywood fashion magazine from the forties or fifties. Kirstin tried not to stare. What had she expected? A stressed-out, rumpled mess? According to Donald's account of what Morag had been through, the answer was a firm 'yes'.

'Morag Ramsay?' The woman said nothing. Kirstin tried a smile and knew immediately it had failed; her nerves were getting the better of her. 'Look, I'm sorry, I know it's a bit early in the day. But I wanted to see if I could get hold of you. I . . . I've just come back. I've been out of the country for a while and . . . well, I've only recently heard about Jamie. I was . . . very, *very* fond of him. I didn't even get to go to his funeral and . . . and I've been talking to his best friend, Donald. Donald Ferguson — I think you met him once or twice? In fact it was Donald who

29

told me where your house was and about the terrible thing that happened at the river. And what happened to you, and how Jamie wanted to help, and well . . . '

She was sounding ridiculous. Her breathless delivery was making no sense, even to herself. She stood back. 'Look, I'm sorry. I probably shouldn't have come. It's too much, I know. I really should g — '

'Why did you?'

Kirstin frowned. 'I'm sorry?'

'Why *did* you come here?'

The voice was low, the Edinburgh accent strong. Stronger than her own. The delivery was clipped and the blank gaze of the woman's sunglasses was disconcerting. Kirstin took a step forward again and noticed the protective reflex before it was checked. Morag Ramsay's inclination had been to push the door to, keeping it firmly in place between her and any intruder. Kirstin retreated, trying to appear relaxed.

'I need to talk to someone about Jamie.'

'I thought you said you'd talked to Donald Ferguson. And what about your husband? Why didn't you hear about Jamie's death until now? None of this makes sense.'

The comment sounded like an accusation. Kirstin immediately felt tense again, as if she'd been caught out in a lie.

'Well, actually, Ross and I are divorced but Jamie and I, we still kept in touch, until the past year or so. And that's just it. I . . . I didn't get the chance to see what might have been wrong with him, maybe to help him.' She stopped abruptly, feeling the rush of suppressed grief. 'I never even got to say goodbye.'

Kirstin looked down at the ground, wishing that she too had employed the protection of sunglasses. She heard the door creak as Morag Ramsay pulled it wide and nodded an invitation to enter.

★ ★ ★

Kirstin was amazed. She'd been here, what? Twenty minutes? And still the woman hadn't removed her sun-glasses. She could obviously negotiate her darkened kitchen wearing them, despite every window being obscured by blinds. And now, thankfully, here they were, sitting on her sun-flooded patio, rays bouncing off the deep cobalt-blue lenses. Throughout their entire conversation, Kirstin had noticed how, despite the glory of the view past lawn and trees, down to the glistening Water of Leith far in the distance, Morag Ramsay had kept her back firmly towards the garden, her face resolutely turned towards the house. She seemed excessively self-contained, tense, her bearing upright. Kirstin couldn't help but notice the clenched fists that were moved quickly from tabletop to knees as she began to speak.

'I heard about Jamie's death when I was in prison on remand. It was a bolt from the blue. He had recently visited me. Said he was keen to help. Assumed automatically that I was wrongly accused, which is more than I can say for my other so-called friends. Jamie's support was unexpected though welcome. But sadly short-lived. As with everything else in that hellhole, the news of his death was delivered by a particularly sadistic warder, with premeditated cruelty and callousness. I asked if I could attend the funeral. My request was turned down point-blank.' She paused to give a low harsh laugh. 'Hah! No surprise really. Let 'The Witch' show her face at such a spectacle of public grieving? That would only serve to humanize her, and that could never be permitted. So. There you have it.' She paused again, her face still unreadable. 'But I am sorry for your loss.'

Morag Ramsay sat back and raised the now looser fists to the table. The oration, infused with dramatic quality, had been articulate, perceptive, honest and dignified. But Kirstin couldn't help feeling alarmed at the clearly painful, iron self-control it had taken to divulge so much. There was obvious, and understandable, anger there, bitterness too, underpinning the clipped, formal mode of speaking. Kirstin had visited her fair share of prisons in her time as a paralegal. On each and every occasion she'd found herself practically sprinting to the front gate, gasping for a breath of freedom. Whoever said there was no punishment in being sent to prison should try visiting one.

Kirstin attempted a smile. 'Thank you. I'm sure you miss Jamie too. But . . . he wasn't a specialist in criminal law. I just wonder what he thought he could do?'

Morag offered her what looked like a wry smile in return. 'Oh, little or nothing of any practical use, I'm sure. But the thought was there. Anyway, as my own legal advisers admitted, the case was complicated. The prosecution couldn't make a case against me for murder and so tried manslaughter.'

Kirstin frowned. 'Why?' She noticed Morag's fists tighten again as she prepared to answer.

'You want to know the details?'

'Please.'

The fists were unclenched. 'Very well. From the outset it was clear that the police didn't have a clue. After the obvious lines of inquiry, which included all of our group, others who were at the river that day, and various associates of both Craig and Iona, the police drew a blank. Then they looked at the killings as a random event. They brought in some silly criminal profiler to help, and still nothing. There was even talk that the killings might be linked to a similar attack years ago in Northumberland.'

Kirstin nodded. 'I see. But what made them change their minds and settle on you?'

'Two words. Fraser Coulter.' The wry smile had returned. 'One of my party 'friends' there that day. He gave a new statement to the police, saying that I had admitted carrying out the killings. I don't intend to go into the details of my previous group of 'friends' but what I will say is that he was lying. Iona's brother, Ally, thought I'd done it and was using his little gofer, Fraser, to do his dirty work. Plus, there were other complications . . . '

'Like what?'

'Quite simply, I had lied to the police in my

33

early statements. But not in the way you might imagine. Let me make clear that we had all had a lot to drink, smoke, snort that day. Frankly, my memory was shot to pieces by the time it came to playing our ludicrous game of hide and seek. Much is blank or fragmentary up to the point where I stumbled across Craig and Iona lying there, and 'woke up' as it were.'

Kirstin watched as the fists were returned to their previous position under the table. 'In the immediate aftermath of it all, I was reluctant to admit to the police the state I had been in. Drinking to excess, using illegal drugs. Despite the shock of the deaths, I still had my life, my career, my future to consider. To admit what we'd been doing was unthinkable. So, I made the earlier part of the day up. Fabricated, guessed what I was doing and when. Later, when I became the subject of closer police scrutiny, this became apparent. And looked highly incriminating.'

She paused, and Kirstin heard the long intake of breath as Morag composed herself for what was to come next. 'I have recently discovered, thanks to Bonnie actually having the guts to admit something to me, that some of these so-called friends had been spiking my drinks for quite a while. To allow Craig and Iona to enjoy themselves behind my back. Nice, eh? Anyway, that is all by the by. I despise all these people now and, Fraser's lying apart, had they not interfered with my memory, I might not be in this position today. A grim fact that would test the equanimity of a saint. But, as regards my useless recollection that day, the police thought I was faking it. After that, I was doomed.'

'I'm . . . I'm sorry. That's horrible. About your friends, I mean. And the police?' Kirstin leant forward. 'They had nothing else on you?'

Morag shook her head slowly. 'They had no forensic evidence against me. Most of us were nearly naked after sunbathing and being in and out of the river all day. So our clothes were no use to the police, although Iona had helped herself to my sarong, which she and Craig were lying on when they died. The police tried to make something of that. You know, there they were, your boyfriend and his other woman, fucking on your sarong. Enough to make you snap, etcetera, etcetera. Crudely simplistic, I know. But that's police thinking for you.'

The corner of her mouth twitched. In a smirk? A grimace? Then, after another long intake of breath, she went on. 'What else . . . oh, yes. No weapon was found, which was doubtless a source of constant frustration to the police. But they did try to hit me with one other thing. In my initial statement I'd said that I thought Craig and Iona had been attacked only minutes before, and that one of them may even have been breathing their last as . . . ' She faltered momentarily and then rallied, 'As I came upon them. That was confirmed by forensics and, no doubt, added to the circumstantial evidence against me.'

Kirstin shifted in her seat. 'And they eventually dropped the manslaughter charges?'

Morag seemed to grimace to herself again before replying. 'Yes. Fraser made a third statement. I don't know why. By then he was a busted flush, his credibility as a witness shattered. Indeed, should I ever be charged with murder, his antics will be a gift to my legal team. Fraser's recanting, coupled with a lack or weakness of supporting evidence, clinched it. But my lawyers have made it plain, I'm not out of the woods yet. No one has been charged with murder *and* the police still view me as their chief suspect.' She sat up even straighter. 'All in all, it's an intolerable position and one I fear Jamie would have been unable to help me with.'

At last, Morag leant back and seemed to relax the muscular tension that had been holding her rigid. Kirstin let the silence lie between them, looking past Morag towards the river. If there truly was no reason why this woman should have been incarcerated, then Kirstin felt overwhelmingly sorry for her. And the actions of her so-called friends were unforgivable.

Morag stood up. The visit was over. Kirstin felt surprisingly disappointed. Her need to talk about Jamie had been far from satisfied. She'd been here for more than an hour but, not surprisingly, as far as Morag Ramsay was concerned, her sorry plight had taken up most of that time. Still, Kirstin felt some vestige of hope. She had made a connection with someone who had known Jamie at the time of his apparent personality change. Although, given the predominantly closed nature of Morag Ramsay, could she gain her trust? Encourage her to open up about how Jamie had seemed during the weeks and months after the Cauldron killings? Face whatever the truth was?

If so, maybe, just maybe, she could lay Jamie to rest.

Sunday, 13 August 2006

Brilliant! Just as forecast. It was going to be a scorcher. All day to work on that tan. Fraser Coulter bundled the last few items into his backpack, adding an extra bottle of wine for luck. It was getting on for noon. He'd probably be the last there. Best plan was to walk down to the viaduct and cross the river on foot. To hell with going the long way round by the official footpath. With luck that old tosser Jamie Munro would spot him and they could have a long overdue set-to. Clear the air before the party began.

Twenty minutes later he had the Cauldron in sight. Only an anxious-looking Morag and a distinctly sullen Craig had arrived. Christ, had they had a row or something? Craig was swigging at a bottle of San Miguel, between puffs of a spliff, while she was two-thirds of her way through a bottle of white wine. It was going to be a party all right. Blankets and mats had been strategically placed to deter other footpath users from coming too near their area. Great! They'd booked the place.

He raised a hand in greeting. 'Hey, well done. We're all set then, eh? Where are the others?'

Morag shrugged and turned away to fiddle with something in her bag. Craig wandered over to welcome him with a handshake and a beer.

'Hi there. Don't know where they are. Thought Ally would be here staking our claim hours ago. You know what he's like. Bet he's first with the towels on the loungers when he's on his hols, eh?'

Fraser twisted the bottle cap, breaking the seal, and slugged down a deep gulp. 'You okay, pal? You and her seem a bit . . . ?' He finished the sentence with a nod towards Morag.

Craig gestured for them to move a few feet further away.

'Yeah. To be honest, this was the last thing I felt like doing today. We're . . . well, it's not so much that we're not getting on. We're . . . petering out, you could say. Though that's what I feel. I don't know about her. I think she's refusing to see or feel anything at the moment.'

Fraser shook his head at the proffered joint and nodded again towards Morag. 'Time to be cruel to be kind.'

Craig frowned. 'What's that?'

'Finish it. Clean cut. Move on.'

'Funny you should say that. I've been thinking about that all morning. For weeks, actually. But look at her mood. I tell you, I'm beginning to lose my nerve.' Craig finished off the remainder of his bottle with a final swig. 'I can't take female histrionics, least of all Morag's. You know how unbelievably temperamental she is. Call me a coward but she's going to need careful handling.'

Fraser smiled his sympathy and slapped Craig on the shoulder. 'I don't envy you, pal. Let's get you another drink. And listen, come hell or high water, we're going to have a great day.'

5

Morag stood on her front doorstep, tracking Kirstin's progress down the cul-de-sac until she disappeared round the corner. Then she removed her sunglasses and headed back to the patio, risking a seat facing the river.

The visit from Jamie's daughter-in-law had left her shaken. Yet, in another way, relieved. She'd surprised herself at how calm, cool, *logical* she could portray herself to be with this stranger. And the encounter marked something new, or at least long overdue — that she could have direct contact with another human being. Recent weeks had seen her relating to only one person: her psychotherapist, Dr Lockhart.

Morag cleared the coffee cups from the table and moved back into the kitchen, picking up Kirstin's scribbled phone numbers that were lying on the worktop. Her visitor had been somewhat dramatic in her need to find out why Jamie died. The hunger for an answer was written all over her. She didn't fancy the woman's chances. Accident or suicide? Either one would leave her feeling guilty that she hadn't been there for him.

Nevertheless, by the end of their conversation she had decided that the woman was likeable. Trustworthy? Well, she'd let her into her fortress in the first place, hadn't she? And Kirstin had seemed genuine when she'd expressed her regret at all that had happened. The killings, the arrest, the aftermath.

Morag stepped back on to the patio, looking more boldly at the distant ribbon of river. It was very, *very* early days, but she needed to build a relationship with someone *real*, not just a shrink. For the first time in ages she thought it might, just might, be possible to break out of this twilight world in which she existed.

With a firm nod, she turned and made her way back inside. As she replaced Kirstin's scribbled details on to the worktop, she heard the sharp rat-a-tat. Swiftly, she moved to the front door, carefully peering through the spyhole and then opening the door six inches.

'Delivery for Ramsay. Sign here, please.'

Morag pulled the door wider, scrawled a barely legible signature and then closed it quickly, turning over the registered letter in her trembling hand. When every second delivery brought final demand letters she couldn't hope to meet, and the occasional anonymous piece of hate mail, she could congratulate herself that there wasn't a stack of unopened envelopes stashed behind the radiator. However, today's delivery had been expected. Court papers. There would be no holding back the repossession proceedings any longer. And with that, the inevitable: bankruptcy and personal ruin. She smiled to herself. Since any vestige of optimism was fast disappearing, what about opting for the sink and the garrotte again?

She threw the letter on to the hall table and moved slowly back through to the kitchen. But

41

this time, the searing radiance of the summer sun had her retreating into the hallway. Hesitating, she searched in a pocket for her sun-glasses. Protected by the dark lenses, she walked out on to the patio once more.

She turned to look upwards, taking in the full splendour of the building. She'd miss this house. Situated on a hill overlooking a wide valley where the Water of Leith snaked through a near rural area of outstanding beauty, she'd adored the location on first sight. Who would believe that less than two miles away Edinburgh's city centre bustled and vibrated with life? But this area was special. No one had been allowed to build here for years. The conservation brigade had thankfully ring-fenced it for good. There were only a handful of houses scattered across the valley. Further behind her, atop the hill and shielded by the woods, was Scotland's premier modern art gallery, converted from a building of faded grandeur that had once housed a private school. Culture on her doorstep, should she want it. And once she had. The area was a true idyll. Best of all, she could stand, sit, drink, eat, relax out here and not be overlooked. No one could see her. Not on her patio and not anywhere in her hillside garden. Nature, *this* part of the world, was there for her, and her alone, to admire. And that was the problem. That was why she hid indoors. Because what couldn't be hidden even in summer, no matter how abundant the foliage, was the glinting silver ribbon of the river below, in the distance. Once the source of breathtaking, uplifting views, the vista was now a source of perpetual torment.

Her heart started to race, accompanied by a shortening of breath. She recognized the symptoms immediately: the beginnings of a full-blown panic attack coursing through her system. She squeezed her eyes tight shut behind the sunglasses, swaying slightly from the exhaustion of yet another tortured and sleepless night. *For God's sake! Let it stop! Let it stop!*

The phone's ring had her scurrying, gratefully, back inside. She stood rigidly to attention over the answering machine and went through her ritual. On the fourth ring, the digital readout reported that it was in 'screen' mode as the familiar voice began her message.

'Morag, it's Isobel Lockhart. Are y — '

She snatched up the cordless handset and inched her way back towards the patio, the sunglasses still wrapped protectively round her eyes.

'Dr Lockhart. Yes, I am screening. You didn't expect me to be out, did you? Not at this time of day. Although I *am* on my patio as we speak. And facing the garden, would you believe?' The fact that she'd received a visitor, and such an interesting one at that, she'd keep to herself for now. Dr Lockhart didn't need to know *all* her business.

'That's good, Morag. Really, really good. A small step forward?' The gentle, soothing voice sounded genuinely pleased.

Morag settled herself on the metal garden

chair, the frame under her thighs already warmed by what was going to be another day of sweltering heat.

'Yes, but I've just been pushed a hundred steps back. The court papers have arrived. I'm going to lose the house.' She paused to let the news she'd been expecting for weeks sink in. But Dr Lockhart was going to let the silence be. A familiar tactic. 'But, you know what, Dr Lockhart? Maybe it's a blessing in disguise because *this* isn't living. I love this house but I can't live here any more. Too many memories. Too many enemies about.'

She could hear her voice moving up a register nearer to panic mode and took a deep breath, the phone clamped against her clammy cheek. Then she felt the tears. Only noticed as they trickled halfway down her face.

'Morag. I think you should come in and see me today. I can always make room for an emergency session. Ten past two. Okay?' Dr Lockhart's voice sounded firmer now, having the force of an order, rather than an offer.

'Yes, yes, fine. Thank you, Dr Lockhart.'

She sighed, moved back into the kitchen to replace the phone, almost managing a smile, but then caught sight of her reflection in the window. She'd forgotten to take off the sunglasses. Slowly, reluctantly, she removed them, immediately blinking against the sunlight bouncing off the white walls. She risked another look at herself. Yesterday she'd looked haggard, unkempt, hair a mess — she'd forced herself to dye it. Today was a distinct improvement. She should try to keep up some semblance of normality, for what it was worth.

On the upstairs landing she paused, not knowing why today of all days she felt the urge to go to the telescope. Hesitantly, she lowered herself on to the comfortable chair behind it, easing the long barrel down from its sharp heavenwards angle, and scanned away to her left. Should she? Could she? Her quivering eyelid made it tricky to get a focus. And then she had it.

The shimmering silver ribbon had lengthened and widened. The river walkway was quiet. One lone jogger, his bright yellow shorts shooting waves of colour back up the lens to her squinting eye. Reluctantly but irresistibly she inched the telescope further to the left. Over the treetops she could see the light froth of the weir's tumbling waters. Shallow and slow on such a warm, dry day. She could almost hear their steady, comforting lilt. Then, just below the weir, in her line of sight, the fringes of the Cauldron appeared. Not a ripple today. Glassy. Smooth. Deceptive. Seductive. But deep, surely still deep. Luckily, the summer trees permitted no view of the nearside bank. All that was left to the imagination.

But she'd seen enough for one day. She returned the telescope to its heavenwards view and sat back in her chair, staring unseeingly through the window. A familiar wave of anger gripped her. The irony of it. The unfairness of it. If the truth be known, she'd almost not gone to the wretched party. It had seemed a good enough idea at first. But come that Sunday morning, she knew by the closed look on Craig's face that he didn't want to go. Or, at least, he didn't want to go with her. Bastard. He hadn't even the guts to say as much. So, why had she even bothered? Simple. To be bloody-minded. Why should he be given free rein to drink and flirt his way through the day without her? On *her* territory. With *her* friends. Except, he had become more at home at the river, more at ease with the crowd than she'd ever been. *His* territory, *his* friends. More unfairness.

She stood up, suddenly craving the darkness of her bedroom. The ever-persistent questions returned to persecute her. *Why did you go? Fool! Just think how different it would all have been if you'd stayed away.*

With stiffened shoulders and white-knuckled fists, she made her way towards the welcome darkness.

6

'I'm sorry. You can't see him without an appointment. Glen's very busy.'

The receptionist looked young. Kirstin guessed he was new to the job; he'd already needed to check the extension list twice as calls had come in.

She tried again. 'Please, can you just ring through and tell him Jamie Munro's daughter-in-law is here. Only a few minutes of his time. Please?'

It was clear Jamie's name meant nothing to him. 'Now, look. I've told you. Gle — ' Kirstin saw the boy's face freeze as he looked over her shoulder. 'I'm sorry, Glen. I told this visitor that she needed to have an appointment be — '

'It's fine, Rory. Really.'

She spun round to see a tanned and beaming face.

'Hi, I'm Glen Laidlaw. Welcome.'

His hand was outstretched, waiting for her to clasp it. A cool, firm handshake. She'd heard a good bit about Jamie's boss at the river association and had envisaged a much older man, in a suit, maybe nearing retirement. Instead, here was a smiling man in his mid-thirties with sun-bleached tousled hair, casually dressed in three-quarter surf pants, a red Abercrombie T-shirt and Birkenstocks.

'Please, come into my office. Rory, can you

rustle us up some drinks? Coffee? Water, sparkling or still?' He looked at her for a decision.

'Oh, eh. Water, please. Still. Thank you.'

'Please, take a seat. I'll be with you in a minute.'

The room wasn't large but seemed double its size thanks to the enormous windows on her right. The entire wall was made of glass and the outlook was spectacular. Panoramic views towards the Pentland Hills rolling gently into the distance, and, just a few yards away, the Water of Leith flowing past, its current swift. She glanced at the other two walls facing her. Behind the desk was a giant map of the river, charted from its source deep in the Pentlands, down through the heart of Edinburgh, to the port of Leith. Along the map's length were various sidebars, dotted at irregular intervals, containing unintelligible symbols and dense unreadable text. The wall to her left held an array of framed photographs: Glen Laidlaw in baseball cap and lumber jacket, leaning out of a Land Rover with a snow-covered pine forest providing the backdrop; waving from a canoe; bare-chested in shorts on a beach that had to be in East Lothian, given the unmistakable outline of the Bass Rock in the background. And finally, a long shot of white-water rafters — including Glen, presumably — with the boat and its occupants tilting perilously down towards some frothing rapids.

She heard the door click and turned round to see him balancing a cup of coffee and a glass of water as he tried to close the door with a backward kick of his foot.

'Done. There we go. By the way, sorry about Rory. He's here on work experience. Shouldn't actually be on reception on his own, but we're short-staffed today.' He placed the water gently in front of her and sidled round the desk to take his seat, still smiling. He nodded at the photos. 'I'm not quite the action man they imply. Those just capture some special memories.'

He took a sip of his coffee and then sat back, his face unsmiling now but still welcoming, eyebrows raised. 'You're Jamie Munro's daughter-in-law?'

She shifted in her seat. 'Yes, well . . . ex-daughter-in-law. I'm sorry, I . . . I should've introduced myself properly. I'm Kirstin Rutherford. I was married to Jamie's son, Ross. I saw Donald Ferguson yesterday and he said I should talk to you. That you and Jamie got on well?'

He smiled. 'Actually, dear old Donald rang me today. Told me about your meeting, and gave me your number. I was going to phone you. I'm really glad you stopped by. Jamie talked a bit about you. Now . . . what was it he said that stuck in my mind? Yes. That he liked to take you on river walks after lunch? Have a good old blether. And then you went away. Left the country.'

The statement felt like an accusation. Once again, the familiar sensation of guilt gripped her. 'Yes, I've been having a bit of a . . . a gap year. Nearer two, as it happens. Jamie and I lost touch and I left the country, so I had no idea about his death. Until just a few days ago. It's . . . frankly, it's been awful. I still find it so hard to believe. Look . . . I'm sorry about just turning up here. But after talking to Donald, it left me . . . confused. Like I said, he was struck by how well you and Jamie got on and I wondered if you had any idea wh — '

She felt the sting of tears and grasped the water, taking a deep gulp, grateful that she had the glass as a distracting prop.

He leant forward, one tanned hand splayed palm downwards on the desk in a calming gesture, a smile still lingering on his face. 'Please. It's okay. I miss Jamie too. A lot. Listen, you wondered if I knew why he'd died? I'm not *entirely* sure. But, I think I might be able to help you understand his last year or so.'

She recovered herself quickly and, replacing the glass, sat back. 'Really? That would help me so much. Because, you see, from what Donald and Ross have said, it seems like Jamie underwent some sort of personality change.'

'Change.' He stretched out the word as if pondering its meaning. And then his features altered. All trace of a smile had gone.

'Okay, three years ago, Jamie came to us here at the association. He was just what we wanted. An injection of enthusiasm from an able volunteer. He transformed the whole volunteer programme, improved the guided walks that, up until then, had been occasional one-offs. He was just great *and* undoubtedly raised our profile, which brought us new donors. We have charitable status so that sort of thing's important. He'd go on local radio and even TV once or twice. Livened up our website too with lots of information and articles. The trustees loved what he was doing. We all did.'

He came to a sudden halt and shifted his eyes from hers.

She leant forward. 'But? I sense there's a 'but' coming.'

The faint smile was back. 'What I'm telling you here is, I suppose, what journalists call 'off the record'. I can see how important it is for you to find out what you can. And Donald says you're all right — very all right. So that's good enough for me. And, speaking of Donald, I've not gone into great detail with him about this. He was too close to Jamie. I don't want to hurt him. But by speaking to you in this way, I'm *trusting* you. Do you understand?'

She began to feel anxious at his change in tone. What was coming? 'Of . . . of course. I just want to know what was going on.'

He held up a hand. 'Right. Things started to go 'off' when Jamie got into an ongoing dispute with the group that Donald told you about. They were, frankly, a bunch of shits *but* they were self-confident, well-off local residents *and* well connected. At least, Iona Sutherland was. And she became their . . . how can I put it? Their cheerleader, their shop steward, in the dispute with Jamie. She could pen a particularly poisonous letter when she liked. And, towards the end, she was threatening Jamie, me, the association, all of us, with legal action.'

Without warning he stood up and moved over

to a filing cabinet, unlocked it, and returned with a bulging suspension file. He flicked rapidly through and stopped to pick out what looked like a lengthy handwritten letter. He offered her the last page.

'This'll give you a flavour of the late Ms Sutherland.'

Kirstin cast her eye over the slender script, picked out with a fine-nibbed fountain pen. The ink was an unusual, idiosyncratic choice: brownish red, like watery, dried blood.

Finally, while it is understandable that an organization such as yours might wish to use the elderly in the community — if nothing else they have the time and the wherewithal to work for free — it really is incumbent upon you to understand the limitations of such people. Infirmity of body and mind are commonplace after a certain age. And while the most infirm would be unable to fulfil the duties of a river association volunteer, the relatively physically fit older person can be masking serious mental health issues such as senility, dementia, depression, delusions, or perhaps just a deep-seated, long-harboured frustration and disappointment with his life. Such a person may find it intolerable to see younger generations enjoying life in the way he never could and never will. Bitterness and envy are deeply unattractive and, at times, dangerous qualities.

In closing, I would like to say that if I, or

*my friends, experience any further harass-
ment, unfounded allegations, or any
impugning of our characters, either verbally
from Mr Munro or in writing from you, I will
have no hesitation in handing the matter
over to my legal advisers and talking to my
local contacts in the media.*

*I understand that Mr Munro's son is a
senior lawyer, like his father once was
before him. Perhaps Mr Munro junior may
be able to offer some wise filial and professional counsel before an already unsavoury
matter becomes irrevocably unpleasant.*

Yours sincerely,

Iona Sutherland

Kirstin shook her head, letting out a long sigh of
disbelief. '*That* is nasty, truly nasty. She must
have really hated Jamie. Why? He was just a
harmless old man.'

Glen slid the letter back across the desk and
replaced it carefully in the file. 'Iona Sutherland
died in a terrible way. No one should suffer like
that. But I will say this. I met her on numerous
occasions, and she was an arrogant, spoilt
woman, clearly used to getting her own way,
even if she was in the wrong. As she most
certainly was over the river and Jamie. But he
had his answer for her.'

He stopped to fish out a small hardbacked A5
notebook from the file and opened the front
cover. 'By the way, did you know Jamie was such
a good artist? He seemed to like to have a sketch

or two at the beginning and end of each notebook.'

The pencil drawing he showed her was of a little bird, the pale chest plumage picked out with delicacy, sitting midstream on a rock. Underneath, Jamie's familiar handwriting.

White-throated dipper. Spotted first on June 2nd. Several sightings. Obviously s/he has found new territory along this stretch. Hope s/he stays! Welcome little dipper!

The page opposite had a sketch of a plant. Both were reminiscent of some illustrated Victorian almanac of flora and fauna, designed for genteel ladies of leisure as they promenaded about the countryside. The second sketch, equally delicate in its representation, was of a tall flowering plant, instantly recognizable to her even though Jamie had provided its name underneath. On their first river walk together, he'd pointed it out to her.

Himalayan Balsam. (Impatiens glandulifera.) I look forward to your glorious pink blossoming!

She lifted her eyes from the notebook, shaking her head in wonderment. She had no idea Jamie had been such a gifted artist. It wasn't as if his house had been festooned with paintings and drawings, as was often the case with those amateurs who had little or no talent but were unashamedly happy to put their efforts on display. The tears stung her eyes again. This was

54

a side of Jamie he'd never revealed.

Glen slid the notebook back towards himself and thumbed through to the page he wanted. 'As I said, Jamie had his answer for Iona Sutherland. Here it is.'

She accepted the opened notebook again.

The bitch! The absolute bitch! How dare she write such a letter to Glen! But I know Iona Sutherland's type. I've had many a client like her. A spoilt bully. Thought they'd bought you body and soul to do their dirty work in court. Morality and ethics alien concepts to them. So, she has contacts, has legal advisers, knows people in the media. Well, that doesn't surprise me. What does she call herself? An 'artist' and 'gallery owner'. Well, you have to have money to swan about doing that at her age. Family money. Old money. Not earned. I'd wager she's never done a day's real work in her life. And that bit about Ross! How does she know about him, about his job? She's been nosing about, but she'd better stay out of my life. I'm trying to get a job of work done and she has shown me nothing but contempt. It's too much. Too much. SHE MUST BE STOPPED.

Glen Laidlaw nodded his head towards the window and the flowing waters outside.

'Strong stuff, but I can't blame him. She and her friends were using and abusing this most beautiful of natural resources as their private playground. Matters would have come to a head eventually.' He turned back to look at her, making a pinching gesture with his finger and thumb. 'I was this far from engaging our own legal advisers on matters. And then Iona and Craig died. After that, I felt wretched. And Jamie felt far worse. Especially after what he'd written about her.'

Kirstin was still staring at Jamie's words, trying to process what she'd just read and heard. The contrast between the gentle delicacy of Jamie the artistic nature lover and the violence of his written words had the force of a physical blow. She deliberately kept her voice even and low.

'It . . . it *is* very sad and I'm sure anyone would feel uncomfortable — guilty, even. I *am* a bit surprised at the vehemence in what Jamie says.' She paused. A bit surprised was an understatement. 'But Jamie had a strong sense of right and wrong. If he *was* in the right about her and the group's behaviour, surely he shouldn't have felt so guilty about it all.'

Once again, she felt there was more to come. Slowly, Glen allowed the thick file to drop open as he looked up at her.

'That's true, if it had stayed at just that. But I'm afraid he had very good reason to feel guilty.'

7

'It's good to see you, Morag. You're looking better than I expected. Tell me about this morning.'

Morag glanced round the familiar room. It always impressed her. Dr Lockhart must have put a lot of time and energy into achieving just the right level of calming blandness. Pale colours — beiges and creams everywhere. The surprisingly comfortable couch, the inviting easy chairs, the tasteful paintings — all originals — and the soothing herbal teas. She let her glance drift back to the therapist and met her gaze with confidence. Not something she always felt able to do. Dr Lockhart, tall, slim, plainly but elegantly dressed in a trouser suit, looked back expectantly, waiting for a response. Morag scrutinized the woman's carefully considered attire, appropriate for her late middle age and her job. Finally, she slid down into the comfortable chair, trying to relax.

'This morning? The court papers had to come one day and now they have. I'm actually feeling much calmer, even relieved. The sword of Damocles has finally fallen. But I don't particularly want to dwell on that today. I'd far rather talk about the hypnotherapy. You said you wanted me to see Professor Beattie.'

Dr Lockhart pulled a sheaf of papers towards her, shifting her glasses back on to her face as she bent to examine a page.

'Okay. I've sent him everything that I told you I would. That's the outline of your court case and surrounding circumstances. And . . . where is it? Oh yes. 'With reference to hypnotherapy I have, on several occasions, attempted to work with Morag in this way but we have been unable to establish the necessary rapport. However, her psychotherapy with me is progressing.' '

Dr Lockhart looked up. 'I have, however, done as you requested, Morag, and withheld a full report about you. Professor Beattie rang me yesterday. He remarked on this and I told him you were . . . reluctant to divulge everything about yourself at this stage. He said that might make things difficult, but he has at least agreed to read and assess the file and get back to me tomorrow. I hope he can be persuaded to see you very soon. You *do* still want to try it?'

Morag nodded and shrugged simultaneously. 'Maybe. But I still don't know why you think he can do something for me that you clearly can't.'

The statement could have sounded insulting or petulant, but she knew Dr Lockhart was used to her difficult ways.

'Morag, I've asked you to work hard these past months and I know it hasn't always been easy. You have anger, anxiety and fear. All of these have been exhibited here, with me, and we can continue to work that out, face to face in psychotherapy. *But*, as regards hypnotherapy, it's my opinion that you are blocking, resisting me in some way. It may be an issue of *trust*, even though we've worked together for a while, and you have been open with me about your past, both recent and distant. But still, some part of you may not wish to go where hypnotherapy with me might take you. Like any therapeutic relationship, success depends on the two individuals working well together. And we do in psychotherapy. But with hypnotherapy, I think it's time to try a fresh approach.'

She knew Dr Lockhart was trying to engage her with one of her kind smiles. But she wouldn't return it. Instead, she shifted her gaze to rest on the floor between their chairs as she struggled to control her rising anger.

Dr Lockhart continued. 'I can't promise that Professor Beattie will be the answer to you remembering events on that day. But he *is* one of the best in the country at dealing with trauma and memory. As such, he's worth a try. I think there is hope, real hope. However, I sense a hesitation in you. I wonder. Is it that you actually don't want to try and recall that day? That would surprise me. You've said repeatedly *that* is your main driving force in working with me. *Or*, is your hesitation to do with other aspects of yourself you may reveal to Professor Beattie?'

Morag groaned inwardly. She knew what was coming and raised a hand.

'All right, let's do this again, shall we? One more time with feeling. I can say it, I can 'own' these things about myself. Right. Eleven years before I met Craig, I fell apart after a particularly shitty relationship breakdown. And yes, I turned to drugs and drink, as I had before when in a crisis. And yes, I had episodes of violence, mainly towards inanimate objects but on occasion towards myself, which the fading scars on my thighs and stomach will attest to. And finally, yes, I have had treatment on and off for that lovely duo, anxiety and depression, for as long as I can bloody well remember. Would *that* be enough for the good professor?'

She barely noticed the silence. It was the uncontrollable trembling enveloping her entire body that was worrying her.

'Morag? Here.'

She forced her eyes to refocus on the paper tissues that Dr Lockhart was holding out to her across the gulf between their chairs. Why did she never know when she was crying?

'You're angry, Morag. You're frightened of anger and you have so much of it. That's understandable. But what we're talking about here is trust. *If* you go to Professor Beattie, you will be giving him your trust. That includes being open with him about your past. And trust is something that you find difficult, isn't it? You shy away from admitting it, but we all need to be able to trust others.'

Morag turned her eyes away from Dr Lockhart's scrutiny. 'It's not about trust. I . . . I'm just getting fed up with us not getting anywhere. I'm not sure this Professor Beattie is such a good idea now. I feel you're pressurizing me into seeing him.'

'Okay, Morag. We can go back to that. But I want to stick with trust. Trust and relationships, friendships. We've talked before about your inability to trust others. Something that has led

you, not so much into friendships, but into
. . . acquaintanceships of convenience. Tell me
again about them.'

She didn't like the way Dr Lockhart had
repeatedly put that to her over these past weeks
and months. But she'd play along. She assumed
a sing-song tone of voice, as if telling a children's
story. 'Well . . . once upon a time I had lots of
friends. In the past, my job and my wider
interests gave me the opportunity to go out every
night of the year if I wanted to. I liked to travel
and would jet off for weekends, give parties, go
to parties. Then things started to quieten down
after I met Craig.'

'Why was that?'

'You know why. I wanted him to myself. And
why not? Yes, I had less time for other folk and
started turning down invitations. And then, I
suppose my world contracted a bit, without me
even noticing it. I still socialized with one or two
people from work but, like I say, I didn't notice it
when it was happening. By the time I had, my
world had shrunk. Until there was just the river
crowd. And that was fine. It was no big deal.'

Dr Lockhart nodded. 'But, as it turned out,
none of them were true friends, were they?'

Morag crossed and uncrossed her legs. She
was beginning to feel uncomfortable. Dr
Lockhart knew only too well the answers to these
questions.

'No, but so what? I knew the river lot were
fair-weather friends. I mean, none of them
exactly invited emotional intimacy. I suppose it
was just a matter of synchronicity. We all met at

the 'right' time, had something in common. Some of us were fighting off encroaching middle age, while others were catching up on missed opportunities. That was particularly true in Fraser's case. He'd married young and was definitely having a second flush of youthful hedonism. Iona and Ally could be . . . well, 'difficult' doesn't go near it. But when they were on form, it was good fun. Bonnie was agreeable enough, though she had her limitations. Bonnie and I are very different people.' She let out an overdramatic sigh. 'Look. My friendship with that lot was never about trust. And I was never one to do 'friends' in that soulmatey kind of way. Nauseating concept. Some people have to do that. I don't. With the river lot, I had a laugh. I wasn't looking for anything more.'

'Except it wasn't quite that straightforward, was it?' Dr Lockhart was leaning forward now, her face serious, almost stern. 'When you introduced Craig to the group, he *did* bond with them. You've already told me how you and Craig had rows about that. You felt left out. Worse, you suspected Fraser and Ally were encouraging Craig to leave you. The murders of Craig and Iona were shocking to you, to everyone. The final straw in a life that had dealt you so many blows. Your distant relationship with parents you believe don't love you, your problems with drink, drugs and self-harm going back to adolescence. It hasn't been easy for you. But matters had reached crisis point before that, hadn't they? You weren't really *that* shocked to know Craig and Iona had been together. Some part of you had acknowledged it already. Subconsciously, semi-consciously, you knew, didn't you?'

At last she felt able to meet Dr Lockhart's scrutiny. The release of volcanic anger came as a blessed relief.

'*What!* All these months of me coming here. You claiming to help me, care about me and what is this you're saying? That I did it? That I killed them both because I was jealous and that I'm nothing but a bloody cold calculating liar!' The urge to wrench one of Dr Lockhart's no doubt criminally expensive paintings from the walls and throw it through the nearest window was almost overwhelming. 'I've told you before, and I'll tell you again. I *did not know* what they were doing behind my back. *I* was the last to know! Trust? You go ask them about trust. The ones that are still alive, anyway!'

Dr Lockhart was leaning even further forward now, practically out of her seat.

'Morag, I am *not* saying that you killed anyone. What I am saying is that if you truly want to have some chance of revisiting that day, you will have to release, admit to, some of your authentic feelings of that time. You are a sensitive person and, like any sensitive person, you have intuition. You might want to deny that, but I believe some part of you knew or suspected what Craig and Iona were doing. And yes, it was a betrayal of trust. You were let down by everyone. By your lover, by your friends. Just as you've been let down before.' Dr Lockhart was looking at her, but not waiting for a response this time. 'We're opening up new ground right now and I want to make a suggestion. Why don't we admit you here as an inpatient? Just for a few days. Let's really do some intensive work, and then we'll talk again about hypnotherapy. What d'you think?'

Morag stood up, control gone at last. 'No. Absolutely not. I don't want to be put anywhere. I want to be in my home. While I've still got one.' She looked at her watch. 'Thank you for the appointment but I'm going to cut it short. You're right. I am angry. With you. Angry that *you* don't seem to trust *me*. Goodbye.'

As she marched down the soft carpeted corridor, half hoping Dr Lockhart would come racing after her, she felt relief and fear. Relief that she was away from the all-seeing gaze of the therapist who could read the rage within her. And fear? At last she was ready to admit a simple yet unsettling truth.

She was frightened of herself.

8

Kirstin was aware of Glen sliding two pages of A4 paper across the desk to her. His voice was low, the tone apologetic.

'This stuff must have taken him hours to compile. If he wasn't out and about on patrol, then he was at home in his study at the computer, typing up his logbooks into these neat notes. It took over his life. Please, read on.'

Sun 30/7/06
18.51 hrs — arrived at Cauldron. Evidence of empty wine bottles, cigarette butts (fire hazard), torn Rizla paper — indicating cannabis use? Heard laughing from other side of Cauldron. Crossed footbridge to search wooded area. Caught sight of the back of a female scurrying away from my approach up towards the Gallery of Modern Art. Looked like Iona (bitch!) Sutherland. More laughter heard. (V frustrating!)
19.12 hrs — cleared up mess. Finished patrol.
Action: recommend letter(s) be sent to at least I. Sutherland — no, to ALL re: littering and (again) fire hazard. Query — check with

police re: lewd behaviour issue (and swearing?) — legal aspects?

Sat/Sun 5 & 6/8/06 — no patrols. Indisposed. (Hip).

Fri 11/8/06
19.55 hrs — late finish at Cauldron. To my surprise met one of the problem group — Morag Ramsay — there on her own.
Went through my most recent log entries (inc those above) and discussed the latest difficulties presented by her friends. She was apologetic but raised question of the letters they had received from Glen Laidlaw/WLRA. She understood why I might be so annoyed but thought it unfair to include everybody. I replied that I had no choice and she quickly dropped the subject.
Ms Ramsay went quiet for a short while, then told me that she and her friends were thinking of having a 'sort of party' this Sunday! Said it was probably the last 'bit of fun' they would be having by the river together for a while as most people would be away for the rest of the summer. With that in mind, she asked me if I would 'turn a blind eye'

for just once if she promised to keep everyone 'in check'.

I nearly exploded but managed to hold my temper. Said I would think about it. Told her to watch herself on Sunday and think carefully whether she really should go.

I have no intention of letting them get away with this! The scum! Morag has no idea who she is mixing with, but I fear she will not listen to me. It will all end in tears. But, whatever else happens — THEY MUST NOT HAVE THEIR PARTY!!!

Action: V worried. Will take advice from Glen.

Sat 12/8/06

Called Glen. Told all, reminding him that I was not going to do patrols this weekend as the doctor had suggested a bit of rest for my hip. (No golfing either — shame!) On his advice, rang round all volunteers. No one available. Summer holidays or work commitments apparently. (V frustrating!) Rang Glen again. Said he'd do the patrols himself but that he too had commitments. (V, v frustrating!) Hip hellish. Please let it be better by morning. THEN I'LL CATCH THEM!!!

Sun 13/8/06
Indisposed all day/evening. No patrols.

Kirstin let the pages drop on to the desk and slid them back towards Glen. Two things had hit her. First, the language. The heat of his anger seeping out of those fury-laden words. Language he'd never used in her company. Language he'd been known to vehemently disapprove of. And second, the dates. He'd wanted to go to the river party on that day. But couldn't. Thank God.

'Kirstin? You okay?'

She realized that she'd been staring, eyes unfocused, at the pages now lying beneath Glen's hands.

'I . . . I'm sorry. I just don't remember him being like this, *ever*. And the language. He's got utter contempt for these people. Perhaps with good reason but . . . it just doesn't seem like him. These read like . . . well, they're almost ravings at one or two points. I just don't recognize him here. Do you know what I mean?'

She knew her look was pleading. *Please agree with me, but help me too. I need to understand.*

Glen offered her another sympathetic smile. 'Yes, of course I do. The Jamie I first met and knew was, I think, the one you so fondly remember. What's here is not what I thought Jamie was doing at the time he was working for me. I knew he had issues with Iona Sutherland and the others. But I didn't realize how far it had gone. I didn't realize it had become so personal.'

Kirstin flicked her hand towards the pages. 'I

don't understand. Didn't you see these? Weren't they written for you?'

Glen shook his head and moved a palm over the typed sheets as if trying to hide them from her eyes. 'Not exactly. You see, it seems he had two sets of logs. The official one, and a set he called 'alternative' logs. Two sets of notebooks, two sets of transcriptions. A double life. It seems he began the practice sometime in the early summer when he'd become increasingly incensed at the group's abuse of the river. I suppose it was a way to vent feelings he couldn't share with anyone else.'

She frowned. 'So, how come you have these now? Are you the only one who's seen them?'

He sat back, glanced out of the window. 'Yes, I am.' He sighed. 'Jamie handed them over to me, along with his laptop and the disks. I suppose he could just have disposed of them. That wasn't in his nature, though. I don't have to tell you that Jamie was an honest man. He was in a dilemma and he chose to put his trust in me. He asked for my help.'

'Help?'

'As you can see, Jamie knew about the party that was planned that day. Intended to go down there and catch them. Luckily, *very* luckily for him, his hip let him down. But he was worried. After the killings he came to me in a panic. What if the others in the group told the police about their feud with him? What if they started looking at his logs? I calmed him down. I doubted very much that the police were going to look at a seventy-year-old overzealous volunteer. Apparently Ross had reassured him in much the same way. Jamie was feeling guilty about being horrible to horrible people. And now some of those people were dead. Also, I promised that should the police ask me about any of it, I would support him unreservedly. I wouldn't divulge the existence of these. He was, after all, in the right, even if he'd gone *way* over the top about things.'

Kirstin leant over the desk, trying to get Glen to look at her. He seemed transfixed by the view of the hills and river.

'So, did you have to lie to the police?'

At last, he tore his eyes from the view and looked directly at her. 'An officer came to see me about the Iona Sutherland letter. It wasn't anything heavy. They were looking at everything then. The group hadn't raised hell about Jamie. I imagine he wasn't on their radar. They were all too traumatized by the killings, I suppose. I told the officer the truth. That Iona Sutherland and her friends had been a pain in the neck and that I, on behalf of the association, was thinking of taking some legal action against them. I praised Jamie's work, showed the officer a sample of his logs. The official ones. And that was that. I wasn't asked anything more. I didn't have to lie.' He paused to finger the file again. 'But had they dug any deeper, I would have. You see, there are more notes. Notes that Jamie didn't transcribe. I think the reason for that is clear.'

Kirstin felt a stab of anxiety. She watched as Glen flicked back through the file. He passed a sheaf of Polaroids across the desk to her, then flicked back through the small notebook. Stopping at the page he wanted, he handed it over.

'Brace yourself.'

<u>Sat 12/8/06</u>
I am almost ready. The backpack is supplied: logbooks (2 including the 'alternative' one), flask (with a wee dram in it!), mini-binoculars (in case the dipper makes an appearance), pen and torch on string, sketch-ing pencil (in case of creative urge), sandwich box, baseball cap. AND my new digital camera. How kind of Ross. Such a practical gift for an old man.

The old-fashioned way of catching them out is gone. The Polaroids had their limita-tions but showed enough: the disgusting Iona Sutherland and her consort, Craig Irvine. Faithless swine! Indulging in a repulsive embrace and worse! By the wall at the weir of all places. Sacrilege! Mouths and bodies locked together. Poor innocent, naïve Morag. Surely it's time for someone to care. Should I show her these? She is far too good for Irvine. He and his bit of skirt — disgusting, filthy, repulsive pair — are making a fool of her.

But no matter. There are far better pictures to be taken tomorrow of the whole shower. They'll be sitting ducks, insensible from their bacchanalian indulgences. Unequivocal evi-dence of them sullying my river.

I WILL CATCH THE DESPICABLE WRETCHES THIS TIME. THEIR GAME IS UP.

9

Kirstin knew Glen was waiting for some reaction. She stood, scooping up the notebook as she rose, and walked to the far corner of the office. It was her turn to look out at the distant view of the hills, and to listen to the rhythmic burbling of the river a few yards below.

Eventually, she wiped at a tear and looked away from the beauty of the vista outside, turning the notebook over in her hands. Part of her wanted to hurl the thing into the Water of Leith. *Let the river take it away to where it belongs!* Another part of her wanted to hold it for hours, know every word within it, and see if somehow she could intuit what had transformed a dear old man into a ranting, obsessive, peeping Tom. What had made him curdle like this? Or was this a part of Jamie that had always been there but he'd never let her see it before? The thought chilled her.

She'd been unaware of Glen standing up and walking towards her. Gently he eased her fingers from the notebook.

'Come on. Please, sit down.'

His strong hands settled her back in the chair and he moved round the desk. Slowly, he gathered the sheaf of photographs, his hand covering the near-naked bodies of Iona Sutherland and Craig Irvine caught in writhing passion by the weir. Jamie had dated the snaps on the back and this encounter was long before their final, fatal coupling. It seemed these two had been enjoying each other's company for quite some time.

Glen began putting the file back together. 'I'm wondering if I should have shown you all this. I suppose I had a selfish motive, in that I've not been able to share it with anyone. It's been burning a hole through me. Especially after Jamie died. So, in an odd way, your appearance here has been something of a godsend. I can share the . . . guilt, I suppose, the overriding feeling that maybe I should have seen more, done more. I don't know. And yet, the real guilt is in eventually having to deceive.'

'De — ' She could barely find her voice. 'Deceive?'

He'd finished with the file and slid it to one side. 'Because after Jamie died, I *did* have to lie to the police. And I don't know if I've done the right thing. By Jamie, by his son. And now, by you.'

She sat up, straining to compose herself. 'Go on.'

This time, his direct look had gone, his gaze straying past her. Seeing something else? In the past?

'After Jamie died, they came to see me. Asked if I could think of any reason why he might have been distressed. The suicide theory was obviously the one they favoured.'

'And?'

'And I told them everything was fine, that Jamie had been absolutely normal. They

73

mentioned the Cauldron killings. Did they upset him? I said that they upset everybody. They obviously didn't appreciate how obsessed he was with Morag's case. But in a way that didn't matter. What I couldn't have them knowing about was the logs, the photos, the hatred of Iona Sutherland. It would just have made everything . . . messy. And hurt people. Ross, the dead people's families . . . it would have been complicated.'

She felt unaccountably cold. 'Complicated.' The word Ross had used.

Glen glanced back at her, waving a hand over the file. 'I should have got rid of all this ages ago. I don't know why I kept it. But at least it may have helped you. Painful as it might be, you can see a bit of what was going on. Jamie changed all right. I'm just not really sure why. I *think* he eventually found life too hard once his career and his wife were gone. Circumstances overwhelmed him. The river work might have helped but the clash of personalities with Iona's group, then the killings, then the accusations against the only one of them he liked.'

'Why was he so eager to help Morag? What made him so convinced of her innocence?'

He frowned, as if pondering the question for the first time. 'Actually, I don't know. He just judged people, didn't he? Took a position on them — for good or ill — and stuck by it. You must know that?'

She nodded, a smile involuntarily returning for a fleeting moment. 'Yes, he was quite a one

74

for first impressions. And he was usually right.'

Glen was trying a faint smile back. 'He was loyal, I'll say that about him. But . . . everything I've just outlined . . . I think it was all too much. I believe it led to a downward spiral. A chain reaction.'

She didn't want to vocalize the thought, but it was there in the air. 'You think he took his own life? I'm sorry, I find that so hard to believe. And it's not what Donald thinks either . . . though he hasn't seen what you've shown me, thank God. But it just doesn't fit with the Jamie I knew. Not suicide.'

Glen's sad half smile was fading. 'I don't know if it was *intentional* as such. But he *would* have known the danger of going down to the Cauldron in those conditions. There had to be some self-destructive impulse involved. I've thought about that every day these past five months.'

Without warning, he sat up straight and banged a palm on the desk, making her jump. 'It's left me sad but, from time to time, so angry. Whatever happened to Jamie, some of those bastards that made his life a misery are responsible. At least in part. To that extent, you could say that the river work killed him. If he hadn't met that lot . . . but maybe that's too simplistic. I can't afford to think that way. I couldn't live with myself.'

He slumped back again, the momentary spurt of fiery energy gone. 'And, as for those sods, it's pointless trying to get back at them. Two of them are dead. And I suppose the rest of them don't really matter. Initially, after his death, I had fantasies of telling all, and then shaming those that are still living. I'm thinking of Alistair Sutherland and Fraser Coulter in particular. They led Jamie a merry dance. But,' he splayed his hands over the file, 'but *this* makes it all too . . . well, as I say, complicated. By shaming them, you forever taint his memory.'

The impulse grabbed her without warning. She needed to get away, breathe some outside air.

'I . . . I'm sorry. I must go. I want to think about all this. It's . . . not what I expected to hear today.'

'I'm sorry. I shouldn't have told y — '

She raised a hand. 'No, no, don't apologize. I'd far rather know what was going on, whatever it was. It's just . . . I need to go now.'

He was at the door before her, opening it and gently placing something in her hand. 'Here. My card. My home number, mobile, everything's on the back.'

★   ★   ★

He walked past the deserted reception area and back into his office. At least she'd allowed him to escort her to the car park. He sat back down at his desk, hands clasped, as if in prayer. It had been a lot for her to take in. But he had done the right thing. He'd thought long and hard about it after Donald's call.

His hands dropped on to the desk and, slowly, he retrieved the notebook. There had been nothing to worry about. Kirstin Rutherford wouldn't have stumbled on it during a cursory look. But he knew exactly where the entry was.

Mon 14/8/06
All hell has broken loose. I am utterly at a loss. I feel sick all the time. I can concentrate on nothing. Every minute of the day I try to blot out the memories. But they are seared into my brain. That is my punishment and I cannot escape it. Ross is worried about me, keeps coming round, phoning. Has offered to come and stay or has offered me the option to stay at his house for a while. I don't want that. I want to be alone. Away from everyone.

Tues 15/8/06
The police are still swarming over everywhere, interviewing everyone again and again.

Wed 16/8/06
Bad news. Two officers turned up this afternoon. I am to be interviewed tomorrow.

Thanks be. Glen has agreed to withhold the logs — or, rather, the 'difficult' logs. 'It's best all round.' He's right. We need to stick together. Anyway, he has little choice. Not only would the logs reflect badly on the association (and Glen) if they came to light, but there is a deeper worry. So I, in turn, will help him.

Gently, Glen turned the page, running a finger down the little notebook's spine.

I will not tell anyone that Glen was there on Sunday.

Sunday, 13 August 2006

Bonnie Campbell ambled along the ground floor of the Scottish National Gallery of Modern Art, easing her way through the throng, and turned right, back out of the main door. She wasn't really enthused by any of it today. Not by art, not by the prospect of a picnic, not by anything. The idea of spending long hours with that lot had depressed her from the moment of waking. She thought of pleading illness — calling Fraser, who was the most likely to be sympathetic without flushing out her lie.

'That was a short visit, Miss. Thanks for coming anyway. Enjoy the rest of your day.'

She smiled at the elderly security guard and walked out into the grounds, choosing a shaded, corner bench. The mobile had been left at home intentionally. To keep her choices open. If she did decide to opt out, then she'd use a payphone and no one could call her back to persuade her otherwise. What was the time? Damn, they'd all be there by now. She listed the options in her mind. Go home? No, she wanted to be out and enjoy some of the day. Go back into the gallery? Go to the picnic? Mentally, she plotted her journey. All she had to do was go round the back of the gallery, down the steps past the wooded area, over the footbridge and she'd have arrived.

Slowly she got to her feet, pushing her sunglasses firmly back into place. The sun's glare was merciless today. She approached the first flight of steps, peering to her left to see when the river came into view. She caught a glint of the Cauldron and veered off the pathway steps to her left. Then she picked her way carefully through undergrowth, trees and fallen branches, until she was satisfied with her vantage point. Ally and Iona were just arriving. Kisses and hugs all round. Morag looked tense, unhappy. Ally seemed in cockier mood than usual. Iona was already taking her clothes off in as close proximity to Craig and Fraser as possible.

'Darling Fraser, spread that rug out for me, would you? Morag, that sarong is absolutely gorgeous. It's new? You must tell me where it's from. I shall copy you. I need one for my hols.'

Her overloud, super-confident tones were carrying easily across the still waters of the Cauldron. Bonnie sighed. Could she bear it? A whole day with Iona, with them all?

She began to stand up from her crouching position, and froze halfway. Surely Ally couldn't have heard her? Nor seen her behind all this foliage. But he was staring directly over to where she was. She caught his frowning look of puzzlement before he turned away to accept a glass of wine.

As she rejoined fellow path-users and gallery visitors on the steps, she made up her mind. She'd go to the picnic. But not yet. Not without emotional preparation. She badly needed a meditation. Somewhere in the gallery grounds there would be a quiet spot.

★ ★ ★

An hour later, Bonnie paused just before the wooden bridge. This was her last chance. She could flee back up the steps to the gallery grounds. Or step on to the bridge and be swallowed up by the revelry, deafened by the drunken yells of greeting. She could hear them clearly now. Fraser was singing a guttural rendition of 'Flower of Scotland', at the top of his voice like some oafish football fan, Ally egging him on at every chorus. Iona's bray could be heard somewhere in the distance, with Craig's answering laughter floating across the water. Only Morag's voice was absent.

Bonnie took up her surveillance position again, peering through the foliage. They were all in sight. Fraser's football was stranded halfway across the Cauldron. She could hear him simultaneously curse and laugh as he stumbled, thigh deep in water, on his way to retrieve it. She smiled. Maybe it wouldn't be that bad after all. Fraser seemed on a high today and . . . well, he was at his best then. She watched his slim, bronzed torso twist as he reached for the ball and turned to throw it back to shore. With a firmer step than before, she moved out on to the footbridge and caught his eye.

He tried a wave. 'Yo! At last. My day is made!' At that, his footing eventually gave way and he fell back, the waters of the Cauldron momentarily enveloping him. She felt a fleeting tug of anxiety as his waving arm disappeared under the water. But, within seconds, he re-emerged, the soaking tendrils of his shoulder-length hair plastered over his face. Laughing and spluttering, he shook his head violently, the halo of spray radiating off him, refracted by the still searing rays of the late-afternoon sun into a rainbow of liquid colour. Bonnie stopped halfway across the bridge, amazed. He looked like some Greek god today. She should be glad to be here.

So why wasn't she? What was really bothering her? It wasn't just the irritation factor of some of the others. No, that was an excuse. She felt something more significant than that . . . wary? Afraid. How foolish. Today would be tense at times. She was certain of that. Surely nothing more than that. But the feeling was there. Niggling away somewhere deep in her mind. A premonition of something fearful?

If so, of what?

'Friends'

10

'You still enjoy coming here, don't you? I think that's a bit weird. But then that's you all over, isn't it, Bonnie lass?'

She ran ahead with a laugh, skipping away from his grasp, and then came down to earth again. Fraser had a habit of doing that to her. Making her momentarily joyful, and then leaving her annoyed, furious even. And guilty. Guilty that she could let out even one little giggle. At this of all places! She watched as he booted a bit of old tree branch along the river path, lost in thought now. In football shirt, shorts and trainers, she could imagine he was half his age. An unruly adolescent, instead of the self-made builder and property developer he now was, with an ex-wife and young son somewhere in the past. She looked at him more closely as he scuffed the branch along the path. His face had changed. He looked downcast, sad, older.

They were at the Cauldron now. She wandered over to the wall by the weir, kicked off her little fabric Chinese slippers, and sat down, bare feet dangling above the water, the golden polish on her toenails causing an array of spangles to sparkle in the sunlight. She wriggled her toes and blurred her eyes, imagining the spangles were shiny-scaled little fishes, leaping salmon-like out of the river. Then she lifted her head and watched as Fraser gave the tree branch one final boot that pitched it into the centre of the Cauldron with a loud splash. He manoeuvred himself on to the low wall beside her, discarding his trainers over his shoulder with a flourish. They watched the ripples from the branch make increasingly wide circles on the previously unspoilt surface of the water. She felt momentarily happy again. Just the two of them. Like children, their two pairs of suntanned legs swaying in unison, relaxed, as if they hadn't a care in the world. All was quiet except for the gentle shushing of the weir, the water low even by summer standards. His eyes were fixed on to the tree branch and she matched his stare. The effect was mesmeric as the branch glided its slow way towards them. Bonnie waited until it reached the weir, where it tumbled over to meet deeper waters, and caught the current for its final journey downstream.

She picked some loose stones from the wall and began tossing them randomly at the weir. 'I've been thinking about Ally, about how it's getting near the anniversary and everything. And I thought it's important to get down here again. I used to come out here quite a lot before I went away. What about you? How many times d'you think you've been here since . . . since last year?'

He didn't answer. Just continued staring at the spot where the branch had gone over. She felt him tense up and noticed that the previously carefree motion of his dangling feet had come to a halt.

'Look, I'm sorry, Fraser. It's just that I haven't seen you for ages and I won — '

Without warning he reached a hand out to her and laid it on her shoulder, his eyes not shifting from the spot on the weir that so transfixed him. 'Ssh, Bonnie. Enjoy the moment.'

She sat, her legs stilled now too, enjoying the light but firm touch of his warm hand. It had been too long since he, since anyone, had touched her. She strained against the urge to turn towards him, to lift that welcome hand and place it elsewhere.

★ ★ ★

Alistair Sutherland stood up from the low log, the movement causing a flurry of scuttling insects to and from the peeling bark of his makeshift seat. A stone's throw away he could see Fraser, head hanging, with a hand on Bonnie's shoulder. He looked nothing short of miserable. As for her? Well, she looked surprised and . . . and, what else? Almost happy, the hint of a smile playing round that surprisingly generous mouth. Yes, for someone so slim, so bird-like, she would have some unexpected charms to offer the right kind of man. To hear what she'd said had been impossible. But, whatever it was, Fraser wasn't responding. Not verbally anyway.

It was a surprise to find them here. Yet, by the law of averages, given how often he visited, it was only a matter of time before he bumped into one or the other. It wouldn't really matter if they saw him, should they decide to cross the bridge into the wooded area. He wasn't exactly hiding. Just making his pilgrimage. But he preferred to do that, *had* to do that, alone. What he was certain about, though, was that he didn't want to see Morag Ramsay here. Fat chance. From what he'd heard, she wouldn't dare cast her shadow. But what he'd do should she turn up . . .

A sound from behind had him swivelling round. Someone was coming down the steps from the grounds of the art gallery high above. Time to disappear. He moved swiftly off to his left, picking his way through the foliage until he was deeper into the wooded area. He could have found his way blindfold to the spot. There was no evidence of anything untoward now. Just the images in his mind. There day and night. Iona. Gone. In an instant. Gone.

He parted the branches in front of him. To his right he spied a solitary walker crossing the footbridge from his side of the river. A gallery visitor enjoying a post-culture stroll? After a brief glance at the figures of Bonnie and Fraser, the walker turned to the right and marched briskly away. Alistair smiled to himself. The two of them hadn't even looked up. Lost in their own thoughts. Thoughts of what exactly?

★   ★   ★

She couldn't stand it any longer. Shifting to face Fraser, Bonnie put her hand over his and moved it down to her lap. 'Why won't you talk to me? I've been phoning and phoning and phoning. Ally too. You've both been ignoring me. Like I don't exist!'

He was allowing her to keep his hand. At last he'd decided to look at her. 'I told you. I've been in Spain, working on a couple of properties. And . . . and I needed to get out of here for a while. Get some sun. Put some distance . . . ' He looked away from her and turned back to his river-watching. 'I'm surprised you have to ask. You've been playing the disappearing act too. The only one who hasn't is Ally, and he's just doing the 'I want to be alone' thing. You're not the only one he's been ignoring. He won't answer my calls, emails, anything. It's absolute shit, Bonnie.'

She sensed he wasn't finished and stayed silent, watching his breathing quicken, his face tighten. He looked close to tears. Suddenly, he wrenched his hand away. Without a word, he raised his legs, spinning his body rapidly through a hundred and eighty degrees, until his back was facing the Cauldron. He reached down for his trainers, hurriedly shoving one on and fumbling with the laces. 'And now they've let that bitch Morag go.'

His outburst had taken her aback. She'd seen him angry, furious, only a handful of times.

'What's been going on, Fraser? With Morag — your statement, or evidence, or whatever it's called? What's happened? Tell me. *Please.*'

The frantic edge to her pleading had stopped him. He dropped the other trainer and turned towards her, lifting his leg to straddle the wall as if on horseback. But he wouldn't meet her eyes, merely looking past her into the distance.

'It's all complete crap. I've been fucked

around by everybody. The police. Clients have gone funny with me. Ally. *Everybody*.'

'Ally? I thought you hadn't seen him?'

'Well . . . I . . . I haven't as such. We talked a wee bit. Just about the Morag thing. He's livid about them letting her go. Absolutely beside himself.'

Tentatively, she reached a hand out and touched his arm. 'Please, Fraser. Calm down. Tell me what's been going on. Why you've been telling all these stories to the police. I don't understand. About that day, about Morag, about any of it. I don't see how you could have said . . . *known* she'd done it in the first place. You weren't with her. You were with *me* for most of the time during that . . . stupid bloody game. This is all making me scared.'

He shrugged off her hand. 'Leave it, Bonnie. Just leave it.'

She was near to tears, and there was something else. She felt fear. His erratic behaviour was more than unsettling. She sat in silence for a minute and then turned to him.

'Fraser, I don't know if you know, or if you care, but Morag is in a bad way. We all know that she's become a recluse in that big house of hers. And I, for one, don't blame her. But things are much, much worse than that.'

She noticed the quiver of his upper lip and thought that he was going to say something. But, instead, he turned his head away from her. The action hurt. Not only was it a rejection of her, but he was, literally, turning his face from the truth. But she wanted, needed, for him to hear her out.

'I may not have seen much of Morag lately, but what I saw was enough. She's . . . well, she's having mental and emotional problems. They're well hidden, but I can tell. Add to that the fact that she's broke. Morag's going to lose that house. She's going to get out, leave Edinburgh completely. Oh, she told me in that typical Morag, cavalier, devil-may-care, cold way of hers, almost in passing. But I can read between the lines. What's happened to her has finished her off.' Bonnie paused again, hoping, praying, that something of what she'd said would penetrate Fraser's now icy exterior. But still he remained silent. She looked down towards the sparkling waters. 'I know it's very late in the day to admit this but . . . but I don't believe Morag deserves what she's got. Unless you know, *really* know something about her that I don't. If you do . . . *please, please tell me.*'

She could feel tears of near panic rising up in her as he continued to stare away from her, unnervingly still.

11

With stabbing fingers Fraser Coulter closed the spreadsheet. He stared for a moment at the glowing computer screen and then logged off. Exhausted, he sat back, welcoming the blackness that the extinguished screen had plunged him into. The afternoon's encounter with Bonnie had been wearing and the evening's grim work trying to balance the books had just about finished him off. He topped up the gin tumbler, his unsteady hand causing the bottle to clink repeatedly against the glass, and then leant back, looking into the darkness of his study and sipping at the drink. A wind had been whipping itself up as he'd worked and now he let himself listen to it ripple through the trees and shrubbery in his back garden. He loved this house. Similar in design to Morag Ramsay's, an acre or two away to the west. The same architect, in fact. But while she'd left hers untouched, he'd made his own modifications. He'd been proud of the work, much of it accomplished by his own sweat and toil plus that of a few skilled craftsmen. Yes, he'd proved to himself that he could still get his hands dirty.

His own home was as good an advert for his skills as any of his commissioned work, and he wasn't averse to displaying countless digital images of it to attract clients, offering them a virtual tour via his website, or even inviting them to see the place in person. There was no doubt. He'd done well for himself over the years. From humble labourer with a burning aim to better himself, his achievement graph over the past ten years had been more or less a vertical rocket. Except for his marriage. Something was bound to give for the twenty-five-hour days of two-hundred-per-cent effort. And his marriage had been unable to take the strain.

After the birth of Sam, his wife had hung on for a couple of years and then boom! She'd gone. Now she was more than comfortably off with another husband, living in Truro. One *not* in the trade. Some dullard who came home for dinner at the same time each evening. Someone who was winning, if he hadn't already won, Sam's six-year-old heart.

He'd got over it, thanks in large part to this place and his decision to settle here. Ally and Iona had quickly made themselves known. Done a rapid social assessment of him — a clever bit of rough made good, with a useful skill. He'd cleaned up on commissions from their circle of well-heeled acquaintances. Then Ally had bestowed on him the ultimate compliment; he wanted to invest in his next development. Two developments, in fact. One in Scotland, the other in Spain. Yes, he'd arrived! His memory of that celebratory evening sealing the deal hadn't survived beyond three in the morning. But he *had* remembered Iona's form of congratulation sometime before that. Hurriedly but satisfyingly offered and gratefully received over this very desk. An offer occasionally repeated but *never* to be experienced again. He pushed away the ever-persistent image of her final day and refilled his glass, trying to rally himself and recapture happier memories of those breathtaking couplings.

Christ, if Ally had ever found out! Iona said it would have infuriated him, though she hadn't explained why. It seemed okay for Ally to know about her and Craig. In fact, Ally had approved of her liaisons with Craig. Encouraged them even. Partly, or mainly, because he couldn't stand Morag. He'd been reasonably friendly when Bonnie had first introduced Morag to them all as a new neighbour. But, once Craig had been brought into the circle, Ally had made it plain that he only tolerated her because Craig was such a hit. A funny, clever guy. And yes, there was no doubt his good looks had turned Ally's head. Ally had been jealous of Morag in that department. But he'd never stood a chance with Craig. Craig was one hundred per cent straight. It was a wonder Ally didn't go through the roof when Iona stuck her claws into him. But maybe he got a sort of kick out of it. Keep Craig in the family, as it were.

One row in particular, between Ally and Morag, still stuck in his mind. It had happened a couple of months before the killings, at one of Iona's lavish private views. Ally and Morag had been down in the basement strongroom, shouting at each other. He was telling her that Craig was too good for her, and that she was too old for him. That she should let him go. Eventually, Ally had emerged with a bleeding lip, which he'd lied about and laughed off to everyone else. But he'd let his real feelings rip when they were alone. *'I'm telling you, Fraser. She's neurotic, uptight. And dangerous. I pity Craig. I think she could be a real bunny-boiler.'*

As for Ally and Iona? They had had their fair share of stand-up rows. Jesus, the fireworks when Ally had been caught at a Christmas party getting it on with the latest in a long line of gallery assistants. Dom . . . Dominic, some poncy name like that. Spectacular! Typical Iona when she was in fiery mode.

God, Ally could be an arrogant sod at times. But that was all gone now. Buried. Under a cloak of something far darker. Fraser shivered as the night's breeze rustled through his garden. What a shitty day it had been. It wasn't just the business worries. He'd had yet another visit from those two detectives just as he was settling down to dinner. They were fast becoming his tormentors. *'As you know, we're still determined to pursue our inquiries into the deaths of your friends. We've been looking at the timings again . . .'*

Like hell they had. It was just another excuse to have a go at him about his statements. It had been a tense, almost threatening, twenty minutes. He had ended up throwing away his uneaten dinner and settling for a liquid one as he wrestled at his computer with the depressing figures. Should he get his solicitor to make noises? Waste of time. They were just rattling his cage. Issuing a warning. *We've still got our eye on the ball, on Morag, and we haven't finished with you.*

95

He shoved his chair back and walked towards the patio doors. All was black outside with just the faintest glow of light seeping round from the front of his house. Gin glass still in hand, he reached to close the shutters.

A rat-a-tat at the furthest window had him recoiling, the glass tumbling on to the soft carpet underneath, the liquor pooling and spreading beneath his bare feet.

'Wh — ?' His peripheral vision caught a movement.

Standing out in the garden was the last visitor he'd expected, or wanted, to see tonight.

* * *

In the space of half a minute his visitor strode confidently in, flicked on the light and took a leisurely glance around the room. Then he helped himself to a stiff gin and tonic before perching on the corner of the desk, to begin fingering the printouts.

'So, Fraser, I'm glad to see someone's working. How are our mutual business interests coming along? Sit. Let's hae a wee chat then, pal.'

He knew Ally was in belligerent mood, putting on that exaggerated tough-nut Edinburgh accent that felt like, and was probably intended to be, a mockery of his own. Fraser decided to ignore the needling. Ally was just too strange nowadays. Immediately after Iona's death, he'd gone into a deep, brooding, silent depression. That was understandable. But over time, and particularly since Morag's release, he'd remained uncommunicative. When he did engage in conversation, it was often a tetchy exchange. He'd frequently 'go missing' for long periods, refusing to answer phone calls or emails. To make matters worse, whatever inner turmoil had taken hold of him was now being reflected on the outside. A previously snappy, immaculate dresser, these days he looked scruffy. The polo shirt and shorts he was wearing were badly crumpled, as if they'd been slept in, and Ally's usual fashionably close-shorn head showed signs of growth. As did the goatee beard. But it was the eyes that gave it away. Bleary, exhausted, reddened. From sleepless nights, from weeping — or both? And he seemed to be losing weight by the day. As Ally brought out his cigarette packet, Fraser noted the tremor in his hands. *Join the club.*

He shook his head at the proffered packet, and quickly snatched up the gin glass from the floor, rubbing a handkerchief over the damp patch of carpet. Then he grabbed another tumbler and poured himself a drink, before wheeling his office chair towards Ally. He sat back, feet on the desk, cradling his gin as if he hadn't a worry in his head. He didn't like giving Ally the advantage of being seated above him. But he was sending out the message he wanted. *I'm okay. Okay enough to let you tower over me. I'm not intimidated, pal.*

Ally leant towards him. 'How's Bonnie, then?'

'What?'

'I saw you both today. By the Cauldron. Deep in thought.'

97

Shit! This was all he needed. Where the fuck had Ally been? Not skulking on the other side of the river, not at the scene? He wasn't still doing that, haunting the place? For weeks, months, after his sister's death, Ally had spent days, and even nights, wandering about the Cauldron. It had been unsettling behaviour. But surely all that had stopped? Evidently not. The realization confirmed Fraser's suspicion that Ally was on a downward slope. He took short sips of the gin, playing for time, before finally deciding to feign an unruffled, casual approach with Ally.

'Oh, so you were down there too? You should've said hello. Yeah, Bonnie and I were just catching up, what with me being in Spain. And she's been away too. She was asking after you. Said you weren't answering her calls. I said I hadn't seen you much either. She's doing all right.'

Ally had shuffled the printouts into a neat pile and was resting them in his lap, hands clasped on top. The now familiar sarcastic stare was there, taunting, goading. Fraser broke off eye contact as he wiped an imaginary drop of gin from his lap. He felt Ally move, the desk creaking under his shifting weight.

'*What's been going on, Fraser . . . ? What's happened? Tell me. Please.*' Ally's tone was a high-pitched caricature of Bonnie's voice.

Fraser whipped his head up. 'What?'

Ally gave a brief smile, stubbing out the half-smoked cigarette before answering. 'You could've heard her bloody wailing and whining down at Dean Village. 'I could only hear her

98

loudest and most irritating shrieks, but I assume she's been bleating on about Morag.'

Fraser couldn't bear the power imbalance any longer and stood up, moving back towards a side window.

'Look, Ally, Bonnie's far from being on an even keel. Not that she ever was, mind. But this has blown her to pieces. She's a nervous wreck. You know she's talking of leaving? And she was asking about Morag. What am I meant to say?'

He risked a glance at Ally, who was shaking his head, a twisted smirk on his tired face. 'You can tell her that you were once a friend, but one that eventually chickened out when things got tough.'

'That's not true. I helped you as much as I could. But it's got out of hand now. At this rate, *I'm* the one who'll end up in prison! For attempting to pervert the course of justice.'

Fraser waited for a response but Ally just sat in silence, his head bowed. Then, there was the faintest shuddering of his shoulders. Was he crying, laughing, or what? The sight was unnerving. A moment later, and with slow, careful precision, Ally slid off the desk, placed the printouts in a neat pile and moved over to the patio doors, his back towards Fraser.

'I feel utterly let down by you. Betrayed. I believed in you as a friend. Gave you *everything*. Contacts, money, a welcome into my world. Now all you've succeeded in doing is making Morag feel safer. That silly, jealous, insecure, drunken, drug-crazed fool of a woman.'

Fraser felt stung by the accusation of betrayal. He moved back towards the desk and began fussing with the paperwork.

'Look, Ally. What do you want? Did you come here specifically to pick a fight? You've been ignoring me for ages, now you suddenly pop up at dead of night and saunter in like old times. I don't have a clue what's going on with you these days and, frankly, I'm beginning not to care. Besides, I don't feel like company right now. I've got a lot on my mind.'

More silence. Fraser turned in time to see Ally's fists clench before he spoke.

'And I've not? I just want to know why you didn't stand by your statement. *I* always said she was guilty. *You* always did.'

Fraser turned back to his paper-shuffling, wishing he had the guts to fling Ally out of the door. He didn't need this, not tonight. 'You're doing a fair bit of rewriting of history here, Ally. You didn't *always* think Morag was guilty. None of us did. The police's random-nutter theory seemed to suit us all at first.'

Ally raised a hand at him. 'Oh, *please*. The police were useless. We were all in shock, incapable of rational thought. But the police should've known better. They were incompetent. They should've done their job. Looked at those closest to the victims — it's usually one of them — and locked Morag up straightaway.'

Fraser gave up on the paperwork and turned round again, gesturing for Ally to sit down. 'All right. Here, have your drink.' He handed over the glass and pulled his office chair forwards, straddling it, his chin and hands resting on the back. 'Look. My second statement to the police, the one that got Morag into trouble, was a pack of lies and you know it. Yes, you'd won me round to thinking she could have done it. Yes, I was happy to do you a favour to get her put away. But . . . but as the thought of standing up in the witness box got nearer and nearer, I . . . I just thought, no way. I'm not up to that, and . . . and I don't know about Morag any more . . . her being guilty, I mean.'

Ally slammed down his glass. 'So, you're standing up for her now, eh?' Raking back his chair, he marched towards the patio doors, hands thrust into pockets, and stared out into the night. 'I never liked Morag Ramsay. That's no secret. Craig was far too good for her. But I tolerated her. Her jealousy and possessiveness weren't my problems. They were Craig's. And her envy of Iona . . . well, Iona could give as good as she got in the catty women stakes. But Morag was more than that. In retrospect, she was a psychopath. It *had* to be her. There was no other plausible explanation. No random nutter running amok. And none of us wished Iona or Craig ill. Just Morag.' He shrugged his shoulders, and continued staring out at the black nothingness of the garden. 'All I wanted from you was to 'help' the evidence, the case, along a bit. How the hell can you say now that she didn't do it? How can you have helped them let her go?'

'Oh, come on, Ally. You're getting things out of perspective. They would have let her go anyway. They didn't have — and still don't have — enough to hold her.'

101

Ally spun round. '*At the moment.*'

Fraser nodded. 'Yes, okay, at the moment. But, listen. I don't know for sure if she did it or not. But what I do know is this. The absolute bloody irony of it all is that if Morag hadn't been drugged and boozed up, she either wouldn't have done it in the first place *or*, if she had, she'd have remembered and admitted it. *That*, I know, is too much for you to handle right now, but it's time it was said. Iona may have brought it all upon herself. And that's why I wasn't prepared to get up in court and lie.'

He knew he was pushing it. 'And we're guilty too for colluding in her stupid childish games. I see it now. You might think I'm some kind of rough, pig-ignorant dunce, but you'd be wrong. I recognize what you and Iona were doing. What you are. What you were. Like some secret, silent virus, infecting us all with your apparent charm when, beneath that charm, you, *both* of you, were eating away at us, playing with us, fucking us around *and* fucking each other around. Oh, you used to be a nice guy a lot of the time, but the arrogant side of you — pumped up by Iona, of course — thought you were a real player. Well, there's a price to pay for that kind of manipulation. And it's been and is being paid right now!' He took a deep breath. 'And, guess what? I can be a bit of a player too, *pal*! You didn't have a clue, did you? About me and Iona. That I too had sampled her charms.'

He knew he'd gone too far. Ally took four rapid steps forward. Fraser flinched. Was Ally going to hit him? But instead, he slammed his palm down on the desk. 'You shit, Fraser. That's it. *That is bloody it!* You're no friend of mine. Just . . . Just keep away from me. I can't trust you, can't depend on you for anything ever again.' With that, he marched towards the patio doors and wrenched them open.

Fraser jumped up. 'Look, stop! Ally, I'm sorry.'

But Ally had disappeared into the garden and was tramping across the windswept lawn, taking a short cut down to the road.

Fraser shouted after him. 'Morag's going to get her come-uppance anyway! Bonnie told me what's happening with her. She's going bankrupt, will lose the house, lose everything.' He began trotting down the garden, desperate to catch up with Ally. 'She's got no family to speak of and she'll be marked out as the killer who got off, wherever she goes. She's broke *and* she's losing her mind big time by all accounts. She's finished, Ally. *Finished, understand?* Whether she ends up in prison or not, one way or another, she'll be gone soon and probably end up selling the *Big Issue*, if not herself, down at Leith docks. Oh, and if it makes you feel any better, I'll be following Morag to the bankruptcy courts before long. Wait, Ally, please! Don't just walk away like that! I'm sorry . . . what I said about Iona and me.'

Suddenly, Ally halted and turned on his heel. It was impossible to see his face in the darkness, but the voice was steely. 'I knew about you and Iona. You weren't important to her. She was just playing with you. She was good at that.'

Fraser swallowed hard, trying to keep control.

'Well, then. It looks like *I'm* getting my comeuppance all round. The business has gone to hell. I'm going to salvage what I can and get out of here as soon as possible. If I can sell the house for a decent sum, I might just break even and I'll pay you back what I can.' He held out his hands in appeasement. 'But . . . I've thought about this for weeks. We have got to let everything from last summer go now. I mean it . . . it's over, Ally. Just . . . just let it go, man. I'm sorry. Sorry that Iona's gone. Sorry for it all. But she *is* gone. Let it go.'

His last few words had dropped to a whisper, whipping away on the wind. Ally wasn't looking at him now. Instead, he'd half turned, ready to resume his journey down the garden. His body was eerily still, the wind flapping at the baggy shorts and shirt, his immobile silhouette like a near-ghost in the darkness. At last he moved his head to speak.

'You can run away if you like. Bonnie too, for all I care. But, I tell you something. *I'm* going to stay. Until I know Morag Ramsay is going to get what is due to her. Bankruptcy? Destitution? They're the least of her worries! She's got two creditors that she *will* honour. She will repay the debt she owes me. And, most of all, the one she owes Iona.'

Fraser shivered, watching as the ghostly figure moved silently away until it disappeared, engulfed by the night.

12

Kirstin approached Jamie's old house on foot, admiring the familiar sight before her. Jamie's home was a magnificent Victorian villa, with the ruins of an old water mill further along the riverbank, at the edge of the property. Halfway up the gravel drive, she caught sight of Ross standing by a ground-floor bay window. In shirtsleeves and suit trousers he'd obviously come straight from work. His right hand was cutting short sharp chopping movements through the air as he spoke into his mobile. Probably making mincemeat of some poor minion who'd been forced to stay late at the office.

Although the day had, inevitably, been another hot, steamy affair, by late afternoon the clouds had descended. Now, the night air was humid and heavy with the threat of thunder. Maybe she should have brought the car. She checked her watch. After nine. She'd allowed Ross to set the time for her visit; he was the one with the busy job, after all. Besides, it had left her free to talk to Donald Ferguson again, though she'd carefully omitted any of what Glen had confided in her. And she had called Glen. He'd seemed to sense her fragile mood over the phone and offered to meet up soon to talk more. She was grateful for the people who'd cared for Jamie. It was making her life easier, a bit less guilt-ridden.

Both Donald and Glen, from their very different perspectives, had reassured her that whatever had been going on with Jamie, she shouldn't blame herself for not being around. They *had* been around for him, and still he'd died.

She paused in the driveway, still gazing at an over-animated Ross. Was she up to this? The day had been stifling, on the emotions as well as the body. The encounter with Morag Ramsay had been draining. There was something insidiously infectious about being in the presence of someone so brittle and tense, with such volcanic, suppressed depths of anger and pain. And here she was about to face another person with hidden depths of bitterness.

She could remember the exact moment when she knew it was over, and that she was going to leave Ross. There had been no drama, no histrionics, no affair on either side. Rather, she'd been aware, by slow increments, of a change in him. He'd become more absorbed in his work, desperate to 'get ahead' at all costs, morphing into the kind of ruthless careerist she'd always abhorred. He seemed to have less and less time for her and her friends. She'd even resorted to going on holiday with *them*, leaving him happily slaving away at the office. And then finally, and most importantly, there had been his refusal to consider having children, fobbing her off with the 'not yet' excuse.

Ross had not seen her departure coming. It was a complete bolt from the blue. He'd tried, variously, pleading with her, stalking her, begging her to try again. And then, almost overnight, he'd curdled. After their separation, he'd insisted she stop seeing Jamie. She had little energy to fight Ross's anger and bitterness. It was time for her to go. Leave Edinburgh, leave the country . . .

She began walking again. *Forget about all that for now. Just keep calm.* As she reached the top of the drive, Ross looked up. He gave a nervous half smile and quickly wrapped up the phone conversation. She watched him jog out of the front room and, moments later, tracked his distorted outline as it approached her behind the frosted glass of the porch door.

'Hi, Kirsty, thanks for making the time. Come away in. Let's go to the morning room.'

His smile and demeanour were unusually welcoming. And perhaps too forced. She had tried not to react to his use of 'Kirsty'. Now was not the time to open old wounds. She nodded her greeting and followed in silence as the familiar sights and smells of a house she'd once thought of as a second home welcomed her back. She'd been anxious that any visit would have her collapsing in tears before she'd crossed the threshold, but she had been wrong. Rather, she felt comfortable, almost happy to be back and slowed her pace to take in the view down the wide hallway, glancing left and right at the few tasteful watercolours — multiple vistas of Edinburgh as seen from the top of Arthur's Seat and Calton Hill. And then, near the end on the left, Jamie's pride and joy. The photo gallery, which included several of her, enjoying various summers in the garden with the in-laws and

Ross. Although they brought back happy memories, she brushed them aside. It was the last two images that held her gaze. One, captioned *Jamie's first day as Head Warden*, showed him uniformed, standing to attention, but smiling. A wide, joyful beam, hiking stick in hand, the weir and Cauldron shimmering in the background. Finally, *My Jeannie*. A simple shot. Jean, caught unawares, sitting under a sunshade in the back garden, homemade lemonade to hand, her nose in a book. '*It's how I remember her, Kirstin. How I'll always remember her.*'

'Wine? I've got some chilled rosé.' Ross had pulled the bottle from its cooler and was waggling her favourite summer tipple in mid-air.

She was determined to sustain a jolly tone. This was going to be a difficult enough encounter. 'That'll be great, thanks.'

She was aware that they were both on their best behaviour tonight, walking on eggshells, and she was content to play the game a bit longer. She wandered over to one of the huge windows that gave a view over the back garden. Unlike Morag Ramsay's house, set high up on the hill a mile down-stream, Jamie's was within touching distance of the river. A short, well-trimmed lawn, with some carefully colour-coordinated bedding plants at the sides, led to a gentle slope down to the river. The waters were running slowly tonight. A gentle summer flow. Nearby, Jamie's black rubber dinghy lay beached on the grass, oars askew.

She nodded her head towards the view as Ross

joined her, wine glasses in hand. 'Who's been doing the garden?'

'Oh, a guy Donald recommended. Actually, Dad went off the garden this past year or so. Only interested in being on the river, so he got someone in. Does a good job. Charges through the nose for it, though.'

Uninvited, she dropped her bag to the floor and sat on one of the two luxurious sofas that formed an outward-looking nook designed to encourage guests to face the river view. She continued staring out of the window, aware that Ross was hovering nearby, unsure whether to share the same sofa. Sensibly, he opted for the one opposite.

'Look, Kirs — '

'Ross, I wa — '

Their openings had been simultaneous, leaving both in a momentary hiatus of embarrassed silence. She was the first to laugh it off, and Ross joined in a second later with an overloud guffaw that left her wondering if he'd been drinking before she arrived. He held up his hand as if pleading to talk first. She nodded for him to continue.

'Listen, Kirsty, I'm pleased, really pleased you came. I wasn't sure if I should call, but I took the risk and I'm glad I did. I want to apologize properly. I was thinking of writing you a card or something, but it's better that you're here in front of me.' He paused to clear his throat before what was obviously going to be a difficult speech. 'I admit, I could've got hold of you somehow to tell you about Dad. But . . . but I was so overwhelmed by everything and I was still so . . . so *angry* at you. I know it's unforgivable, I do. And I know it's one of many, many, *too* many, unforgivable things I've done. You leaving me . . . it changed me. I knew, *know*, I can never get you back. I know, or think I know, why you left. Shit, I'm so crap at this! Look, I've lost Mum and Dad. To that extent I'm like you. I now understand when you used to talk about how it felt to be orphaned. After your mum died, when both parents had gone. I agree, it doesn't matter how old you are. When they go, you feel alone.'

He paused, giving them both permission to take some refuge in their wine. She wasn't enjoying this. He looked tired, almost on the verge of tears. His face was drawn and haggard, and it occurred to her that he probably wasn't eating. She half smiled at him and offered another, barely discernible nod to continue.

'Kirstin . . . I . . . I'm not sure how to put this, but I don't want you driving yourself mad over Dad. The truth is . . . he'd been going a bit funny since Mum died. And I *don't* mean senile. I mean he became very introverted. Oh, the river work helped, up to a point. But then . . . then he got everything out of proportion. The river became an obsession. Completely out of hand. I don't know where to begin. You probably don't know much of what I'm talking about. There were rows a — '

She held up her hand this time. 'I do know. I've been to see Donald. Met Glen Laidlaw. And I even got to see Morag Ramsay.'

110

Ross's glass stopped halfway to his lips. Eventually, he took a sip and then, slowly, leant forward to place the glass back on the coffee table between them. 'Right. I'd no idea. What . . . what have they been saying? Glen and . . . and Morag Ramsay. *Incredible*. Rumour is, she's effectively a hermit.'

She wanted to discuss everything Glen had told her, but he'd asked her not to. And anyway, it was a lot to dump on Ross, whatever she felt about him. Besides, she'd been unable to erase the uncomfortable, creeping feelings of disquiet that those photos had sparked off in her. Explicit. Pornographic. Taken by Jamie — the Voyeur? Or by Jamie — the Crusader for Moral Justice? A misguided act but with honourable intentions? Glen never seemed for one moment to have considered them sinister.

She was aware that Ross was staring at her, waiting for an answer. 'Morag Ramsay . . . eh, yes, she doesn't venture out much. I presume you know that your dad was trying to get involved in her case? Had been to visit her in prison?'

Ross gave a slow pitiful nod of his head. 'Oh, yes. We had a big bloody row about it. And that's just an example of what I was talking about. To try and sympathize with this Ramsay woman as a . . . an acquaintance, and I'm loathe to say that she could've been a friend, that's one thing. Maybe even to visit her, though I was taken aback by that. No, it was this *interfering*, these offers of 'help'. Dad didn't know the first thing about criminal law! He was a property and

111

commercial law man through and through, just like me. The last thing he knew about was murder, for goodness' sake!'

'She was charged with *manslaughter*, Ross. There *is* a difference.'

He shrugged, knocking back the last of his drink and pouring himself a refill. 'Yeah. But watch this space.'

'Meaning what, exactly? I take it you don't like her?'

He shrugged again, glancing out towards the river, now barely visible as night approached. 'I don't know her as such. Just seen her knocking about the river. I advised Dad to let her own legal team get on with it, and to be careful in his unquestioning trust of her. Dad painted this glowing picture of her. That she was really nice, vulnerable, even though she could seem a bit cold and unfriendly on the outside. I wasn't convinced. I wondered if she was just a good actor. Charming and 'nice' when she wanted to be, but inside really a bit of a calculating, cold fish. In fact, from what I know now about her and her so-called 'friends', I wonder if she was using him. Trying to get him to soften his stance on her group, where she wasn't exactly popular, and so gain some admiration from them.' His eyes flickered towards hers, looking for some reaction, and then he glanced back to the river. 'It obviously didn't work. Dad was faithful only to the river's needs. Though once she was arrested, she knew she could count on him for unconditional belief in her innocence. No, I wasn't convinced. After all, the most unlikely people can do the most awful things.'

'I don't know, Ross. Jamie was a pretty good judge of character. And, having met her myself, I don't agree with you. I think Morag Ramsay's a genuine person. I'd guess she's got a lot of problems, emotional ones, some of which I think were there long before the deaths of her boyfriend and Iona Sutherland. The only credence I could possibly give to her being guilty is if she did it and can't remember.'

He laughed. 'Hah! Barely credible.'

'Not so. I don't know what that lot were on, but they were having a high, and I mean *high*, old time together. It's perfectly possible that she had amnesia. I've known you to have memory lapses when you've overindulged.'

'Hardly comparable.'

'Oh, come on, Ross. Did you know that some of these so-called friends of hers had been spiking her drinks? They sound a bloody unpleasant lot. With the exception perhaps of Bonnie Campbell. But she hasn't exactly rushed to stand up for Morag. It's a shame. If even one of that group had stood by Morag, she'd be in a better state than she is today.'

Ross clattered his glass down on the table with more force than was necessary. 'And doesn't that tell you something? Maybe her friends knew her better than anyone else. I told Dad as much. Warned him. Maybe I should warn you too. Be careful with this woman.'

She shook her head, exasperation taking hold at last. 'I'm not stupid, Ross. But, my first impressions of her made me think she was okay.

113

The thing is, I don't see how she could have done it anyway, even if she did have genuine amnesia about the event. There would've been other evidence. Actually, I feel sorry, very sorry, for her. She reminds me of some of the poor souls I used to meet when I was a paralegal. Some really sad cases. Victims, dumped on by all and sundry. Morag Ramsay's one of them. She just hides it a bit better than most. Her brittle, defensive attitude makes sympathy hard to come by. In fact, if it came to court, I reckon a jury wouldn't take to her one bit. And that would be bloody unfair.'

Ross was shaking his head in disbelief. '*God, Kirsty!* You were always such a soft touch. Just as well you never thought of being a prosecutor. You'd be letting them all off!'

The comment stung but she let it pass. He wasn't intending to be offensive. He was just being his usual patronizing, insensitive, infuriating self.

She shook her head back at him. 'Just being humane. That's all.' *You should try it sometime.* She accepted another refill and dropped her eyes, toying with the glass.

'Look, Ross. I'm glad you called. Really I am. And I'm glad I'm here. But I *don't* want to talk about us tonight. I want to ... ask you ... something. Something we only touched on at the cemetery. Tell me, what *exactly* do you think happened to your dad?' If she couldn't discuss her meeting with Glen, she could at least try to unearth what Ross was really thinking about the death of his father.

Ross didn't react immediately. Instead, he turned away towards the window, seeming absorbed in the blackness of outside. She wondered if he hadn't heard her. She felt the irrational urge to lean over and touch his arm, check if he was still breathing. Then he inhaled — a loud, deep breath — and turned to face her, full on, his eyes locked on hers.

'I *have* thought about it. Almost endlessly. And I *do* have an idea. It's not one you might want to hear . . . To find an answer, you need to go back four years. You'll remember some of that time, I'm sure. Dad's retirement was the start of it. He had great plans for doing all the things he and Mum hadn't done because he'd worked so hard all his life. The 'wonders' of retirement. Not in his case. The truth . . . the *bitter* truth for Dad was something else. The fact is, Mum was happy doing her stuff at home. The garden, reading, her coffee mornings, evening classes, and all the rest of it. All that stuff well-to-do, middle-class older women do. I'm not knocking it. Just stating a fact. Mum didn't want her life turned upside down by Dad's retirement plans. And once he recognized this, I think he quickly became disappointed. In short, their marriage worked because they had separate lives.'

He paused to break eye contact with her, and she thought he'd never seemed so sad, so weary. But within a moment he'd rallied and met her gaze once more.

'It's an age-old story. Mum's domestic life was already full and fulfilling. Dad felt a huge gaping hole in his. No work, no business lunches, no client dinners. All that he used to fill his days and nights with had gone. So it didn't take long for him to start drifting back into the office, 'on the off chance'. Once or twice at the start was fine. I and some of the more senior partners would take him out for a good lunch. But it wasn't long after that when he started quizzing me and others about cases, about old clients of his. And thereafter it was one short step to offering 'advice'. It was a very tricky situation. A bit of a nightmare, frankly.'

She looked at him, puzzled. 'Why didn't I know any of this?'

'I didn't want to worry you, and I freely admit I was a coward. I hadn't the balls to tell Dad where to get off. One or two of the older partners tried, but it was useless. They were old buddies of Dad's, still played golf with him. So they bottled out. Can't blame them. In the end it was down to poor old Mum to dish the dirt. And she didn't pull her punches. I came round for one or two Sunday lunches just after. Dad was depressed. The GP had put him on some tablets.'

'What? Antidepressants?' This was news to her.

'That's right. They helped. A bit. Mum had a private word with me about it and asked, *insisted*, that I didn't tell you. Dad wouldn't want it. He'd be embarrassed if you knew. Anyway, the medication worked up to a point. He and Mum were learning to coexist. Donald was helping too. He'd take Dad out, keep him occupied many days of the week. I don't think

116

Donald cares much for me, but I will say he was good for Dad.'

She watched Ross momentarily close his eyes, as if composing himself for the next words. 'And then, out of a clear blue sky, the worst happened. Mum died. Gone. And you know the rest. Well, most of it. Up until you left, that is. To bring you up to date, the last two years have been a nightmare. I believe Dad became mentally ill. He refused to see the GP or take any more tablets. I'm no psychiatrist but I think, in addition to his depression, there was the trauma of sudden bereavement. And there was tetchiness, and paranoia, and — I'm sorry, Kirstin — I think Dad finally got very, *very* tired of living. And remember, before you remonstrate with me about this, you *did not* see him during the last year and a half of his life. I did.'

She watched as he sank back into the deepest corner of the sofa. What had been a dignified and painfully frank speech had left him clearly exhausted. Ross was right. She had not been around. The Jamie she *had* known might not have killed himself. But there was another Jamie being described here now. Another Jamie that Donald, Glen and Morag had described to her also. Many Jamies, maybe. But not all of them were bad.

She shifted her position to lean towards Ross. 'Donald told me something about Jamie that both surprised and heartened me.'

'Oh?'

'Yeah, during the last couple of years before he retired — and for a while afterwards, I think

— Jamie was apparently helping some small wildlife and environmental groups in their struggle against a building development on the east coast.'

'He *what?*' Ross shook his head in astonishment.

She nodded. 'Yes, and that . . . well, it seems to go against this notion of him being terminally depressed, not engaged with the world. It suggests quite the opposite, actually.'

'The bloody fool.' Ross was still shaking his head. 'I hope to God it wasn't one of our clients he was advising against. He would have got us, the firm, into so much trouble. But . . . that doesn't matter now. It just underlines a spectacular loss of judgement . . . of *balance*. The fact is, after he retired, after Mum died, he got depressed, clinically so. Until the river work came up, but then he . . . mucked that up. He changed, went downhill. I'm sorry, but it's the truth.'

Kirstin leant back and glanced out towards the river, barely visible now through the darkness. A year and a half had led to untold change in her own life. For the better. Why couldn't the reverse be true for Jamie? To his credit, Ross had not tried to instil any guilt concerning her absence while Jamie deteriorated. He didn't need to. She was carrying enough of her own. Perhaps what Ross *was* trying to say as gently as he could was 'leave it alone'. But how could she? She was still left kicking against her ex-husband's firm belief in his father's suicide. Ross believed what he was saying. No doubt. But Ross didn't know what she knew. And if he did? Like Glen, he'd still come up with the same conclusion. That Jamie was somehow responsible for his own death.

She suddenly felt alone in it all. Glen might be troubled, but he'd already decided what had happened. Ross too. That left her and dear old Donald. It would have been laughable in other circumstances. Jamie's flag-carriers — a directionless divorcée and a seventy-odd-year-old man who missed his best friend. Oh, and maybe there was one other she could recruit, to complete a ridiculous trio. A vilified, furious and depressed woman. A woman everyone, except herself, thought was a ruthless killer.

13

Morag knew it was madness. Coming down to the Cauldron at dead of night. But she'd had a restless time of it since her disastrous session with Dr Lockhart that afternoon. Things were calming down again. Dr Lockhart had called her, obviously worried that she might rush into some foolish, self-destructive action. And here she was. *Morag, the Bitch-Witch-Cauldron-Killer, is out, at night, on her own, by the river!*

As she passed along the path, atop the hill opposite she could see the reassuring lights of her own house and the window where the telescope stood, pointed right towards her at this very moment. She imagined looking down at herself. Here she was, Morag the hermit, padding along on this surprisingly bright moonlit evening, leaving the heavy torch swinging redundant by her side. The occasional scuffles in the undergrowth, and the owls hooting above, were reminders that other creatures were keeping her company tonight.

She gathered the long-sleeved cotton shirt around her. The night was warm but with the gentlest of cooling breezes scudding along the wide river valley. All the nearby houses were in darkness. What hour was it? She'd left her watch behind. Unusually, *uniquely*, since her descent into hell, she'd stayed out on her patio until well after sunset — how proud Dr Lockhart would have been of her — listening to the radio, flicking through an old *National Geographic* magazine but taking little in. That morning's encounter with Kirstin Rutherford had been playing back and forth in her mind, eventually to the exclusion of all other worries: money, the house, Dr Lockhart, hypnotherapy.

There had been something heartening about Kirstin's visit. She felt believed. Kirstin had said that during her legal work she'd come across all sorts of injustice, and she had seemed to genuinely sympathize. That was important. Useful, maybe. Somehow it was more significant to be believed by her than by Dr Lockhart. And then there was Jamie. It was important to talk with someone who had really known him. Bonnie and she had talked about him after his death, but only in passing.

Morag shook her head. Bonnie had been a let-down. Just a couple of meetings, a meditation and a few phone calls were all she'd offered. She knew why. Bonnie was simply deeply uncomfortable in her company. She wished she'd asked the question the last time they'd met: 'Do you think I did it?'

Perhaps that's why she'd found Kirstin's visit so emboldening. Here was someone who was not quite saying but implying, 'I am, or might be, on your side. Let's see.' That, in turn, had freed her from the paralysing anxiety that had become her default mode of existence. And here she was taking a nocturnal jaunt to the Cauldron. Foolish? Maybe. Liberating? Certainly.

Morag heard the weir long before it came into

view. The familiar sound was welcome, almost making her smile. The freshwater scent drifted towards her as she approached the fringes of the Cauldron. She let the torch beam rove from side to side across the pool's glassy surface, eventually settling the silver disc of light on a point opposite. Where it had happened was too far in the wooded area to pick out. Should she, *could* she, cross the footbridge? She swung the torch to her left and ran its beam to and fro along the wooden structure. She swivelled to her right, the light flickering off the low wall where the game had begun. She took a few tentative steps towards it. Gently, she lowered herself on to the wall, swinging her legs over to dangle on the weir side in forced playfulness. But she knew her smile was no more than a bitter curl of the lip

The wretched irony. How she'd loved to stroll along to this very spot on a summer's evening and let the whoosh of the weir sweep her everyday woes away as she cooled her feet in the waters. And it had worked. Just like magic. Now look what she was reduced to. How long had it been since she'd dared to come back here? There had been regular pilgrimages soon after it happened. Some with the others. Then she had come alone a few times. She'd preferred that. Not having to deal with the others' reactions to the place. But this was her first visit since prison. Strangely, it was Jamie's presence she felt here tonight more than anything else. He'd died near this very spot. But on a very different night. The place transformed, the topography practically unrecognizable thanks to the power of fast-running water. Water he must have known would be a danger. And yet he came. She shook her head again, aware that her mouth was still twisted into a mock smile.

Jamie. Silly, stupid Jamie . . .

★　★　★

Morag felt tired now. How long had she been sitting here? She fought off the urge to lie along the broad flat surface of the wall and sleep until dawn. That could be done more comfortably in her home. Enjoy its comforts while she still could.

She began swinging her legs over on to the path when she heard it. Another scuffle. But louder, nearer than any of the previous ones. She grappled for her torch lying nearby on the wall, and listened. Again! That was no wild creature. Fumbling with the torch in her trembling hands, she pushed the 'on' switch.

14

Her beam caught the figure full in the face. Standing ten feet away.

'Turn that bloody thing off. You're blinding me.'

It took her a moment to recognize who it was. The voice didn't fit with the vision before her.

'Get it out of my face!'

She kept the torch on but shifted its beam to his side so she could keep him in clear view. It was Ally all right. But he was different, completely altered. Shirt and shorts were crumpled, his chin showed several days' growth, and she noticed that his left hand trembled as it toyed with a half-smoked cigarette.

'Ally?'

He took a step backwards, to escape the torch's glare. 'I'm astonished that you have the nerve to be here. I still spend a lot of time here, and I've not seen you. Well, not since they were foolish enough to let you out. Why have you come now? You've got no right to be here.'

Immediately, she felt the need to get away. What had she been thinking of, coming down here? It had been a mad idea. She knew Ally used to haunt the place, so why hadn't she thought about that on her way here tonight? She'd never known him to be violent, though she'd had her fair share of rows with him. But he looked so different now. Like he'd lost control of . . . everything. She had to leave but there was no room to back off. Her heels were jammed against the wall. Instead, she took two steps sideways as he approached.

She held up a hand, suppressing the instinct to flee. 'Ally, look. Wh — '

'I consider this to be a sacred place. For Iona, her memory. I can't believe you've got the nerve to be here. I tell y — '

Without warning he lost his footing on the bumpy ground and fell to his knees. The impact must have been agony on his legs, but he seemed not to feel it. The cigarette had gone flying. He ignored it as he scrambled to stand up.

She saw her chance and made a run for it, dodging round his body, the torch flickering wildly in front of her as she tried to avoid hidden obstacles on the uneven ground. But she hadn't given him enough clearance.

'Wait! I want to tell you something.' His right hand grasped her ankle and she felt herself falling, the torch arcing away overhead, its bright beam illuminating a useless path through the long grass as it fell to earth. He'd managed to get to his feet and was pulling her by one arm. 'Get up, Morag! I want to talk to you.'

He released her arm and stood over her. She began lashing out at him with both feet, scrabbling backwards out of his grip, thanking the gods that she'd worn stout trainers tonight. In a moment she was on her feet. He seemed momentarily dazed by the ferocity of her attack and backed off a couple of steps.

'For Christ's sake, Morag! Wait! What the hell are you do — '

'Get away from me, Ally! I mean it!' She spotted the torch and grasped it in her fist.

He was shaking his head. 'You are absolutely fucking mad. Go on, then. Piss off. But I want to tell you something before you go.' He began inching towards her as he spoke. 'I don't want our paths to cross here again, *ever*. You have absolutely no right to be here.' He was getting too near now. 'And I want you to know that I'm going to do *everything* in my power to make sure that the police get you. I swear to that.'

With her full strength she aimed the torch at his head, and hurled it, catching him on the left temple. 'Just . . . fuck off, Ally! Leave me alone!'

The blow had caught him off balance, and she watched as he staggered the few feet back to the edge of the Cauldron. The loud splash told her what she needed to know. She was tempted to move forward and see where he was. But fear took over. She turned on her heel and began racing along the path. As she sprinted away, one thing cheered and worried her in equal measure. He couldn't run after her now, but why had she heard nothing after the initial splash? Ally was a good swimmer. His instinct would have been to reach the riverbank. *Christ! Had it happened again?* Was this to be her justice? Damn it all, there was irony indeed! Seeing herself facing a prison cell for accidentally plunging her bitter enemy into the Cauldron. That would be too much to bear. Too much of a punishment to endure. As she hammered along the path towards the exit, she took one final glance backwards. Nothing. Had he got out and given up? Or was he lying at the silty bottom of the river?

Yet another victim of the Cauldron?

15

'*I . . . I want to go back down there to the Cauldron to see!*'

Kirstin held up a restraining hand and pressed Morag back into the passenger seat. They were parked, out of sight, near to Ally Sutherland's house.

'Please, Morag, we can't do that. Just wait. *Please.*'

The call on her mobile had woken Kirstin in what she thought was the middle of the night. In truth it had been just after midnight. She'd thought for a millisecond that it was a dream, but realized only too quickly that it wasn't. She'd driven to Morag's, breaking every speed limit, and arrived to find her a dishevelled, scratched and sobbing wreck, babbling almost incoherently that she thought she'd killed Ally Sutherland. But, as she calmed Morag down, the picture became clearer. He had, in some way, made her feel threatened, and she'd retaliated. In truth, Morag's actions had sounded like an extreme overreaction to Kirstin. But they were understandable. Morag had ventured out to the Cauldron, at night, for the first time in an age, to confront her inner demons. Instead, what she'd been confronted with was an all too real demon in the shape of Ally. If anything, Morag's relatively unprovoked attack underlined to Kirstin just how vulnerable the woman was. She should be helped, not condemned.

Morag had wanted to go back to the Cauldron to see what had happened to Ally. Kirstin couldn't think of a worse idea and suggested a compromise: that they drive over to his house to see if he'd come home. But they'd been waiting for twenty minutes and still there was no sign of him. Kirstin glanced outside. She was worried they might attract the wrong sort of attention in this sparsely populated and exclusive area. Two women, one in a clearly distressed state, parked late at night, seemed to be asking for trouble. But all was quiet. She looked again at Ally Sutherland's property, hoping to see some signs of life.

The house was of a modern, split-level design, like something out of a luxury car advert. The garage door was open, and, sure enough, there it was; the rear end of a top-of-the-range BMW. At least he wasn't in his car, then. The entire place was in darkness except for the faintest glow coming from somewhere on the ground floor.

'*Kirstin! Kirstin! Look!*'

She followed Morag's outstretched finger as it pointed through the windscreen and down the lane. Their wait had paid off.

'*It's him! He's alive! I must talk to him.*'

Morag had released the passenger door, illuminating the interior for a second, before Kirstin had time to switch it off. 'No, Morag! *Shut the door! Now!* Think what's happened, for goodness' sake. No one's going to talk to him tonight. *Look at him!*'

The tall shambling figure approached. Kirstin

touched Morag's arm, indicating that they should both slide down out of sight behind the dashboard. It was an unnecessary precaution, since Ally Sutherland was keeping his eyes directed firmly down towards the ground. Kirstin peered through the darkness, grateful that streetlights were few and far between in this area. Another couple of faltering paces and he'd reached his front door, where the porch light held him in its dim yellow pool.

Kirstin heard Morag's loud intake of breath and knew what had caused it; the state that Alistair Sutherland was in, plain for all to see. His clothes stuck to him, obviously still damp. His head had a deep gash near one temple, and there were a number of scratches around his shorn scalp. The left arm seemed to be causing him some pain and both knees were bleeding. He had certainly come off worse in his encounter with Morag. That apart, he had been lucky to reach home at all, and apparently without attracting attention. Presumably his homing instinct had taken over and got him back safely. He'd know the back routes and deserted streets of this quiet area. Now he was fumbling with a zipped pocket at the side of his shorts.

Kirstin thought it would have been comical under other circumstances. 'He must be looking for his key.'

Morag nodded in agreement, her eyes terrified, but she seemed transfixed by the swaying figure a few yards away. His repeated curses of frustration filtered down the drive and through the open driver's window, rising in volume with every failed attempt to undo the pocket. The struggle was obviously hurting his left arm and forced him to make a one-handed attempt. At last the zip gave and he wrenched out the jangling bunch of keys. Kirstin was waiting for the next stage of the pantomime. But by the second attempt he'd undone the locks and disappeared with a slam of the door.

Morag turned to her. 'What if he calls the pol — '

But Kirstin was already getting out of the car. 'I know. I've thought of that. Stay here. I'm going to see if I can hear or see what he's doing. If he's going to call the police, he'll do it straightaway. Now, wait. And lock the doors!'

She scurried up the short drive, half running and half crouching, until she reached a side window, praying that he'd not turned on some fancy security system that would suddenly flood her in its unforgiving glare. But there was nothing, only the continuing glow from the porch and a trace of faint light coming from somewhere deep inside the house. The window she'd settled by looked into what had to be a games room. A pool table held pride of place, cues neatly lined up in order of length, standing in a rack on the far wall. The door to the room lay to her right. It was ajar and the light was coming from what looked like the main hallway.

His sudden appearance in the doorway had her almost tumbling backwards into the shrubbery. He stood naked except for a white towel round his waist. After a moment, he turned to his left. The bar was small with two high stools situated either side. With his back to her, he switched on a wall light, immediately illuminating an array of bottles. Through the closed window she could still hear the clanking of bottle against glass. Without warning he turned round, forcing her to duck. With her back pressed hard against the wall, she was struggling to control her breathing. What the hell had she got herself into? This was sheer madness. It was time to go. If Ally Sutherland was going to call the police surely he wouldn't be behaving so damned casually, would he? She raised her head for the final time. He'd lit a cigarette and was standing at the far end of the pool table, slowly rolling the cue ball back and forth to the far cushion with his right hand. In his left, with some difficulty, he held a whisky tumbler and cigarette. She watched as he carried out the ritual five, six, seven times.

And then, without warning, he paused the white ball, trapping it under his palm. She noticed the shoulders first. Shaking. Then his upper body bent over the snooker table as he half collapsed on to the green baize. The whisky tumbler slid from his hand as he stubbed out the cigarette in an ashtray perched on the edge of the pool table.

The light behind him made it impossible to see his face, but she could guess at his expression. His entire body was wracked by powerful yet silent sobs as he pressed both palms against his eyes to staunch the flow of tears.

* * *

Kirstin's tired eyes squinted against the late-morning sun. Hard to believe that eleven hours ago, she had been peering nervously into Ally Sutherland's house and observing the most unexpected sight of him breaking down. Kirstin had kept that piece of information from Morag, for the simple reason that she had no idea what it meant. Had he just experienced the fright of his life and was sobbing with relief at his narrow escape? Or, was it a deeper expression of grief at the loss of his sister and his meeting with the person he genuinely thought had killed her? She didn't know what to think.

But now, here she was, back at Jamie's grave. Morag was bending down to place a loose bunch of white lilies, clutched tightly in both fists. Kirstin tugged gently at her shoulder.

'C'mon, Morag. Let's sit down. There's a bench over that way, in the shade.'

The wrap-around sunglasses were back, hiding the eyes, and Kirstin watched as, almost painfully, Morag got to her feet and stood hugging herself, fists still clenched. A muscular tension seemed to encase her entire body as she stood ramrod straight. Kirstin gave her a moment and then guided her towards the nearby bench, settling her down carefully, as if she was an infirm old woman, before taking her own seat. It was clear to her that Morag was in a bad way. Perhaps she should suggest they go round to her GP immediately and get an emergency appointment?

But Morag seemed to sense her concern, and turned to her, offering the hint of a smile.

'I'm okay now. Much better this morning.' The clipped, defensive delivery was back.

Kirstin nodded. *She doesn't want to appear vulnerable. Okay, let her be.*

'But I want you to know, Kirstin, to believe me. The truth is, I really thought he meant me harm. I know what you must think. The look of him last night. What I did. But Ally's a different person now. I can see why that should be, given the level of his grief. But, I think he might wish me real harm.'

'I *do* believe you, Morag. It was just the worst thing that could have happened. Him turning up like that. But . . . from what he said to you, it seems that he wants you charged with murder . . . that implies he wants to do things the official way. He may wish you ill, but that's a far cry from taking matters into his own hands. And he obviously hasn't reported last night's incident to the police or you'd have heard from them by now.'

Morag turned down her mouth in a doubtful mouse. 'Or, he's waiting to get his own back in some other way. I wish you could meet Ally. You might understand what I mean. But . . . mmm . . . maybe not. Anyway, I want to thank you. For bringing me here but also, mainly, for last night. We're effectively strangers, I know, but . . . I . . . just thought of you and I remembered having your number and . . . to be honest, I had no one else to call.'

Kirstin sighed. Morag was confusing her. One moment she seemed fully in control, the steely exterior deflecting any attempt at sympathy, yet the next moment she seemed to be worrying obsessively, adamant that Kirstin should believe her.

'It's fine, Morag. You did the right thing. Really. Just steer clear of Ally and try to forget about last night. It's over.'

But those few hours of the early morning had stayed stubbornly with Kirstin, the traces of fear and anxiety still clinging to her. Added to that was her sheer puzzlement at Morag's excessive behaviour and Ally's tearful reaction. But she was determined to hide her feelings and tuned back into Morag's voice, trying to shrug off the image of Ally Sutherland's injured, sobbing figure.

' . . . I *do* feel ashamed to say I had nobody else to call. It's . . . it's barely believable, but true. I used to have a wide circle of friends, far beyond the river crowd. But now? Who would want to befriend the 'Cauldron Killer Witch'?'

In a rare gesture of vulnerability, Morag raised a hand to wipe under her sunglasses with her fingertips. The last sentence had been said without trace of melodrama or self-pity. Indeed, Morag had almost whispered it, as if to herself.

Kirstin shifted in her seat, trying to see Morag's eyes. 'I know there's not a lot I can do to help, but I'm going to be around for a while longer. We can meet up, talk any time. Tell me, what's next for you?'

'Well, there's a hypnotherapist who is going to try to help me with my memory.'

'Really?'

Morag nodded. 'Yes. An initial session has

been arranged for next week. I'm dubious, though.'

'Dubious?' Kirstin frowned.

'I'm not convinced about it. I just want to get away from here and start a new life. *With* what, *as* what, I don't know. I don't even know if that's possible. The shadow of what's happened is not going to miraculously disappear. The police won't give up trying to get me. They just won't. It may sound a bit dramatic but I'm thinking of changing my name, my appearance, and then trying to get a job somewhere. England, maybe. Or I could go to one of the cities up north. Maybe not Aberdeen. Craig had links there. Possibly Inverness? I don't know. It all sounds so . . . so unachievable. Maybe it's an outlandish notion, d'you think?'

Kirstin shrugged. 'Not really. It's what you need, isn't it? To start a new life? But . . . with this hypnotherapy thing . . . don't you *want* to know what happened, find out what you can remember and wipe the slate clean, as it were? Then you can move on to your new life.'

Morag leant forward, elbows on knees, and stared at the ground. She wasn't answering. Kirstin caught her breath. Had she offended her by prying too deeply?

At last Morag looked up. The sunglasses were still locked in place, keeping her eyes invisible. 'I think I'm reaching the stage where I just want to run away from it all. The thing with Ally has pretty much decided me. I'd probably be better off trying to put everything behind me. And yet . . . he and the police will *never* be off my case.

It's bloody hopeless.' She let out a sharp, bitter laugh. 'Hah! Even though I don't have bars on the windows, I've pretty much been given a life sentence anyway, haven't I?'

'Yes, and I'm sorry for that. But if the hypnotherapy works, and even if the police won't recognize the outcome, at least *you'll* know, within yourself, what happened that day. Isn't that the most important thing?' Kirstin tilted her head and smiled, trying to encourage Morag to open up about the memory issue.

Without warning, she stood up. 'The bastard! How dare Ally threaten me! Say I can't go to the river! If he and the rest of them hadn't buggered about with my drinks and all the rest of it, I wouldn't be in this wretched position.' Anger at the memory of their betrayals almost crackled like an electrical current around her. 'I tell you this, I know now that Jamie was trying to be more of a friend than I realized at the time. And certainly more than all the rest of them put together. *Bastards!*'

She paused to take a deep breath, clearly trying to control her fury. 'You know, when Jamie visited me in prison, he said, 'I'm no longer in touch with her, but I wish you'd known my former daughter-in-law. She had a firm sense of what was just and unjust. Shame she's not here right now. We would have made a good team.' ' Morag straightened her hair and pushed the sunglasses more firmly into place. 'But it's too late for all that now. Far too late. Look, I want to make my own way back home. I'll . . . I'll see you.'

137

To Kirstin's astonishment, Morag bent stiffly and gave her a tight hug before pulling away and wandering along the dusty path. She gave a last turn of her head. Was that a half smile trying to cover the sadness and anger? It had been too fleeting to be sure. The mask of brittleness had been drawn down again before her final wave of farewell. Kirstin tracked the slim figure's progress, the warm breeze catching at Morag's light summer shirt, her words from Jamie's prison visit still hanging in the air. 'We would have made a good team.'

Kirstin slumped back on the bench, overcome by an overwhelming sadness that caught in her throat. She glanced over towards Jamie's gravestone shimmering in the morning heat. The tears came easily once she let them. She pitied Jamie, whatever change had overtaken him. She pitied Morag. And some compassion had to be left over for that wretched couple. What a way to die.

Despite her steely, defensive exterior, Morag had no power — it had all been lost long ago. No friends or supporters. Indeed, she seemed to have lost control over everything. Even the will to live. After all, hadn't she tried to end it all in prison? All in all, it was a surprise that Morag wasn't a gibbering wreck. And yet, wouldn't it be best if she tried to remember? But . . . who was she to say what was best for Morag? Thank God, she wasn't in her shoes.

Kirstin eased herself up from the bench and wandered over to Jamie's gravestone. Gently, she laid her fingers on the deeply chiselled letters of his name and began tracing them one by one. If Jamie had lived, Morag would have had a worthy ally in him, fearlessly championing her cause. No doubt he'd have ruffled feathers. Morag's cause would likely have become an obsession to replace his river work, irritating everyone: Morag's lawyers, Ross, the police. But so what? That was his nature. Jamie would have given his all. And perhaps that was the point. Discovering how or why he died might not be possible. But helping Morag was. Therefore, in honour of Jamie — the Jamie she wanted to remember — maybe that should be where she directed her energy?

She bent down to rearrange the lilies that Morag had left. An elusive thought that had been niggling away since last night returned to her mind. It was that frantic phone call from Morag. The first words. About Ally. *'Kirstin! Kirstin! I've killed him. It's happened. Again!'*

Again.

Sunday, 13 August 2006

Ally pulled his T-shirt on over his head. It had cooled down. The sun would be leaving their picnicking spot in shadow soon. Still, everyone seemed happy to play on. He checked his watch. Jules would be well on his way. Good. Time to get this party going.

He jogged up to the group, clapping his hands. 'Okay, you lot! Enjoy your last bit of indulgence for now. It's games time! Right, Morag, this'll be base, here at the wall. You count to a slow hundred. The first one caught takes us all out to dinner after the holidays. Or you do, Morag, if you can't find us!'

He watched as Morag gave a half nod and finished her drink. Wearily, she got to her feet, helped by Bonnie and Fraser. Ally moved back as Iona stepped forward, swinging something from her hand.

'And just in case you feel like cheating . . . '

He smiled as his sister tied a soft cotton napkin across Morag's eyes. 'There you are. Oh, and can I borrow your sarong? Don't want to get my legs, or back, scratched up. Thanks.'

Ally waited for some reaction to Iona's cheek, but Morag's only answer was a shrug and another nod. Boy, was she out of it. He moved forward again and began turning an already

140

unsteady Morag round and round.

'Here we go!'

Morag immediately staggered on being released, but somehow kept her balance. With both hands outstretched behind her, she found the wall and managed to lower herself on to it. Ally swivelled back towards the others, a forefinger held to his lips.

'Ssh. Right, Morag. Start counting!'

He was relieved to see that his childish pantomime actions seemed to have infected the others with equal mirth. Even Bonnie was stifling a giggle as Fraser held a hand over her mouth. About time. She needed to lighten up. Iona was evidently enjoying herself, leaning against Craig, pointing exaggeratedly and repeatedly between them and the area beyond the footbridge, leaving no doubt about where they intended to hide.

Slowly, Ally backed away from the others, nodding down the path towards his rendezvous, and mouthed a 'good luck' at them all. Then he was off. As he sprinted away, he heard Morag begin to drone a slow, monotonous count. By the time he was nearing the bend in the path, he risked a final glance back. Morag was rocking herself to and fro, like a small child, as she recited the numbers at a snail's pace. Beyond her, in the distance, he could see Iona and Craig, hand in hand, skipping over the bridge.

He smiled after them. Fine, off you go, as far away from me as possible. Enjoy yourselves. For now. It'll be short-lived.

16

Ally Sutherland looked at himself in the bathroom mirror. A hot bath and long-overdue shave had made him feel a shade better. But he was looking old, and very much the worse for wear. He knew the cause. It wasn't just the nightmare-infused sleep or the encounter with Morag Ramsay. No, the root cause was Jules. Yet another relationship had bitten the dust. But this one had hurt hardest of all. He'd lost him. The final blow had been delivered in the early hours of the morning. He recalled making it through the front door and ridding himself of his damp clothing. Thirty seconds under an icy shower had pummelled some sense back into his aching mind and body. But not enough.

Jules's phone had been answered by someone else. Someone who sounded as young as Jules. English accent. Sleepy, as if he'd just been woken up. But there had been soft, chill-out music in the background. The guy had been in bed all right. More likely, it had been some post-coital spliff and drink that had accounted for the lazy slur in his voice. But Jules had sounded far from relaxed.

'Stop calling here, Alistair. I mean it. It's harassment. I'm sorry for you, you know. You need help. You need to sort your head out. But listen, I don't want to have to tell you again. If this doesn't stop, I'm going to make trouble for you. I mean it. This is the last time I'm going to tell you. It's been over for a long time. I've moved on. So should you.'

The phone had been put down and, after a dozen failed redials, he knew Jules had left it off the hook. But why did it really only hit home last night? Maybe he'd just had enough by then. He frowned at himself in the mirror, gently fingering his injured temple. *Morag Ramsay. At the Cauldron! Unbelievable!* She had finally lost it. She could have really hurt him. He still had half a mind to report her to the police. But no, that was a waste of time. In fact, she'd probably revel in it. Accuse him of lying and instruct her lawyers to tell the media that she was being harassed by the police. Best not alert them. However, he *did* want to talk to the police again about where the investigation was going. The last conversation with the senior investigating officer had left him frustrated. '*We are still actively investigating the death of your sister and Dr Irvine. But you have to realize, Mr Sutherland, that we need evidence, concrete evidence that will stand up in court. We simply do not have that against Ms Ramsay at the moment. But please, be assured that we are determined to see justice done . . .* ' He'd probably be fed more of the same placatory drivel and that would just make him angry. Best to leave that conversation for another day.

He wandered through to the bedroom and gazed out of the window, looking down at the front lawn. How he'd made it back last night he didn't know. It was a miracle no one had seen him. He cast an eye over his shoulder. Yes, there they were: his clothes from last night awaiting washing. In the sober light of day they screamed disapproval at him. What a fool he'd been. He had no one but himself to blame for what had happened with Morag Ramsay. He had taunted her, and you only had to see the look in those blazing eyes. She was utterly unstable. And despite his vowing to her — and to Fraser — that he would ensure the police charged her, he knew those were hollow threats. He turned away from the window. How far he had sunk now. Look what he had let happen to his life since last summer. He might as well have inhaled the silty waters of the Cauldron last night and been thankful for it. A release from pain, from anger, from fear. *I've got to stop this. Stop haunting the Cauldron. I can't reverse things. What's done is done. Iona's gone. It's too late. All too late. Now stop it!* And he would stop it. He had other ideas now.

Slowly, he moved into his dressing room and began rifling through suits. He felt like being formal today. He'd give some semblance of order to his life, even if it was just for one day. His fingers hovered over the suit that had always been Jules's favourite, and then he shoved it far along the clothes rail, out of sight. To hell with Jules, to hell with everyone. He was utterly alone now. He'd never been a great one for friends, anyway. But even those he could call acquaintances were not around now. Same with his various business contacts. He'd pushed them all away. Initially, they had been understanding. Iona's death had dealt him the severest blow, of course, and they understood. It'll take time to get over. *Get over!* You never, ever get over something like that! The dolts! And, after a while, he could sense their thoughts. *Ally should be pulling himself together by now. He's changed. He's quiet. He's surly. Monosyllabic. Quick to take offence. Paranoid, even.*

And he was neglecting his work. But what did that matter? He'd decided. He was selling up. Leaving. To go . . . he had a few places in mind, but he'd definitely go . . . somewhere. He wouldn't tell or warn anyone. Just disappear. His parents wouldn't care. They were practically estranged now, hunkered down further into their narrow lives in the back of beyond, to grieve over their favourite child. They'd always given Iona the benefit of the doubt, since her mode of making money was 'artistic'. Christ, you'd think she'd painted every bloody work she'd sold! In truth, despite a promising art school beginning, she'd been a disappointment artistically. *'Those who can't, sell, dear sister.'* It had been an unforgivably cruel remark from him, made what, over ten years ago? When his parents' bias and favouritism towards Iona had just about driven him to despair.

But she'd found her rejoining barb in no time. *'Yes, but at least I don't have to lie about what I am, dear brother. Or perhaps you're too scared they'd disown you? And remember, they certainly would have long ago if I hadn't kept your grubby secrets.'*

He pushed the thought away and brought

145

back the image of his parents' stony faces as they sat at the solicitor's last year. The meeting was to discuss Iona's estate, and included a frosty exchange over selling the gallery. That was the last time he'd seen them, and the underlying message had been clear. He was to blame for Iona's death, one way or another. He should have been looking after his sister. And there was a final message in their disappointed and anguished looks: they had no other child. He was, essentially, an orphan. Alone.

Fine. He could live without them. What mattered was what he was going to do with himself. Leaving, clearing out was the only option. Fraser was taking flight and so was Bonnie by the sound of it. Deserting the already sunken ship. So, why not him? Each day here made him feel sicker. But what was he going to do about Morag? He couldn't have her followed from now to eternity. He needed to think things through. She was getting kicked out of her home. Good. But where was she going? The police just couldn't be trusted to keep an eye on her, of that he was certain. Bonnie might know. Time for a visit.

TRANQUILLITY COTTAGE. The River-side Sanctum of Bonnie Campbell. All Are Welcome If You Come With Peace And Love In Your Heart.

As always, Ally shook his head at the gaudy, amateurishly painted sign. The creaking gate had caused the usual fluttering of the ground-floor

146

curtains. She'd better not try pretending she was out. The way he was feeling right now, he'd kick the door off its hinges if she tried that game. But she wasn't going to. The door was opened and there she stood. Thinner and paler than ever, despite the sunny weather, her bony face was trying to give the impression of a surprised, welcoming smile.

'Ally! Eh, hi, I . . . it's lovely to see you. Please, come on in.'

She hadn't approached him with the offer of a warm hug or kiss to the cheek. Those days were long over. He slid past her into the gloom of the hallway.

'Go on down to the back room. Make yourself at home.' Her voice was unusually high-pitched, the tension getting to her.

He gave a nod without turning his head and marched down the narrow hallway in front of her. Although she called her house a cottage, it was more idiosyncratic than that. Bonnie had made some quirky decisions when renovating it. The room sizes were uneven. A pokey front room, which he always avoided spending any time in, was balanced out by the back room, where he now stood. It was low-ceilinged but long, giving the illusion of more space than it actually contained, and its windows looked directly out on to the river, flooding every corner with natural light. And the final triumph of this room was that it remained mercifully cool in summer. Even so, he could feel the sweat breaking out under his shirt. Perhaps he too was nervous? Through her very oddness, Bonnie had

147

the ability to unsettle. He surveyed the room with one glance. No change. Still the obligatory cushions and burnt-out candles.

'Tea? Coffee? Something cold? I've no alcohol in at the moment.'

Even though he'd kill for a cold beer, he ignored the lie, selecting a seat with its back to the garden and the river.

'Sit down, Bonnie. We've something — two things, actually — to talk about.'

She was standing awkwardly in the doorway and making a fluttering movement with her right hand. 'Oh? Okay, I'll just get myself a cup of t — '

'Bugger the tea. *Sit down!* There.'

The rebuke had been as good as a slap in the face. Meekly, she slumped down into the chair opposite and tried to settle herself. 'Ally? I've been mean — '

His look shut her up immediately. He leant forward, elbows on knees, wiping trickles of sweat from his brow with his thumbs.

'I want you to listen to me very carefully, Bonnie. I've seen Fraser and I know you've seen him too. I saw you both at the Cauldron the other day.'

He waited for some show of denial. Nothing. She was sitting rigid but compliant.

He went on. 'I'm also damn sure you've seen Morag Ramsay recently. An act of betrayal so disgusting I can't tell you how furious and utterly let down I feel. Both *you* and Fraser have betrayed me. Betrayed Iona.'

As expected, she pushed her chair back and

started waving her skinny arms. 'It wasn't that recently. Honest. I just did a meditation with her, that's all.'

He dragged his chair forward to counter any further retreat. 'I don't care about your meditations. I've come to *tell* you two things. First, I'm liquidating my business and I want out of your clinic. I want you to get things in motion first thing on Monday and organize paying me back the remainder of what you owe me. I know it won't be too much of a hardship for you, clever Bonnie. But I want it done, fast. Second.' He inched forward again, the back legs of the chair gouging their way through the carpet. 'I want to know where Morag's going. I know she's going bust. But I want to know her plans. And I think *you* know them.'

He sat back, pulled out his cigarettes and lit up, daring her to remonstrate.

She was swallowing hard, her thin neck convulsing with the anxiety. Nervously, she tucked stray straggles of thin hair behind her ears. 'Look, Ally. As far as the business goes, that's fine, fine. I'll get things going on Monday. But with Morag. I don't, I really *don't* know where she's going.'

'But you could find out.' His voice was a soft whisper, but he knew she was getting the message.

'What d'you mean? I ... I don't know anything. I don't see anyone. Yes, I saw Fraser the other day. But that was the first time in ages. And, anyway, we rowed. You must have seen that if you were at the Cauldron.'

'What did you row about?'

She'd had enough, and he let her stand up and move towards the window. She kept her back to him as she stared unseeingly towards the river.

'I don't understand, Ally. Why Morag? Why are you so convinced? Why is Fraser? Why *did* he say those things to the police and then change his mind?'

She spun round to look at him. He stayed sitting, but swivelled his chair to face her, shaking his head incredulously.

'You mean you honestly don't think it was Morag? You must be joking!'

She was shaking her head just as vigorously. 'I don't get it. You never seemed to think anything about it being Morag at first, and neither did the police. Until Fraser said those things.'

Giving up on the cigarette, he stabbed the butt out in a nearby plant pot. '*I was too much in shock to think about anything but my loss, for God's sake!* It had to be Morag. Underneath that cool, calm exterior, she was burning with insecurity about Craig. It was a no-win situation for her and somewhere, deep down, she must have known it. You capture a good-looking guy, it's good for the ego. But other people will always want to get their hands on what you've got. And with someone like Iona around, you'd better watch out. Morag was always on tenterhooks about Craig. She tried to hide it, but I saw it. If you didn't, then you're blind. And it made her such a bore. The only way she'd lighten up was if she had drink, or some chemical, inside her. But I began to wonder if she knew about Craig and

Iona and was just biding her time, ready to lash out.'

He paused to draw breath, trying to control his increasing anger. 'And Morag could lash out all right. Still can.' He pointed to the healing gash on his temple. 'Look, she did this to me last night. She had the cheek to be down at the Cauldron last night, saw me, freaked, and lashed out. And it's not the first time. Morag has a problem with violence that you know nothing about. Believe me.'

Bonnie frowned. 'I . . . I don't believe you, Ally. If, *if*, she did anything like that, then you must have provoked, threatened her. You don't know Morag. I've been thinking a lot about what happened last summer. If she did it, she did it as a reflex thing. But no one will ever prove it one way or the other.' She turned back to her river-watching. 'I . . . I'm sorry for you, Ally. Really. What happened has had . . . well, a catastrophic effect on you . . . on your personality. I'm sorry. But, if you won't get help for your anger and your grief, then I don't know what to suggest.' She sighed heavily, her back still turned rigidly towards him. 'I want you to leave now. You're disturbing me. Tainting my house. Please go.'

He pushed back the chair roughly and walked up behind her, his breath on her cheek. 'I don't want any amateur psychoanalysis, thanks. But . . . I'm speechless. Morag's pulled the wool over your eyes all right. I want you to find out where she's going or at the very least *when* she's running off. I don't want her just swanning off

151

into the world. I don't trust the police to keep her in their sights. I mean it, Bonnie. I know you could find out.'

She surprised him by spinning round, the light cotton shift swirling about her legs. 'Don't use that threatening tone on me! Two can play that game!'

'What are you talking about?'

'I know about Jules. Does that surprise you? I can see it does. I know he was there. Know you hid that from the police. That's a serious matter, Ally. *And* I know you were going to humiliate Iona that day by producing Jules as yours. It could get a bit grubby and unseemly, if all that got out, couldn't it?'

He moved swiftly towards her. 'Don't ever, *ever* talk to me again about Jules. Christ, this is the worst betrayal. You've let me down, you've let Iona down. *You're despicable!*'

As he headed down the darkened hallway, he heard the first of her sobs, and nodded his satisfaction before slamming the door behind him. Moments later, he felt the onset of his own tears.

17

After Morag had left, Kirstin sat in the graveyard car park wondering what to do about lunch or if she even felt like eating. She needed to clear her mind of Morag Ramsay. The woman exerted a powerful but exhausting presence. All that pent-up emotion. And she desperately wanted a rest from thoughts of Jamie. Just for a while. So Glen's phone call had been a welcome distraction: *'I'm thinking of taking a very long lunch hour. I wondered if you'd like to join me?'*

She'd agreed to drive over to his office and they'd taken the association's Land Rover high up into the Pentlands, eventually settling on the fringes of a pine forest, offering magnificent views towards Glencorse Reservoir. He'd brought a selection of fruit, sandwiches and a flask of coffee.

The picnic was perfect timing. She hadn't realized how hungry she was until he'd laid out the food. It had been a happy, almost carefree, hour chatting about herself. Glen, in return, had told her about how he'd ended up at the river association after years working for the Forestry Commission in Aberdeenshire. They were both steering clear of any serious talk about Jamie. Glen had obviously decided to strike a lighter note and had even made her laugh with a few affectionate anecdotes about him. Lunch over, they'd finished the last of the coffee. Now they were enjoying a moment's peace in the sunshine.

Sitting against a tree, she handed Glen the empty cup, shading her eyes to look at him as he cleared up.

'When are you due back in the office?'

He paused to sit back on his heels, squinting out at the view and at a distant group of hill walkers. 'I've got another half hour or so. Eh . . . actually, I wanted to talk to you about something else to do with Jamie.'

'Oh?'

She waited while he tidied everything away and carried the picnic box back to the Land Rover. He returned carrying a blue plastic document wallet. She frowned at it as he sat down cross-legged opposite her.

'What have you got there?'

He smoothed a hand over the cover and began unconsciously unfastening and refastening the white plastic popper on the front, looking away over his shoulder again towards the view, as if suddenly anxious or embarrassed.

'Glen? What is it?'

He let out a little cough and then turned to look directly at her; a piercing, disconcerting gaze.

'Kirstin, I don't want you to think I brought you up here on false pretences, just to discuss this. But I did want to talk to you at some point and our first meeting wasn't appropriate. And I wouldn't want to talk over the phone. I suppose, I *hope* these are better surroundings than any other.'

She felt the beginnings of tension tugging at her stomach. *God, what else is coming?*

He fidgeted, as if trying to get comfortable. 'I, we, well the association's getting a bit worried

about when we can get into Mill House. We
don't want to be pushy, but I wondered if you
could have a word with Ross about it? We're
talking beginning of September. That'll have
been a good six months and more. I thought that
would be plenty of time, but I get the feeling that
Ross is . . . well, not really *motivated* to leave.
Don't get me wrong. I can totally understand
that. It's just that time's getting on. D'you see?'

She looked at him as if he'd just spoken to her
in another language. 'I'm sorry, Glen, but I
haven't a clue what you're going on about.'

But he'd worked out as much from her first
look of puzzlement.

'You don't know, do you?'

'Know *what*? What's all this about Mill
House?'

He looked away again and restarted the
popping and unpopping of the folder, eventually
pulling the envelope out and handing it to her.

She recognized the handwriting immediately.
Slowly, fearfully, she pulled out the two pages of
stiff, dove-grey notepaper.

The Mill House
off The Wynd
EDINBURGH
EH12 QA6

23 November 2006

My Dear Glen

I have left this, together with a copy of my
will, at my solicitor's for you to receive once

I have passed on. I might still discuss this with you in life (though I have told no one yet about my plans) and so this letter may never be read by you.

I am and will be eternally grateful for what you, yes _you_ as an individual, have done to help me. The work you have given me, indeed honoured me with, has been life-changing and, just when I needed it, life-saving. Although I have always loved the river, it is my respect for you that has prompted me to leave Mill House to the association.

There is only one hard and fast proviso: that my house be used for new conservation offices. And, if the board see fit, perhaps the old water mill could be refurbished and used to hold an exhibition space that will keep visitors up to date with the latest work and the history of one of this city's most wonder-ful assets.

The other suggestion, and I stress the word _suggestion_, is that the board consider Ross for trustee status, should there be a vacancy in the future. However, if the board decide that this is not what they want to do, then that in no way alters matters. Equally, it may be that Ross will not find my suggestion regarding trustee status inviting. (I have a feeling he may not.) So be it.

Finally, I want to thank you again for all that you have done for me. True friends can be trusted with everything. Can accept the good and the bad in each other. You have

*done that for me, and I, hopefully, have
done that for you. You have been a true
friend. I hope I was one to you.*

All the best, always,

Jamie

She let the letter drop into her lap, one hand
holding down the fluttering pages as a cool
breeze rushed through from the forest behind.
Glen moved sideways to shield Kirstin from the
sun and to make her look at him.

'I'm sorry. I thought you'd know. *Shit*, I've
upset you. I . . . I'm so — '

She was finding it hard to swallow but she
didn't want any more tears. Not today. She'd
had enough of them.

'It's fine, Glen, really. It's a very touching
letter. And it's some of the old Jamie back again.
I would've been happy, thrilled, to have received
such a letter. He admired you. As for the house.
Actually, I think it's a lovely, really lovely idea.
Generous. To the association, to river users,
present and future generations of them. And it's
fitting too. Thinking about it, I'm not at all
surprised.'

She took a deep breath, pondering carefully
her next words. 'I'm sorry you were embarrassed. I think I might have assumed the same,
that I would have known. It's not as if Ross and
I are estranged. But I didn't. And I'm furious
that Ross hasn't told me. However, that's
between him and me. But that letter. I don't
know how to say this. It's got the th — '

157

He shuffled forward. 'It's got what, Kirstin?'

She tried to stem the snuffling by putting a hand to her mouth, the words coming out in a slow whisper. 'Given . . . everything we've talked about before. I'm wondering. It's got such a tone of finality about it. Look when it was written. Last winter. When he surely wasn't doing very much on the river. Instead . . . he . . . was maybe brooding over his life, over the past year or so. It's ju — '

'What?'

'It's just that I can't help thinking that it *feels* like a suicide note.'

18

Kirstin sat parked at the entrance to Mill House, toying with the baseball cap. Two shades of green with electric-blue lettering: 'Water of Leith River Association. Head Volunteer. JAMIE MUNRO.' Glen had insisted she have it as a memento. A touching gesture that had completed a wonderful evening, two days ago.

After the Friday picnic, he had insisted on having her round for dinner. The simple meal had been set out on his small balcony overlooking the river at Dean Village. And then, over coffee, allowing the inhibitions to be finally released by the sweet but potent dessert wine, he'd walked round behind her to place the cap lightly on her head. He'd stood back, head cocked at an exaggerated angle to admire the view, and then moved forward to kiss her. No surprise. She knew it would happen. Wanted it to. And what joy-filled hours they had been.

Thinking back over the past few days, of course she'd been aware of the signs, from him and from within herself. She was hardly immune to the appeal of an attractive, charming and personable man. But it wasn't only that. He was sensitive to what she was going through with Jamie. Shared her own feelings of guilt and puzzlement. And he'd obviously had a burning need to reach out. To tell someone what he'd known of Jamie. In turn, he'd picked up on her own need and had decided to trust her. That was a bond.

She checked her reflection in the rear-view mirror. Slowly, her smile sparked by the memory faded and she threw the cap on to the dashboard. Her gaze moved through the windscreen towards the entrance to Jamie's house. Ross thought she was stopping for a quick drink, had seemed positively enthused by the idea. Little did he know.

Five minutes later she was settled in the garden. She didn't feel nervous or anxious. Just angry and let down. Again.

Ross was throwing back the wine as she sipped at a mineral water. 'Shame you're driving, Kirsty, this rosé's a cracker. I thought you might have left the car behind since you were coming for a drink?'

It was an awkward opening from him. He sensed something was up. She took a final slug of the icy water. 'Actually, Ross, I'm not in a drinking mood. I saw Glen Laidlaw at the weekend.'

'Oh, yeah?' He feigned unconcern, swirling his wine round and round and holding it up to reflect the evening sun's last orange rays. He didn't know what was coming, but he knew something was on its way.

She kept her gaze steady on him while he refused to take his eyes from the wine. 'I know about the house, Ross.'

It was almost comical. His hand and glass had frozen in mid-air.

She continued staring, willing him to look at

her. 'I may not have any rights in your family, but I thought you might at least have told me what Jamie had done. It's a wonderful, generous gesture and may in some way have softened the blow of his death. It was mean of you not to tell me.'

He gathered his wits quickly, the wine glass discarded and forgotten on the table. 'Glen Laidlaw had no right telling you.'

She held up a hand. 'He thought I knew. He was just wanting to get some idea of when you were clearing the house. Don't blame him. He assumed we were on good terms. Tell me something, Ross. Are you angry at him? Your dad, I mean. For doing this and not warning you? Is that why you've done your best to ruin even his death?'

'*What!*'

'You know what. Not telling me about his death, not inviting me to the funeral. Having the briefest of services with a handful of words from you and not even a proper wake. Donald told me what you'd organized. Thinking about it now, I understand. You're furious at your father, aren't you?'

He scraped the metal garden chair back and stood up, walking to the top of the grassy slope to stare at the river flowing sluggishly past the bottom of the garden.

'Fucking hell, Kirstin, you've got a nerve! I did my best for Dad about the funeral. How dare you even think that somehow I was enacting some form of revenge on him! He might not have been the perfect father to me, but it is so

161

low to suggest that somehow I'd try and ruin his funeral. I did what I could. And actually, I don't give a damn about the house. The river people can have it, for all I care. I *do* care that Dad didn't have either the guts or the consideration to warn me what was going on in his mind.'

He turned to face her, his eyes blazing. 'But then, that's it, isn't it? This bequest is one more piece in the jigsaw that was his — and I *will* use this word, Kirstin — his *madness*. It's my view that he was mentally ill at the end. Though I *do* think he knew what he was doing. His decisions on the house were made last winter. He *had* thought about his plans, but told no one else, and I think I know why.' He turned to her, his eyes squinting with suppressed fury or sadness, she couldn't be sure which. 'Yes, I'll tell you why. *That bequest is a suicide note!*'

The silence was absolute save for the quiet trickling of the river in the background. Kirstin shifted her chair backwards, but remained sitting. Ross hadn't unleashed all the anger she knew he was capable of. But she could also feel the waves of genuine hurt flowing from his now immobile body. He had turned away from her again and was standing rigidly to attention, seemingly mesmerized by the water. None of what he'd said was any surprise. What had startled her had been his analysis of Jamie's actions, an analysis that had chimed so perfectly with her own thoughts on reading Jamie's letter to Glen.

She watched as Ross made his way back to the table, dragged a chair over and threw himself into it. 'You wonder why I didn't tell you? That's why. Dad was . . . had lost it. I don't know for sure what happened that night by the Cauldron. But one way or another, his death was caused by his state of mind. Either deliberately or through some dark mood he was in that drew him there at dead of night, and in those conditions. Maybe I should have seen it coming. Maybe I was neglectful. I'll have to live with that. I *do* live with that. Every day. Every hour.'

His last words were delivered in a choked whisper and she heard him give out a quiet sob before reaching for his drink. 'But, contrary to what you might think, I've tried to live a better life. Professionally and personally.' He poured more wine and flicked a quick, furtive glance at her, before looking away again. 'And I think I've got my reward. I'm getting married. To Annelise. Bob Linklater's daughter. We've been seeing each other seriously for a long time and . . . and she's pregnant. We're very happy. I hope *you'll* be happy for us.'

The faint glow of confidence that she'd started the day with evaporated. Ross was going to marry one of the senior partner's daughters. Kirstin cast her mind back to various parties and social events. Annelise Linklater. Yes, she remembered her now. A good catch. Looks, brains, and now a baby. A baby. Fine. He'd never wanted one when married to her. This was another piece of news he could have, should have, told her before. Had he saved it up to use at exactly a time like this? When he was feeling vulnerable and put-upon? Was it to punish her for leaving him?

163

Well, good luck to Annelise Linklater!

Reluctantly, but with a showy flourish, Kirstin lifted her glass of now tepid water to toast him and tried a smile. 'You'll be glad to know that for once I am actually speechless. But yes, congratulations. You kept that one quiet. Did your dad know? About the marriage plans?'

'Yes. But he couldn't stand Bob Linklater, so it was just one more disappointment. And about the baby . . . Annelise is just over three months gone. Dad would have been pleased about that, though. I'm sure.'

He looked uncomfortable. The talk of second marriages and babies was too much. 'Look, Kirstin. *Oh, God!* I *always* seem to be apologizing to you. Maybe I should have told you about the house, but I didn't. I've got a lot on my mind Perhaps you can understand that a bit better now. And maybe you can help me.'

'Help you?'

He nodded. 'With the house. I'm way behind. You know I've been thinking about this since you came back. I wondered if you wanted to move in for a few days. You'll have the place to yourself. And maybe go through some of Dad's things? I . . . I, well, I've not really made any start on his study. I tried but it was just depressing. I've been through his personal papers, all the ones related to probate. And I've sorted out a couple of filing cabinets. But there's still a ton of river material piled on his old desk, and God knows what else to go through. I've skimmed through some of it but, well, I'd feel bad about just throwing it all away. Either that or I could hand it all over to

Glen Laidlaw. It would serve him right me dumping a ton of paperwork on him. Get him back for all those years ago.'

She gave a quizzical frown and he offered her a half smile in return. 'Didn't Glen tell you? We knew each other when we were, what? Twelve, thirteen maybe? He lived down near the Cauldron. Not sure which house . . . I *think* it was that cottage the other woman . . . not Morag Ramsay, Bonnie Campbell lives in. But it was only for a short while and then his family moved away, something about his father getting transferred. Our gang from this part of the river used to come down to the Cauldron area now and again and there was a bit of a territorial feud. I never knew his last name and, in truth, I forgot his first until we met again. Me and Glen had a big fight once. He won.'

He smiled at the memory. 'Funny, it was only when I met him to discuss Mill House that it clicked with both of us. I'd talked to him on the phone, but it obviously didn't register with either of us. He was amazed — and sad too. Said that he didn't put two and two together about Jamie. Of course, he never knew my dad then. We were just two bunches of kids that bumped into each other now and again. Small world, though. I understand why he's so passionate about the job now. He loved the river even as a child, that I do remember.'

Ross paused to tilt his head. He looked puzzled.

'I'm surprised he didn't tell you.'

19

'Morag, believe me. There is nothing to be frightened of. You'll know what it is like from your sessions with Dr Lockhart, but I want to reassure you anyway. Modern hypnotherapy is not the trickery of the Victorian music hall. Not some cheap vaudeville act. I'm not going be dangling a golden pocket watch in front of your eyes until you succumb and lose your reason. Rather, I'm going to place you in a relaxing environment and we will talk. So, are you happy to continue?'

She knew he was watching her every move.

'Professor Beattie, I just want to find out what happened. What I did or didn't do.'

'I know. I know. This is just the beginning. Let's give it time.'

★   ★   ★

'I can feel the blindfold. A napkin. Soft. Iona's putting it on. She's saying . . . what is that? Sounds like, 'Just in case you feel like cheating.' And she's laughing and saying something else. 'Can I borrow your sarong? Don't want to get my legs, or back, scratched up.'

'Okay, Morag. Just let your mind be still for a moment. Relax.'

She shifted slightly, enjoying the comfort of Professor Beattie's deep, enveloping sofa. He'd been right. She hadn't lost her reason. She knew where she was. And it was the most relaxing of environments. Low lighting and so quiet. She allowed her attention to drift back to the professor's voice again, enjoying his gentle, reassuring tones.

'Iona thought you might cheat. How do you feel about that?'

'I don't know.'

'Iona's taken your sarong. How do you feel about *that*?'

'Don't know.'

'You don't know? But it's yours!'

'I'm going to get it back. After this stupid game. I didn't even want to play the game in the first place, did I? And now I'm going to be left behind. And I don't want to be left behind, alone. It's not fair.'

'What's happening now, Morag?'

'I . . . I don't know. I feel woozy and . . . and Ally's spinning me round now. I've almost lost my balance but I'm okay. I'm sitting on the wall now. Counting. I can hear some giggles, whispers, quite loud even above the sound of the weir. And . . . now, I can hear the rustling of feet in the grass and someone running past me on the path. They're all going to hide.'

'And you're still counting?'

'I must be at about twenty now.'

'That's very slow. You've got to get to a hundred. They'll be very well hidden by the time you finish.'

'That doesn't matter.'

'Why?'

She felt herself shake with laughter. 'Because Iona was right. I *am* going to cheat. I'm going to look. They won't know. They've got their backs to me. Running away.'

'And what do you see?'

She could smell the river now, feel the residual heat of the day, even though the sun was casting long shadows. 'I can't see Ally. Maybe it was him I heard running past me. But I *can* see Fraser and Bonnie. Far in front of me, running up the hill into the undergrowth. Bonnie's giggling. I can hear it drifting back to me. Oh . . . I feel sick. Really sick.'

'And the others. Where are Craig and Iona? Have they gone?'

'Yes. No! My sarong. The colour. A vermilion flash at the other side of the bridge. They've gone over the footbridge. Are they going up the art gallery steps? No . . . no! I can see the red. It helps me to follow their progress. And it's fine, just fine.'

She could feel herself trying to pull the non-existent blindfold back down.

'Why is it fine, Morag?'

She could feel a smirk twitching at her mouth.

'Because I know exactly where they're hiding.'

Sunday, 13 August 2006

Craig Irvine inched out into the busy summer holiday traffic on an already nose-to-tail busy Queensferry Road. It was a shitty way to start any Sunday morning, let alone the blistering scorcher this one was going to be. But he had to get away from Morag, so an excuse to go in and handle a phantom 'emergency' at the office was perfect. Who cared if she didn't believe him. Sleeping in, mildly to moderately hung-over, the echo of Morag's grumpy voice ringing round and round in his head had decided him. Escape for the morning and then go on to that afternoon's river party.

It was crystal clear that Morag didn't want to go — or rather, didn't want him to go without her. She was being bloody-minded. If he went, then so would she. If he didn't, then neither would she. A limpet. That's what she'd become. He'd suspected for some time, despite his and Iona's best efforts to keep her boozed or drugged up, that Morag knew about them. And maybe that was no bad thing.

He revved the engine to catch the lights before they turned to red and then found himself stranded in a box junction, being tooted at by irate drivers. Wonderful! He scrabbled on the floor of the passenger seat footwell to retrieve the half bottle of stale mineral water that had been rolling about there for days. God, he was feeling more awful by the minute. Still, he could hide in his office all morning and recover. Morag had insisted that he come back and walk her down to the river. Fine. He would. And maybe, just maybe, it would be the last time. In fact . . . yes, somewhere in his unconscious he knew he'd been hatching this plan. After all, he'd been thinking about doing it for weeks. Today was the day. He'd tell her at the party. It was over. He and Iona were together now.

Morag would no doubt make a scene, go ballistic. But Bonnie would be there. She was good at the calming down bit. And if Morag tried to have a go at Iona . . . well, she could look after herself in any cat fight. But he'd have to pick his moment. Not straightaway. No, the best time would be late on. When — and he'd have to ensure this — Morag was well tanked up. Then he and Iona could disappear into the sunset. He slugged at the tepid water and sighed, grateful that the traffic was flowing at last. It was a good plan, wasn't it? Not just the fucked-up desperation of his hangover talking to him? After all, he'd not talked to Iona about any of it. She'd go along with it, wouldn't she? Come to think of it, Iona hadn't had any serious conversation with him about 'them', where they were going, how they felt about each other. But they'd been together a while now, she had to feel the same. Otherwise, why hang around with him?

Of course, at the start, Iona had targeted him, just like he'd seen her target other men. And 'just topping up Morag a little bit more', be it with booze or drugs, had been her idea initially. Then it had become a habit. No, it didn't leave him feeling very proud of himself. But . . . it had just happened. The same way that deceiving Morag had initially been almost by accident. But who could resist Iona? No, he didn't need to talk with her about their future together. About her feelings for him. Words didn't matter. She showed what she felt. How she showed it!

The glinting slab of the company building was in sight now, the morning sun striking off his tenth-floor office windows. He pulled into the deserted car park and switched off the engine. Slowly, he made his way towards the main entrance, nodded at the security guard and passed through the barrier. Inside the empty lift he stared at his reflection in the mirrored walls. *Once upon a time you were just a bit of a vain lad. Good-looking lady bait, who did science but didn't look or behave like a nerd. Now you're looking a bit the worse for wear. The shitty part of you is beginning to show on the outside. Time to do something about it, lad. Be with who you really want to be with.* He drew a hand down over his hungover features and then turned away, slamming the side of his fist into the tenth-floor button. Then he leant his head back against the cool wall, eyes closed, a smile twitching at his mouth. *Only a few more hours. Then he and Iona would be together . . .*

★ ★ ★

171

He felt Iona's hands lightly touching his back as he picked his way through the undergrowth. It was the perfect place. Enough cover to do what they had in mind.

'God, Craig, is it much further? These bloody trees are determined to attack me.'

He stopped and turned round to embrace her, rubbing the invisible scratch. 'Hey, it's great here. We can keep an eye on everyone else but they'll not have a clue where we are. I promise you. Everyone thinks you can't get along here. But I saw the river association work crew doing some clearing a couple of months ago. The entrance is overgrown again, but we can get through. Come on.'

He kissed her lightly on the mouth and put an arm round her waist. 'Now, just a little bit further . . . a few steps and . . . here we are. The perfect place to chill out.' He signalled for her to crouch down with him, his arm still round her waist. 'We can spy on them, but they can't see us. Look. There's Morag still counting.'

He felt a suppressed giggle tremble through Iona.

'Ssh. Sound carries here.'

'All right, all right. But I was wondering.' She clamped a hand to her mouth to muffle the laughter and then went on. 'I was wondering what number she's at. And whether she's made it out of single digits yet!'

He joined in the stifled spluttering while, very slowly, unwrapping Iona's body from Morag's sarong.

Oblivious to the eyes observing them.

20

Kirstin felt ill from exhaustion. She'd risen at six, grateful for another sunny morning and a return to reality. Her night's sleep had been peppered with almost schizophrenically opposed images and dreams. Glen: smiling, holding her hand as they walked by the river. Ross: angry, drunken, taking a sledgehammer to Jamie's gravestone. And then turning towards her, eyes blazing, a ghostly Annelise Linklater approached from behind, babe in arms.

The news of Ross's impending marriage had come as a complete surprise. If nothing else it showed that, despite his original protestations when she'd left him, he most certainly could live without her *and* thrive. She wasn't envious. The last person on earth she'd want to be married to was Ross, though she had to be honest, her ego was just a bit dented. But then Glen was an effective antidote for any bruised ego.

And what about Jamie? In the space of one short week, her feelings, her motivations had shifted. There were two Jamies to grapple with now. Should she even try? Jamie was gone. Maybe by his own hand, maybe by pure accident. Should she just remember him as he was? Ross had delivered his painful and now increasingly persuasive analysis. Glen too, despite all he'd confided, seemed to be warning her off. For her own sake, and for the sake of Jamie's memory.

Donald Ferguson was the exception. He didn't offer any other explanation for Jamie's death. All he knew was that his oldest friend had been behaving increasingly oddly. Of course he wouldn't want to admit that it had been a prelude to suicide. Poor Donald would never be able to live with himself if he thought that. Maybe it *was* time to close the book on Jamie and maybe it was right not to dig any deeper. If she did, what else might she find that she didn't like?

But there were two things she had to do. First, she *would* take up Ross's offer of moving into Mill House for a few days to go through Jamie's office. Besides, the lettings agency had a booking for her flat, so Ross's offer was timely. Secondly, she was going to spend some time with Morag Ramsay. Sit down with her and see what help she could offer. Even if it was just putting the poor woman in touch with her friends in Devon who ran a seaside hotel business. Perhaps it was time for her to talk to Morag's former river friends too. She sighed, feeling weary. Or maybe she could at least talk to Ally Sutherland? Try to reason with him about Morag. Though, if the other night was anything to go by, she couldn't imagine Ally appreciating her interference on Morag's behalf.

And what of Morag? Should she drop round to that immaculate — almost too immaculate — house? With its clean yet stark, even clinical, character that echoed the rigid and brittle side to Morag's nature. It was, indeed, the perfect house for her. Or should she just give Morag a call instead? But Kirstin knew she didn't have the energy for either a visit or a phone call right now. Though she did want to know how things had gone with the hypnotherapist. Kirstin frowned and shook her head. Morag's reluctance to try the technique puzzled her. As did her disproportionate reaction to Ally Sutherland's presence at the Cauldron. But how could *she* judge? Thankfully, she wasn't in Morag's position. Besides, normal rules of behaviour and rationality just didn't apply in her situation, did they?

★ ★ ★

Morag glanced at the wall calendar in the kitchen. *Damn.* This was all she needed. She'd known for weeks that Dr Lockhart was going away. But the time, running unusually slowly most days, seemed to have galloped away with her. Now she was going to be alone for two whole weeks. She could feel a relapse coming on.

The session with Professor Beattie had left her depressed. In contrast, he'd seemed almost jubilant. '*You have a new memory. Of cheating. That's progress, Morag. I thought you were going to start blocking, but we got there. Well done.*' She'd initially felt fine sitting there, fully aware. In control, and yet not. But, afterwards, she'd felt sick, physically sick. As sick as she had that Sunday last August. The entire hypnosis episode had stayed with her. She'd been feeling strange ever since . . . detached, dreamy, unreal. As for the cheating? That wasn't a new memory. She remembered only too well tracking the

175

colourful sarong on its weaving progress over to the wooded area. But she'd have been a fool to admit that to anyone, even Dr Lockhart. The fact that Professor Beattie had got the information out of her may have been progress to him, but it wasn't to her. It was disturbing. She wasn't going back to him, and there was nothing Dr Lockhart or anyone else could do about it.

Morag crept from the darkened kitchen. With a final glance over her shoulder, she checked that all the blinds were down before heading into the hallway. Might as well go back to bed, even though it was late afternoon. She'd take a pill, try to get something approaching dreamless, nightmare-less sleep, though her waking time now seemed like a dream. Almost as if she was floating above herself, existing apart from her physical body. Or even as if she didn't exist at all, leaving her with the feeling that this was all a dream. She'd felt like this before. In adolescence, when it had been the precursor of severe depression. *Derealization, depersonalization*, the shrink had called it. A terrifying experience. But now, she had to fight it, hold on to reality. Yes, she was in trouble. Yes, she was going to lose her — very real — home. And yes, her feelings of anger, of fury, were only too real. But . . . still the remote, airy feeling persisted.

As she reached the bottom of the stairs, the rat-a-tat of the door knocker had her clinging to the banister, white-knuckled, heart racing. Who was this? The rat-a-tat rang out again, this time more insistent. Tentatively, Morag moved forward and put an eye to the spyhole. With a sigh of surprise and relief, she released the array of locks and bolts.

Bonnie stood on the doorstep, her head turned slightly to one side in a gesture of uncertainty. She pulled off her sunglasses. Her pale eyes looked worried.

'I'm sorry for just turning up like this, Morag, but I couldn't sleep last night. I need to talk to you.'

She looked more wan than ever and her body in the light cotton shift was now stick-like, as if she had no muscles, nothing to support that delicate frame. Had she stopped eating completely? Morag stood to one side and beckoned her in.

'I was just going back to bed, but it's better for me not to. Come in. Take a seat in the front room.'

Odd. Her voice sounded unnaturally loud in her head. Like another's voice. The heavy curtains made it impossible to see. Better switch on a light. As she reached out towards the table lamp, she stopped midway. Whose arm was that?

'Morag? You okay?'

Morag felt the shudder run down her body. *It's your arm. This is your house.* With trembling fingers she clicked on the lamp. *Stay grounded, keep calm.* She turned towards Bonnie.

'Do you need anything? Tea? Something cold?'

Bonnie shook her head as she lowered herself into an easy chair that seemed to swallow her entire frail body. Sitting back obviously felt wrong and she inched forward, both hands in her lap, her back rigidly straight. It was very nearly her meditation posture, but not quite. She seemed far from composed.

Morag took the seat opposite, thankful for the protection of the gloom. She pulled her dressing gown round her. *Try to be normal. Speak to her.*

'What is it, Bonnie? What brings you here?'

Bonnie momentarily pressed three fingers to her dry lips, as if she was unsure how to begin.

'I should be at work right now, but I've cancelled everything. I've been thinking about this all day and I wanted, *needed* to see you. I had a visit from Ally last Friday, and I'm worried. Very worried. About you. He knows about you losing the house, having to move. I'm sorry, that's my fault. I saw Fraser recently and told him. I wasn't gossiping. I was defending you'

She paused, and her fingers strayed back to her mouth. A moment later, Bonnie's hand dropped to her lap and she began to fiddle with the thin fabric of her dress where it covered her bony knees. *So frail, pale, thin. She could almost be a ghost. A ghost in my living nightmare.*

'Oh really?'

Morag's voice was sounding loud yet remote — disembodied — again. *Be strong, keep control.*

'You need to know this, Morag. He's leaving. Says he's liquidating the business. I'm wondering if he's planning some . . . a . . . a *spectacular* before either he goes, or you move on. Doing some harm, real harm to you. Ally's . . . changed. He's out of control, I think. Consumed by grief

178

and anger. An incendiary combination. He's beginning to scare me. I just wanted you to know.'

Morag let the silence lie, wondering if she could be bothered to explain her encounter with Ally at the Cauldron. What did it matter now? She was pleasantly surprised that Bonnie should care enough to come round. That's if she really was here. *Keep talking.* She shifted in her chair.

'You said you were defending me to Ally. Why?'

Bonnie looked up, her twitching fingers suddenly frozen in her lap.

'What d'you mean, why?'

Morag felt herself shrug. 'Oh, I just thought you'd washed your hands of me. Didn't want anything to do with me.' She paused to glance round the darkened room. It was a comfort to be so shut off from the outside world. The dreamlike state had taken hold. She barely noticed Bonnie's presence but continued in a low voice, almost talking to herself. 'I mean, actually, it doesn't matter now, you know. I'm past caring about it. Past caring about much. Life's dealt its blows and will aim a few more at me, I'm sure.' She stood up abruptly. 'Thanks for coming, Bonnie. Will you see yourself out? I have to go back to bed now.' She felt herself trying to get up, but her legs failed her and she slumped back down.

But Bonnie wasn't stirring, had made no move to help her. Instead, she was handing her a tissue. Why? She touched her cheek. Tears. Odd. There was no accompanying feeling. No choking sensation in her throat. No prickling of her eyes.

179

Bonnie had moved nearer, perching on the side of the chair. 'Is there someone I can call? What about your doctor?'

'Doctor? Don't be silly. I'm fine.' She felt herself scrabbling at her cheek, trying to dry the unwelcome tears. 'I'm fine, I'm fine. But, as I said, I need to go to bed now, though. So will you *please* make sure you pull the door to? I can't have it left open.'

She felt Bonnie's light touch on her shoulder. 'Okay, but I'll just make you a nice up of herbal tea. You'll have something in the cupboards, won't you? I won't be a minute.'

'I'm fine I don't want any t — '

But Bonnie had disappeared through the door. How dare she come here and take over, acting all concerned and proprietorial after treating her like a pariah for so long? The hypocrisy! *I don't want any bloody tea. I don't want you here. I just want to go to bed! Or am I in bed? Dreaming? Or am I dead?* She began rubbing furiously at her face, almost tearing at her cheeks. *I will not cry. No! What is happening to me? What?* She shut her eyes tight and stared into the blackness, studying the distorted shapes behind her eyelids. *Count yourself down. Hah! You're good at that. One hundred, ninety-nine, ninety-eight . . .*

She was barely aware of heaving herself up from the sofa and marching down the hallway to the kitchen. The trembling started as she saw the unwanted mug of tea thrust towards her. It was as if another's hand reached out to swipe the mug away, scalding liquid spattering the far wall.

Somewhere in the background, she could hear Bonnie's yelp of fear and surprise as the mug shattered on the tiled floor.

'*I told you. I don't want any tea!* I don't want help. *I want to go to sleeeep!*'

★ ★ ★

Kirstin stood halfway down the stairs, cradling the cordless phone in her hand as Bonnie stood looking up at her anxiously. 'Well?'

'She's sleeping now. The tablets Dr Lockhart recommended should knock her out for a good few hours.' Kirstin opened her fist. 'But just for safety, I've taken these away. They're the rest of the pills out of her bedroom. I'll keep them for now. Dr Lockhart's just about to leave for a fortnight in America, but her colleague will see Morag first thing tomorrow. I've agreed to spend the night here and be around when Morag wakes up. I'll drive her over for her appointment in the morning.'

Bonnie nodded. 'Good. Thanks. It's been an odd way to meet, but I'm glad I found you. You know, I don't think Morag was going to let me help. I had the devil's job calming her down. She seemed to want to smash the place up, given half a chance. I suppose it was some sort of panic reaction caused by what she's been going through. And then she just went . . . well, cold, stiff, catatonic really. I started looking around for her address book but I couldn't find it, so I grabbed the phone. It was quite pathetic, sad. She had only two entries programmed into the

181

numbers list. Dr Lockhart. And you.'

'Yes, I gave her my number the first time we met.'

Bonnie nodded. 'Thank goodness you did. Anyway, I called both and got you first. It was alarming, to put it mildly. I've never seen her like that.'

Kirstin made her way down the stairs. 'It's probably the tension and frustration. Everything getting to her. She's been a volcano waiting to blow. But don't worry. I'm just glad you were here. Okay. I've left her a note in case she wakes up before I get back. You said you needed to look in at your clinic. Want a lift? We can talk some more on the way.'

Bonnie nodded her agreement and Kirstin ushered her out of the door, hesitating for a moment before she locked up.

'What is it?' Bonnie was looking puzzled.

Kirstin shrugged and then allowed the lock to turn. 'Oh, nothing. It's all right.'

As she followed Bonnie to the car, she felt things were anything but all right. And, with her anxiety levels rising, she asked herself what else could go wrong?

21

Kirstin sighed with exasperation. The rush-hour traffic was hopeless. They were stuck in a seemingly endless queue of hot, steaming cars. Beside her, Bonnie was sipping at a bottle of mineral water, talking quietly, unworried by the heat or traffic.

'So, it's true. Morag actually shoved him into the Cauldron? He told me she was violent, but I didn't want to believe him. He must have been threatening. He's a big guy and the way he's behaving at the moment, I'd probably have done the same thing.'

Kirstin nodded. 'Yes . . . though, I watched him after he got back home and . . . he cried, he actually broke down and cried. It just seems strange. Like two people. I hear he's big, threatening, all that, and yet, there he was crying like his world was at an end.'

'Well, I think it is.' Bonnie raised her water bottle again and glanced back at Kirstin. 'He's a classic case of the bereaved male. Can't talk about his feelings, doesn't even *understand* his emotions. And he's angry. Furious at the world, railing at fate. But he wants, *needs*, to give fate a name and a face. Morag Ramsay.'

'I'm sure you're right. I was thinking of going to see this Ally myself. Reason with him, if that's possible?'

Bonnie was staring ahead again, frowning. 'I'd

183

be careful, if I were you. I came to warn Morag and I'd issue the same warning to you. When someone's on the edge like Ally is, you just don't know what they'll do. Harm themselves? Harm others? Do both?' She turned back to look at Kirstin. 'But it's very kind of you to help Morag out. It's what Jamie would have done. I feel very ashamed of how she and Jamie were treated. By us, by *some* of us. I didn't actually know for sure, but I suspected, that they were spiking her drinks, giving her too many drugs, all that. I think the prime mover would have been Iona. And Craig was besotted with her, so he'd have followed her lead. Ally would have thought it a bit of a 'jolly jape'. But then he couldn't stand Morag. At first he got on okay with her, but he quickly decided that she wasn't good enough for Craig. So, there you go, they could spike her drinks unchallenged.'

Kirstin turned her gaze from the line of cars to look at Bonnie. 'Not exactly the actions of friends?'

Bonnie shrugged her thin shoulders. 'But that's just it. The group dynamic was weird. I've thought about this a lot, believe me. The glue — the *magnets*, if you like — were Ally and Iona. They were very spoilt people. No doubt the product of their privileged upbringing. But they had charm. Charisma. Very dangerous qualities, in my view. To those taken in by them. And they had money, of course. But . . . I don't want you to think Ally is just that. Ally is . . . *complicated*. I don't know for sure, but I get the feeling that he's had things happen to him in early life, and he's just never dealt with any of it. You can just sense these things, can't you? Buried pain. He's overcompensated in other ways, though. For example, he's a very astute businessman. Pounces on an opportunity if he thinks it's a good bet. My clinic, for example. Fraser too. He went into the property business with him. And Craig. He got a tip from Craig about some pharmaceutical research and bought a load of shares in this small company. That was one deal that went belly up, though. Still, he didn't seem to hold it against Craig.'

Kirstin nudged the car forward. They were moving at last. 'And Iona?'

'Oh, she had looks *and* money. She was a failed, or rather, talentless artist, who could buy her way to the top table of the rather parochial art world here in Edinburgh. Her gallery, egotistically entitled 'The Sutherland Gallery' of course, was gaining a reputation. Give Iona her due, she had a keen eye for new work and ran a stable of young, pretty, male artists, art college graduates and the like . . . actually, thinking about that . . . you should talk to Jules.'

'Jules?'

Bonnie glanced at her quickly. 'Jules Moncrieff. He was Iona's star protégé *and*, unbeknown to her, the love of Ally's life. Jules has left him now, though.' She turned to look at Kirstin again. 'It was one of the reasons I went round to see Morag, though I've not had a chance to talk to her about it yet. I've already asked Jules if he'd meet up with Morag and he's agreed. I'll speak to him again and let him know what's happened.

Morag should meet him. He was there that day.'

Kirstin was surprised. 'I've not heard anything about him. He was at the river party?'

'Not exactly. He was there to meet Ally. A lovers' tryst. But he's got quite a good take on events later in the day.' She took another sip of her water. 'It's a bit delicate, actually. He never went to the police but, a year on, he's more relaxed about it all. His current partner is a long-term client of mine, so I've got to know Jules quite well lately. It might help Morag to meet him. And he's thoroughly sick of Ally, so that's a little incentive for him to help her.'

Kirstin smiled. 'Sounds like a good idea. Should cheer Morag up. Okay, here we are.'

Bonnie fumbled about in her bag and scribbled down a number on the back of her business card. 'Here. I've given you my home number too, just in case.'

Kirstin nodded her thanks as Bonnie slid the card on to the dashboard. They were double-parked outside Ross's office. 'I've just got to pick up the keys to Jamie's house and then I'll run you over to your clinic.' Kirstin reached for her mobile. 'Let me get Ross to come down before I get a traffic warden on my case.'

Two minutes later, there he was, shirtsleeved, looking harassed and grumpy.

Kirstin tried a smile. 'Hi. This is Bonnie. You've not met before?'

'Nope.' He gave a cursory nod to Bonnie. 'Kirstin, I'm with a client, I can't hang around. Here are the keys. I have to go.'

Kirstin cursed under her breath as she traced

his rapid retreat up the office steps. 'Rude sod. Sorry about that. Right, where's your clinic exactly?'

But Bonnie had already opened the passenger door. 'Actually, it might be quicker for me to walk it. Look at the traffic. It's rush hour now. I . . . it's been good to meet you. I'm sorry about Jamie. Really. Maybe we'll meet again. I must go, I'm so late. Bye.'

Kirstin stared after her until she disappeared down a side street. Funny woman. But she'd been far friendlier, more forthcoming, than she'd expected. If Morag didn't think Bonnie had been much of a friend to her up to now, that looked to be changing.

★   ★   ★

Clearing the flat and picking up her bags had taken longer than she'd anticipated. Kirstin squinted through the darkness at her watch as she pulled up outside Morag's house. Nearly eleven. *Shit. Please don't let her be awake yet.*

She struggled with the various keys and then stepped into the dark hallway. Silence. Good. She wandered through to the kitchen and flicked on the light switch. No sign of any disturbance other than the dried tea spatters on the far wall and a couple of shards of shattered mug on the floor that Bonnie must have missed. Except? She noticed a low cupboard door was slightly ajar. Probably Bonnie when she was making tea. And had that back-door blind been rucked up like that before? Taking the stairs two at a time, and painfully slowly to avoid any creaking floor-boards, she made it to the first-floor landing. Morag's bedroom door was open wider than she'd left it. *Damn!* She'd woken up. Kirstin hesitated before putting on the landing light. Morag may have fallen asleep again, and the last thing she needed in her state was to be woken with a start.

'Morag? I'm back.' She kept her voice to a near whisper, just in case.

She nudged the door fully open. There was nothing at first glance to show that anything had changed since she'd left. But she waited in the doorway for a moment until her eyes became accustomed to the dark. Still, all seemed as she had left it: Morag huddled under the bedclothes, the note by her glass of . . . but wait a minute! That wasn't water and that wasn't her note. It was an envelope clearly marked 'Kirstin'. She raced the last few steps to the bedside and lifted the glass to her nostrils. Brandy. Then her eyes fixed on them, shining almost luminous through the darkness. A heap of coloured capsules and white tablets spilling over the edge of the bedside table, a handful lying scattered on the carpet underneath.

22

'Bonnie, Bonnie? It's Ally. Call me. We nee — '

Bonnie stopped the message and hit the delete button. He could wait. Tonight was not the night. She was still feeling deeply unsettled from the events at Morag's a few short hours ago. Morag had seemed in such an odd mood. Perhaps Kirstin had talked some sense into her by now. She was staying the night with Morag, so all would be well. And as for Kirstin . . . there were more important things she had to discuss with her than Morag. But for tonight, that could wait. *I need to block everything out for now. I need my solitude.*

She turned away from the phone. Every window was wide open and even though the night breeze was picking up, it remained warm. Time for a walk in the garden. Her stretch of the river was running shallow and slow tonight. She could easily wade across to the other side should the desire grab her. But tonight it didn't. She felt the need to be in the cocoon of her home after such a strange and disturbing day.

She stifled a yawn and looked up to the sky. The stars were twinkling, it was a glorious evening. And yet, hard to enjoy. Perhaps if she had someone, or something, to share it with? She turned from the river view, its freshwater scent strong tonight, and made her way slowly up the garden, nodding to herself. Yes, when she made her new life, she'd get a couple of cats. Always far preferable to human company.

Something in the shrubbery to her left momentarily stopped her. A movement? A faint rustling? Breathing? Speaking of cats . . . or maybe it was one of the foxes or badgers coming out earlier than usual. She smiled and sauntered on up to the house.

It was time for a meditation. To ease her mind for whatever was to come and for whatever she decided to do. The candles were lit — a wide dispersal this evening. She felt that she needed their protection tonight. Settling into the chair, she began her breathing exercises, and then the clearing, the stilling of her mind. Readying it to allow whatever wished to come forth. Free-associating visualizations . . .

It came up in her mind's eye as a wall calendar. Date: Sunday, 13 August 2006. Suddenly, a gust of wind tore at its edge and the page flew away. She followed the ragged paper, since she too could fly. And then she was looking down, miles below. At first they were ants, the river a piece of long, winding string. Then, she was coming in to land, the Cauldron, the weir, both looming large and shimmering below her. Picnic blankets, towels, all laid out on the riverbank, the group looking upwards, agog, mouths open. Craig and Iona were standing side by side, arms waving. In welcome? Or warning . . .

She had gone so deep that she was oblivious to the entrance of the intruder. Her eyelids flickered. Captivated by her other consciousness.

She might as well have been blind, deaf and dumb to any unwarranted entry to her home.

It would be some time before she became aware of the candle flames being held to the muslin curtains.

And perilously late when she felt the fabric of her dress ignite.

Sunday, 13 August 2006

'Just like a couple of lovebirds today, aren't they,
Morag?'

'Iona! God, you gave me a fright, sneaking up
like that.'

Iona directed Morag's gaze to the sight of
Fraser and Bonnie cavorting at the fringes of the
Cauldron. His slim, deeply tanned torso was
wrestling with the bird-like Bonnie as he
threatened to throw her into the river. Her
squeals drifted over the water to where Morag
was lying.

Iona held out the champagne, watching
Morag's eyes trying to focus on the bottle.
Excellent, she was half gone already. 'Fancy
some more bubbly? C'mon, get it down you,
girl. Not much left, but there'll be another one
along in a minute.'

Morag held out her glass and accepted the rest
of the bottle with a nod. Iona hovered for a
moment and then sat down, handing her a
freshly made spliff, lighter at the ready.

'You know, Morag, I'm so excited.' Morag
accepted the light and took a long drag before
speaking.

'Excited? What, today? Here?'

Iona shook her head, ruffling a hand through
her short damp hair. She looked down, running

a finger to and fro across the fine fabric of
Morag's sarong, spread out beneath them, and
then stretched out her long, bronzed legs before
answering.

'No, not today specifically. I mean, generally.
I'm going to be making changes to my life. It's
all got a bit samey. But I feel on the cusp of
something more exciting. The gallery's doing
well and I have, at last, found the genius that will
make my name. Have you heard me talk about
Jules, Jules Moncrieff? No? Well, you'll be
hearing a lot about him everywhere soon.' She
accepted Morag's offer of the joint and sucked at
it, staring out at the Cauldron. 'And, that's not
all. My sex life is as thrilling as ever. Like you,
I'm no spring chicken and you do get to wonder,
don't you? But, it seems I've still got what it
takes. So I'm grabbing everything I can! Let me
give you a bit of advice. So should you. See you
later, Morag. Hang on in there.'

Spliff in hand, she skipped off, smiling away to
herself. Job done. She could feel Morag's stare
burning into her back, wondering what all that
was about. She'd work it out. But not today. Not
in her state. Now . . . where was Ally . . . over by
the booze.

'There you are, Iona! Come here!'

She beamed at her brother, who was waggling
another bottle straight from the icebox.

'Right, little sister, what have you been doing?
I've not seen you exchange that many words
with Morag since I don't know when.'

She patted him on the shoulder. 'Since she
became a total pain in the backside. No . . . I

193

was just preparing the ground.'

She was glad that her brother was in better spirits today. He'd been absent recently, never available, and when she'd managed to get him on the phone, he could barely utter a word. But he seemed normal today. More than normal. In fact, he was almost euphoric. Good. They were going to have a fun day.

'God, Iona. What are you up to now?' He was shaking his head in mock disapproval.

She could see that he was intrigued, and aimed a punch at his chest. 'Oh, not a lot. Craig and I are going to slip off for a while, but that's by the by. It's just that I get the feeling from our gorgeous Dr Irvine that he's going to give our Ms Ramsay the push sometime soon. I know the signs and I was just getting her in the mood. A subtle warning, if you like.'

Ally refilled her glass, smirking. 'Oh, yeah. So, are you running off with the lovely Craig, then?'

'Pah! Hardly. If he is going to leave her, it'll be for his own reasons. You know me, no ties, no baggage. I'm off for a dip. See you later!'

As she slid off her bikini top and slipped into the blissfully cool waters of the Cauldron, she gave a jaunty wave to Fraser and Craig, standing close together, like conspirators, on the wooden bridge. They waved back, grinning, and then burst out laughing, clearly enjoying their no doubt smutty joke. Gently, she lay back, naked breasts facing up towards the sun, and let the water hold her body. Ally's remark picked away at her thoughts. She hoped Craig wasn't harbouring any happy-ever-after feelings. For

194

fuck's sake, he was a grown-up. Surely he could recognize adult fun — and only fun — when he met it.

She squinted against the sun. Was that Craig's silhouette still up on the bridge? Yes. Fraser must have gone elsewhere. Didn't he want to enjoy the view too? Fraser had been the perfect example of no-ties fun. Their casual encounters had been pretty spectacular, but he knew when the end was the end. Although . . . he was looking so good at the moment, maybe she might try a little . . . reprise with him? And maybe too she might have to think about retreating from Craig sooner than she'd planned. A slow retreat. She hadn't had enough of him yet. But he wasn't the only one she needed to get out of her hair. There was other unfinished business. She'd need to think about how to handle that. Then, once free, she could make an all-out assault on the one she really wanted. The one she just might like to be tied down with.

Jules Moncrieff, here I come . . .

Hide and Seek

23

Dear Kirstin

I have had enough. Nothing can justify me being thrown into the hell I have been living in. I can no longer endure it. Whatever I may or may not be guilty of, the reviled 'Witch' is about to pay for it.

Morag

Kirstin couldn't stop blinking. Her eyes felt dry and gritty, from tears of shock and from the overwhelming, cloying heat of the hospital. She'd managed to find a darkened corner in the waiting area away from the infectious anxiety of others. For the umpteenth time a middle-aged man stepped up to the reception desk, worry etched deep into his exhausted face, only to be told quietly to sit back down and wait. She closed her eyes, fingers still clutching the note. Waiting: *the* nightmare.

'Kirstin Rutherford?'

She blinked and brought the figure standing over her into focus. A tall woman, in her fifties, smiling gently and handing her a plastic cup.

'Machine coffee. All I could get downstairs at two in the morning. I'm Isobel Lockhart. I've a lot to thank you for.'

Kirstin sat up, feeling her nerves subside, reading the woman's smile as a message of hope.

She accepted the cup. 'So, she's okay? Really? I'm so . . . so relieved. This note . . . I must've read it a thousand times tonight. Here.'

Dr Lockhart smiled again, nodding and sipping at her own coffee as she scanned the brief few lines. Her eyes too, behind the smart designer frames, were desperate for sleep. 'I see. Okay, don't worry. I'll keep this if I may? And yes, Morag is all right. You got to her in time.'

She moved to sit beside Kirstin, the smile now gone from her face. 'You'll understand there is very little I can say about Morag professionally. Because of patient confidentiality. But I know she's told you a fair bit about herself, the problems she's having. I'm going to put her in the care of one of my colleagues, with the full support of my entire team, for the next two weeks. I have to go away to the US tomorrow.' She snatched a look at her watch. 'God, today actually. I've suggested to Morag that, when she's released from here in the next day or two, she be admitted to a short-term unit, attached to my clinic, a kind of halfway house if you like. Just for the first couple of nights. The environment there is calm, there's therapeutic help on tap. It's not the first time I've made this suggestion to her. However, she's adamant that she wants to get back home. I'm not going to stop her, as long as I know she'll have outside support.'

The woman paused, obviously giving careful thought to what she was about to say next. Kirstin realized she looked more than tired. Worried. What was going through her mind

200

about Morag? Whatever it was, she couldn't ask her and wouldn't be told.

Dr Lockhart finished her coffee and looked again at Kirstin. 'As you know, Morag is extremely isolated. Both from her past friends and from her family. I realize that you've known her for only a short time, but she's told me some of your background. You've been very supportive to her.' She paused to take a deep sigh. 'So, I wondered if you felt able to take on any further responsibility, above and beyond what you've already done? I'm talking really about being prepared to call her, drop in on her regularly this next fortnight while I'm away?'

Dr Lockhart was raising a quizzical eyebrow, awaiting some response. Kirstin leant forward, her lower lip pouting as she gathered her thoughts.

'You're right. I . . . I don't know Morag well. But if Morag is happy for me to be her 'minder', then that's okay by me. I'll be staying further up the river from her, in my ex-father-in-law's house, so I'll be reasonably close by. But . . . I do have one reservation. Do you think she'll have a relapse?'

Dr Lockhart pinched at her tired eyes and pushed her spectacles back up into place. Kirstin sensed a hesitation. 'Do I think she'll try it again? Huh. It's always *the* question in these circumstances. Well, I'm neither God nor a prophet. But what I will say is this. If I considered Morag to be a serious danger to herself, then I *would* have no hesitation in having her sectioned until I got back. However,

I've just spent some time talking to her, assessing her. It's tricky. Let me put it this way. I believe that the . . . how can I put this? The *conscious, self-aware* part of her *did* believe that she intended to kill herself. It's common knowledge that she tried suicide once before in prison. So it *is* part of her make-up. *But* from speaking to the medical team here, it's clear that she didn't consume nearly enough tablets. I think part of her unconscious *didn't* want to end it all. Somewhat oversimplified, but there you have it.'

Kirstin frowned. 'What? You mean she didn't *mean* it? Could've fooled me. Morag's either a brilliant actor or just lucky, surely?'

Dr Lockhart sat back and removed her glasses. 'It's a hard one to get your head around, I know. Put it this way. She did *and* she didn't mean it. Look, let's leave it at that. We're both too tired. But you can be sure of this. Morag is incredibly resilient. A real fighter. Frankly, I'm astonished that she's survived so much pressure. I've had other patients who have gone under on far less than Morag has suffered. She *is* psychologically strong. Very strong. But everyone has their breaking point. I think Morag is testing herself to the limit.'

Dr Lockhart leant forward again, replacing the spectacles. 'So, no. I don't think Morag will try this again, given the professional support I'm leaving in place for her. And whatever you can do for her personally will be a great bonus.'

Kirstin stood up and wandered to the nearby bin to discard her cup. Was this too great a responsibility? What Dr Lockhart was asking was a lot, especially since she wasn't being given the whole picture about Morag. That felt slightly uncomfortable, although it wasn't really her business. And there was professional support in abundance. All things considered, it wasn't that much to ask. She sighed, exasperated with herself. *Come on, Kirstin, all you've done for the past two years is be self-indulgent. Where's your natural altruism gone? The Jamie you knew would be disappointed in you.*

Kirstin stepped back to the waiting area, suddenly ashamed at having even considered baulking at Dr Lockhart's request.

'Okay. Can I see her tonight?'

Dr Lockhart held up a restraining hand. 'No, I'm afraid that's not possible. She's asleep now. Call in the morning and they'll tell you how she is. Now, I wonder if I can ask you a last favour? I'd do it myself, but I have to be at the airport in a few hours. Morag needs some bits and pieces from her place. You know, toiletries, a change of night-clothes, and something to wear when she gets out. Is there any chance you could fetch some and bring them when you visit tomorrow?'

'Of course. I've still got her keys. I'll swing by her place tonight.'

They walked in weary silence until the cool night air of the car park hit them.

Dr Lockhart held out her hand. 'Thank you again. You have the number of my clinic. And I have your mobile number, which I'll pass on to my colleague if that's okay with you? D'you need a lift?'

Kirstin smiled her thanks and accepted the

outstretched hand with a firm grip. 'I'm okay. I drove here after the ambulance took Morag away. Good to meet you. Enjoy your trip.'

The tall figure strode over to the far side of the car park and disappeared into the shadows.

Kirstin sank into the driver's seat of her darkened car, head back, gritty eyes closed. Morag, Jamie, Ross, Glen. Her life had become so busy and complicated. Busy with other people, complicated with their emotions, their despair. And a little joy of course, when it came to Glen. After nearly two years in self-imposed exile, with only navel-gazing and herself to consider, now her emotional life was full to brimming. Her crusade to race up here and mourn Jamie's death had turned into something quite unexpected. And yet, wouldn't he be doing just the same for Morag? Probably more, in fact. He'd have installed her at Mill House, warding off all the evils that threatened her.

She jumped at the mobile's raucous ring. Glen. Damn. She'd forgotten all about him. He had been the first person she'd thought to ring after the ambulance had taken away Morag's near-lifeless body. She'd rung off promising him an update.

'Kirstin? What's happened? How is she? You never called me back. Is she . . . ?'

'No, she'll be fine. Long story. Look, sorry I didn't call you again. It was all a bit of a panic. I left the phone in the car and I've been in the hospital until now. Listen, can I call you tomorrow? I'm shattered. I've got to go back to Morag's and then I must sleep.'

He offered a brief goodbye and was gone. She knew her tone had been impatient and harsh. Too bad. She couldn't take on his hurt feelings as well. She felt at breaking point tonight. But there was one more call to make. She should tell Bonnie what had happened, no matter how late it was now. As far as Bonnie was concerned, she had left Morag sleeping it off in the safety of her own home. Kirstin fumbled in her pocket for Bonnie's card and punched her home number into the mobile. Strange? One single tone. Unobtainable. Kirstin tried again. And once more. She shrugged. It would have to wait until the morning. Finally, she pulled out of the car park, barely able to keep her squinting eyes open.

The last thing she would notice was the car waiting at a safe distance from Morag's house, headlights dimmed, the driver patiently intent on choosing their moment.

24

As soon as Kirstin entered the house, she knew. Staying the night was the only option. In her state it would be impossible to drive safely the mile or two back to Jamie's house. Morag wouldn't mind. The best thing was to go straight to bed and organize what Morag needed in the morning.

The hall and kitchen lights were on, just as she had left them. She searched through a couple of cupboards and then tried the living room. There *was* a drinks cabinet. In the corner. An eclectic mix. Some of the liqueur bottles looked sticky and ancient. At least this wasn't one of Morag's current problems. Stuck at the back was what she was looking for: a decent cognac. She sloshed a double shot into a balloon glass and made her way to the stairs. The nightcap was essential. She was so tired, yet wound up. Sleep wouldn't come without a bit of help. She reached the bathroom. Shit, she had no toiletries, no nightclothes. Brilliant! And then she remembered her bags in the car.

The cool air outside was welcome. She hauled a bag out from the back seat. Heading for the house, she paused and turned round, momentarily tense. Was it the faintest of noises or a movement that her senses had picked up? Forget it, she was tired. Letting nerves get the better of her. It was probably some night animal. This place was semi-rural after all. She shrugged off the worry and stepped back inside the house, securing the array of locks behind her.

Minutes later she was settled. She'd chosen a top-floor spare room at the back. Night sounds flowed in through the open window; an owl's cry, the light breeze rustling the trees. But the river was silent. Out there, flowing, but silent. The cognac was having its effect. She managed to switch off the bedside lamp before her eyes closed again and the night sounds faded away.

★ ★ ★

He'd gained entry easily. Morag might have thought she lived in a fortress, but she'd never even noticed the dodgy catch on the utility-room window. It had been some time since he'd set foot in here. In those days, although not exactly a welcome visitor, he'd been included in all her party invitations. Craig would have insisted on that. And what parties they had been! Now, life was so very different. He could have, maybe should have, invited himself in months ago. Had it out with her face to face. But, even until recently, there had been a modicum of caution and control left in him. Not now. He paused halfway across the kitchen to listen. Nothing, she wasn't stirring. The drinks cabinet was already open and welcoming as he padded into the living room. He eyed the unstoppered cognac bottle. So, she was on the booze, eh? Not exactly a surprise. He raised the bottle to his lips and took a long satisfying pull. And another. Replacing the bottle soundlessly on the sideboard, he turned, looked up at the ceiling and nodded.

He knew where the creaking stair was and heaved himself up and over it with ease. Her first-floor bedroom door was wide open, but the light from the landing couldn't reach into the far corner where he knew her bed lay. Slowly, silently he crossed the threshold. He could feel his heartbeat rising, breathing quickening, leg muscles flexing. With a lightning last few steps he was on the bed, its frame complaining under his weight as he leapt on to the firm mattress. Immediately he knew she wasn't there. Only a handful of pillows lay crushed beneath his white-knuckled fists. Where the hell was she? He'd seen her. Spied her shadow moving behind the blinds. This *was* her bedroom. He knew the layout of her house. Suddenly, a wave of panic shivered through him. What if she'd seen or heard him entering and was cowering in some cubbyhole calling the police? *Shit!* He strained his ears, willing them to pick up her frantic whispering. Nothing. Slowly, he released his grip on the pillows, backing off from the bed until he was standing, hands hanging loosely by his sides. Again, he craned his neck back and looked up at the ceiling, his visual memory sketching the layout above him. *The top floor!* She was hiding up there.

This richly carpeted flight gave out no creaks. Confidently, and with a firm hand on the banister, he hoisted himself up to the top, two steps at a time. The upper-landing light was far dimmer. A mere glow-worm. Good. Instinctively he knew which room she'd chosen, and then he heard it. Even, gentle breathing. The rhythm of sleep.

He had her.

25

Swim, Kirstin! Swim for your life! Try as hard as she could, she was unable to make it. The sheer weight, as the waters of the Cauldron pressed down on her, was too much. She could feel her lungs collapsing under the pressure. Only one or two seconds of air left. And what was this? Some long, slim green tendrils. Reeds encircling her throat, squeezing the life from her, wringing out the very last breath. Above, through the shimmering water, she could see them. Lined up along the riverbank. Jamie, Morag, Ross, Glen. Their bodies bent at the waist, leaning over, staring down at her quizzically. As if she was some curious specimen in a fish tank. Why wouldn't they help her? Please . . . please . . .

Kirstin tugged at the reeds — no, *hands*, iron-strong *hands* — welded to her neck, and kicked off the duvet, struggling to free herself, nails clawing at the strangling paws.

She gasped out the words. '*Stop! Please . . . please!*'

Without warning, the hands were released and the bulky figure jumped back, almost toppling from the bed.

Kirstin slid off the other side of the mattress and backed away, keeping the king-sized bed between them. But it wasn't enough. Alistair Sutherland had the advantage of her. He was guardian of the door. All she had behind her were locked windows and a two-storey drop. Her shaking hands were still wrapped protectively round her neck. She was beyond coughing. Instead, she bent forward, gasping for each precious, painful breath. Her chest felt crushed. He must have been levering his full weight on her at one point.

'Who the hell are you?' he barked at her. 'Where's Morag?'

After two more heaving breaths, she tried to respond, her voice a rasping whisper. 'I . . . I know you, you're Alistair Sutherland. My name's Kirstin. I was Jamie Munro's daughter-in-law. I'm . . . I'm sorry about your sister. Really. But look, Morag's in hospital.' Kirstin paused, trying to swallow. Although the room was warm, she shivered in her skimpy vest and shorts. 'Morag tried to kill herself today . . . whatever you wanted to do tonight she almost did for herself already. And I know what happened a few nights ago by the Cauldron. I saw you coming back to your home afterwards. Morag and I drove to your house. Please, please stop all this. If I can help you, I will. But, please, leave Morag alone.'

She tried to stand up straight and failed. Instead, she backed further away, eventually finding support on a windowsill. The words had come out as a weak and pitiful plea. But she'd tried her best. And somehow, the atmosphere had changed. He seemed less threatening, less frightening. In fact, he seemed . . . *glazed*. As if he was in shock.

He took a half step back, frowning. 'When? *When* did she try to kill herself?'

Kirstin returned the frown. His tone was measured, inquiring, as if he was trying to work something out. She shrugged. 'I don't know exactly when. Yesterday afternoon, maybe early evening. I don't know *exactly* when. Why?'

He began shaking his head violently, muttering more to himself than her. 'She's dead. But she still could have done it. She's dead. *She's dead! Dead!*'

Kirstin stood up at last. What in God's name was he gibbering about? She tried to keep her voice light, conversational. 'Who's dead? Morag's not dead. I told you, she's in the hospital.'

His head was shaking and he was simultaneously fumbling with and cursing at a cigarette packet. At last his trembling fingers struck the match and he drew heavily on the first drag, the acrid stench of exhaled smoke making her feel instantly nauseous.

He swallowed a lungful of smoke and looked at her, his head stilled again.

'Bonnie. Bonnie Campbell's *dead.*' He looked down at the burnt-out match still clamped between his fingers and thrust it towards her face. 'Burnt. Like this! Gone. She was going to see her. She was going to see Morag, I'm sure of it. She must've done it. Destroyed Bonnie so she couldn't tell me where that witch was running away to. I'm going to get her for it.'

He stumbled backwards until his legs hit a chair. Slowly, he slumped into it, muttering, 'I'm going to, going to.'

Kirstin took a step forwards, her brain straining to take in the information. 'Bonnie?

No, that's not right. I saw her, here, today. She was here visiting Morag, before she tried to take her own life. Bonnie's fine, really.' But somewhere the first flicker of anxiety was stirring. *Remember . . . Bonnie's number . . . unobtainable.*

He flicked ash on to the carpet, his head drooping. 'Her cottage. Further up the river, round the bend. Burnt out. Bonnie was in it. Didn't you hear sirens, see fire engines? *She's gone.* The police say it was an accident. All those candles. She always had *bloody* candles on the go, hundreds of them sometimes, silly woman. But no, it was that . . . that *witch*, Morag. Going to get her, going to . . . '

His voice had faded away, head still drooping, the glowing cigarette hanging loosely from his fingers. Kirstin moved forward, keeping a safe distance, one hand reaching out for the cold brass of the Victorian bedstead, her mind reeling at his news.

'Oh, God . . . no, look, I'm sorry, sorry about Bonnie. I . . . I don't know what to say. But whatever you've got in your mind, I can tell you Morag was nowhere near Bonnie's. She spent most of the afternoon in bed and took her overdose sometime between then and when I found her late last night.'

She took a long, slow breath, trying to think carefully about what to say next. 'I . . . I don't know these people like you do, but I've seen both of them today . . . well, yesterday now. Morag isn't, *wasn't*, an enemy of Bonnie's. There is absolutely no reason to think she was. Bonnie helped Morag yesterday, when she was upset, and Morag was grateful. Believe me. It's true.'

He jumped up, cigarette butt ground out beneath his foot, the reek of burning carpet filling the air. 'No, *I don't believe it! That lunatic did it. Somehow. She did it.*'

He was moving towards her, gripping the other end of the bedstead as she looked from his face to the doorway and back again. She steeled herself to make a run for it, momentarily forgetting the aching in her chest and throat. *One, two, three.*

As she made her move, he caught her, his fist encircling her arm and pulling her to him in a mock embrace. 'Tell me! What hospital? What ward? *Then* I'll let you go.'

Suddenly, they both heard it, their eyes darting to the door. A heavy thud of running feet hammering up the stairs. A second later, the tall figure was silhouetted in the bedroom doorway.

'You'll let her go, *now.*'

Kirstin gasped at the sight of Glen, relief bringing on the tears she'd been holding back since the attack. Alistair Sutherland dropped her aching arm and turned to meet Glen's approach. Instead of stopping when he saw her arm released, Glen kept marching across the room and hurled himself at Alistair Sutherland, pushing him against the wall with such force that she heard the breath winded out of him.

'What the fuck are you doing here, Sutherland? Eh? Eh?' Glen's tone was belligerent, needling, spoiling for a fight.

She stepped forward, wiping the tears from

her eyes, hands outstretched in appeal. 'It's okay now, Glen. He was leaving. Let him go. I'll tell you about it all in a minute. Just . . . just get him out of here.'

It was as if he hadn't heard, or was ignoring her. He pushed a struggling Alistair Sutherland back against the wall. 'I said, what the fuck are you doing here? Eh?'

But this time his opponent had found his breath again. 'It's got nothing to do with you, Glen. Let go of me! I'm warning you.'

Ally Sutherland lashed out with a kick and headed for the stairs. Glen made to follow, but Kirstin grabbed his arm.

'Leave him. Leave him! He doesn't know what he's doing.'

Again he ignored her, and raced out towards the landing.

'No, Glen! No!' She swung out of the room and on to the top landing just in time to see the push and Ally Sutherland crashing down the stairs, flailing arms unable to break his fall. For a few chilling seconds, he lay inert on the first landing. Had Glen killed him? Broken his neck?

She could feel the hysteria rising in her. 'Stop it, Glen! Stop! *Just stop!*'

By now Ally was on his second wind, and though bleeding heavily from his mouth and forehead, he made one final effort and staggered to his feet. The single, powerful punch connected with Glen's jaw and felled him. In one clumsy movement, Ally stumbled towards the front door and threw a poisonous glare at Glen, the sound of his running feet fading away as he fled down Morag's drive.

★ ★ ★

Kirstin turned for the umpteenth time in the uncomfortable bed. Two hours ago she'd managed to settle Glen, face bruised and battered, in one of Morag's other spare rooms. The memory of the fight had left her feeling . . . what? Shaken, obviously. But worse than that . . . uneasy. Uneasy about Glen. She loathed violence. He might have killed Ally Sutherland. And the deliberate push down the stairs was simply appalling. What the hell had possessed him?

Of course, she was thankful that Glen had been concerned about her, that he'd turned up on the off chance of seeing her. He had saved her from God knows what. But it had come at a price. There had been something . . . excessive, *gratuitous*, about his violent response. After all, Ally seemed more . . . more *unbalanced* than dangerous. He was, quite simply, at the end of his tether. No, Glen had been excessive. She could never in a million years imagine Ross, for example, wading in like that. He'd never have displayed the sheer raw ferocity she'd witnessed from Glen. She had to admit it, Glen's behaviour had made her think differently about him. Yes, he'd been kind, considerate, sensitive to her this past week. Seductively so. But this violent reaction had compromised her feelings.

She turned to look at the luminous display

glowing out from the bedside clock. Ten past five. There was going to be no sleep tonight. She kicked off the duvet and fumbled about for her jeans and T-shirt. Two minutes later, she was padding down to the next landing. His door was open and she could hear the steady breathing. Lucky sod. She wasn't going to be that fortunate. The last couple of hours had been spent tossing and turning, reliving the fight, worrying about Morag and, most persistently, pushing away the image of Bonnie Campbell.

As she backed out of his room and shut the door quietly behind her, she glanced at the room opposite; Morag's study. Once she'd packed Glen off to bed, she'd entered Morag's study and helped herself to the computer to see what, if any, news there was of Bonnie's death, but nothing was available. She should try again. Settling herself down, Kirstin started her search. Details were still sketchy, but there was enough to confirm Ally Sutherland's story.

breakingnews/latest/Edinburgh/05.00hrs/ update/

EDINBURGH WOMAN DIES IN COTTAGE BLAZE

A 34-year-old woman died last night in a blaze at her home. The woman, who has yet to be named, lived in a cottage by the Water of Leith to the west of Edinburgh. Fire services were alerted to the blaze last night after a neighbour became concerned. The neighbour noticed flames and smoke and went to investigate, thinking that a barbecue or garden fire was out of control. But on arrival, it was clear that the interior of the cottage was engulfed by the blaze. Early reports suggest that the source of the fire appeared to be the unusually large number of candles that the victim had lit.

breakingnews/end/next update 06.00hrs/

Horrific. A dreadful way to die. And what would this do to Morag? Kirstin wished now that Dr Lockhart had insisted on Morag spending the next fortnight in the halfway house attached to the clinic. Maybe there she could have been kept away from upsetting news. In any event, the clinic would have to be informed. She'd have to call Dr Lockhart's colleague and talk it through. More worry, more responsibility. She glanced over her shoulder, imagining that she could hear Glen making his way down the stairs. But that was all it was; her imagination. With a heavy sigh, she crossed the room to the small but inviting settee, and leant back, eyes closed, realizing that she was beginning to regret returning to Edinburgh. So far, all it had achieved was to bring her into contact with death, despair and danger. For the first time since involving herself in this misery, she realized that the emotions, the *vibrations* surrounding these people, these events, were more than unsettling.

They were frightening.

26

Kirstin tried to ignore the morning sunlight seeping through a chink in the curtains, but failed. She kicked off the light cotton throw and sat up on the settee, remembering where she was. Morag's study. And then she saw the piece of notepaper float down from the settee to the carpet.

Hi,

Didn't want to wake you. I've got an early meeting. Hope you're okay and didn't get too much of a scare last night. Either from that sod Sutherland or me. I know I went at it a bit gung-ho! Sorry. But I thought he looked dangerous. Considered calling the police, but haven't. Can we talk about it all? Tonight? I'd like to take you out.

Hope today's better than yesterday!

G x

PS: found where he broke in — utility room — have screwed lock back on — botched job but will hold for now. x

The flippant tone should have annoyed her. Yet, with the light of day and a few hours' sleep under her belt, she could now manage a wry smile. At least Glen recognized that he'd gone way over the top. She felt achy and under the weather as she wandered through to Morag's kitchen. Surprisingly, it was filled with morning sunshine. Glen must have pulled up the blinds. She unlocked the door leading to the patio. The sky was a perfect, cloudless mid-blue. In the distance, she recognized the ribbon of river and cast her eye over the entire landscape, enjoying its morning freshness. And then she remembered. Somewhere, out there, hidden by trees, was the burnt-out shell of Bonnie Campbell's home. And somewhere, in a mortuary, lay her charred remains. She reached for a chair and sat down, feeling nauseous. *You must eat something soon. Look after yourself.*

An hour later, the shower and stale toast had dulled the nausea but not her exhaustion. As she parked near the hospital entrance, Kirstin felt the anxiety start up again. She'd been unable to make direct contact with Dr Lockhart's colleague. All that could be done was leave a couple of voicemail messages and try to convey to an infuriatingly unflappable assistant that the matter was extremely urgent.

She grabbed the holdall containing Morag's things and headed for the lifts. As she pressed the button, a fresh worry presented itself. Would she be allowed to visit? She hadn't even rung in, like Dr Lockhart had suggested. Too bad, she'd just have to wing it. She stepped out into the familiar stifling heat that seemed to pervade all hospitals, her anxiety levels rising by the second.

Morag was barely recognizable. She seemed to have become paler and more frail during the past twelve hours. Her fan of dark hair, spreading across the brilliant white pillows, created a tableau reminiscent of some Pre-Raphaelite portrait. Kirstin nodded her thanks to the nurse and took the plastic chair that was offered.

The nurse was hovering. 'Just talk to her. She's in and out of sleep. But on the mend. Physically, that is. She'll need a lot of rest. Dr Mackeson has been to see her and is due again sometime today. Anyway, if you need anything just make yourself known to the nurses' station over there, okay? Now, I'll draw the curtain across and let you have some privacy.'

'Morag?' Kirstin caught the flickering of an eyelid. 'Morag? It's Kirstin. Hello? You're all right now.'

The blinking was rapid and then, abruptly, it stopped. A moment later, Morag offered the quiver of a smile. 'H . . . hi there. God, I've been dreaming. So much. You were in one. Down at the Cauldron. Saving me from Ally. And the flooding waters at the weir.'

Kirstin leant forward and laid her fingers on Morag's slim, surprisingly cold hand. It was a bad start. If she wasn't even getting some respite in sleep, what refuge *could* she find? But Morag gripped her hand back and struggled to sit up.

'It's okay, Kirstin. It had a happy ending. You saved me.' She blinked again, casting her eye around the surroundings as if still trying to work

221

out where she was. 'How long have I been here? And . . . and, oh, Jesus.' She tightened her grip on Kirstin's hand, the fingernails unintentionally digging too deep. 'Look, Kirstin, I'm sorry, so sorry. About . . . all *this*. And . . . the letter. I didn't . . . want to make you feel responsible.'

Carefully, Kirstin removed Morag's hand and began rearranging the sheets round her, anxious to ensure she was as calm and relaxed as possible.

'Morag, you didn't make me feel responsible. Just very, *desperately*, worried about you. I'm not going to ask you why. That's a stupid question. I just want to know, how do you feel now? Please, be honest with me.'

Morag was struggling to sit up straighter, reaching for the beaker of water and holding up a hand in protest at Kirstin's efforts to retrieve it for her. 'No, I can manage, thanks.' The clipped delivery and sharp manner were back. She took a long suck on the straw. And then another. Finally, she seemed ready.

'The *honest* answer is that I'm not sure how I feel, *what* I feel. I'm numb, my head's like cotton wool, thick, dense. I *feel* nothing. At the moment. Dr Lockhart's colleague was here this morning in time to see me wake up. She's pleasant. Obviously knows her stuff. She's still trying to get me to stay at the clinic's residential unit. Dr Lockhart was trying that last night. I don't want to, Kirstin. You must understand that. *I don't want to!*'

The last few words were a near shout. She was obviously becoming distressed. Kirstin half expected a nurse to come bustling in asking what was going on. She shuffled her chair closer to the bed, her own voice a whisper.

'Ssh, Morag, okay. No one's going to make you. Dr Lockhart assured me of that. It's just that those who are caring for you must think it's a good thing for you right now.'

But Morag was shaking her head, and squirming in the bed, almost kicking the sheets off. 'I don't want to be incarcerated *anywhere* ever again. I couldn't stand it. Can you imagine what it's like? No freedom, your every move watched, controlled. I want to go *home*. While I've still got one, that is. *I won't be locked up!*'

Kirstin offered her the water again, hoping that any displacement activity would be a welcome distraction. It was. With relief she watched as, biddably, Morag took the plastic beaker from her and drank greedily, suddenly calm again.

She smiled. 'You know, Kirstin, it was you . . . you and Bonnie who saved my life, one way or another. It's funny. Last night wasn't like when I was in prison. I planned that one down to the last. Checked out the sink and the plumbing, assured myself that the strips of clothing would be strong enough to strangle me. But . . . but yesterday, it was like I was some sort of automaton, sleepwalking through it all. Detached and, again, strangely numb, unfeeling. Certainly, I knew what I was doing. I didn't take the pills you gave me. After you and Bonnie had gone I unearthed my secret stash. I even found time to write to you, believing that this was the end. But

223

I didn't take enough. And . . . and Dr Lockhart left me with this thought last night, and I think she's right. Some part of me must have wanted to live. Otherwise, why didn't I take the whole lot?'

She stopped, breaking her gaze from Kirstin and looking into the middle distance. The vulnerability was back. 'The fact that I want to go home, be in my garden, see the trees, even the river again. That must be a good sign. A sign that I prefer life, any sort of life, over oblivion.' Kirstin offered her a sympathetic half smile before Morag continued. 'I'll never be able to thank you enough for helping me. And I'll never, ever be able to thank Jamie, except through you. I hope we can become friends, you and I. Somehow I think Jamie would approve, don't you?'

Kirstin smiled her agreement, feeling the tears welling up. 'Of course I do. And . . . maybe we need to start thinking about your new beginning, eh? Time I made a few phone calls, checked out the possibilities.'

That brought a matching smile from Morag. 'Definitely. You know, I've always loved the sea.'

Kirstin felt the lurch in her stomach. Now was the time. There could be no escaping the moment. She leant forward, offering another reassuring squeeze to Morag's hand.

'Morag? I need to tell y — '

Suddenly, the curtain was drawn back and the friendly nurse from earlier popped her head round.

'Ms Rutherford, can I have a word?

Kirstin moved into the middle of the ward as the nurse pulled the curtain across.

'Morag's therapist is here. Dr Mackeson. She wants to see you.'

A surprisingly young woman, dressed in jeans and casual shirt, stepped forward. She was slightly out of breath and unsmiling, her face grave as she offered her hand. 'I'm Liz Mackeson. I got your message and have literally run round from visiting another patient. Tell me. About Bonnie Campbell. Have you told Morag?'

Kirstin shook her head. 'No. But it'll have to be done.'

Dr Mackeson laid a hand on her shoulder. 'Don't worry, leave this to me. Are you going to be okay? I'll call you later, if I may?'

With that, she stepped away and made for Morag's bed. Kirstin stood, marooned in the middle of the busy ward, and then turned on her heel. It was as she shouldered her way through the swing doors that she heard it.

Morag's agonized animal wail.

27

Kirstin reached across Jamie's desk to switch on the lamp and paused, taking a final look through the bay windows down to the river. The rest of the day had left her tired and downcast. Dr Mackeson had rung. Morag had been persuaded to enter the clinic's residential unit, just for a day or two. There they could help her deal with Bonnie's death. As for Bonnie, the local news had eventually turned its attention to the fire. The reports had been scanty: a tragic accident probably caused by candles. They told of an incident the previous year, when the fire service had been called to Bonnie's address to deal with curtains that had caught alight, again from candle flames. So that was that, then. A life snuffed out through carelessness.

After Dr Mackeson's call, Kirstin had spent much of the afternoon in the garden, desperate for some space. She didn't want to think. She didn't want to feel. She just wanted to relax. But she'd ended up falling asleep, dozing fitfully and unsatisfyingly. The study was nearly in darkness now. She remembered popping her head into this room countless times throughout her marriage to Ross. Cosy in winter, with a glowing hearth to sit by, watching the flames. Or, like now, enjoying a warm summer evening, the windows thrown open, sipping wine, listening to the sounds of nocturnal creatures emerging to face the night.

She clicked on the desk lamp, immediately extinguishing her view of the river, and looked around the familiar room. It was conventionally furnished for a man of Jamie's age and background: all leather and wood panelling but with lighter, personal touches. Photos of Ross from boy to man, images of Jean throughout the years, and more recent additions of Jamie as a river volunteer and guide. She wondered who had taken those. Glen?

As she bent to start sorting the papers piled on the desk, the sound of a car horn from the front of the house made her jump. Ross was expected, but not yet. She trotted down the hallway and opened the front door. She recognized Glen's Land Rover, its full-beam headlights momentarily dazzling her, and walked over to meet him as he cut the engine.

He gave a jaunty wave through the driver's open window. 'Thought you might like some company. I was passing and wondered if you fancied a bite out? I've been trying to call you all day. Your phone down?'

She stood at the driver's door, looking up at him. Finding a smile of any sort was hard. 'I've had it switched off. I'm very tired. Look, I've got a lot to do tonight. I need to settle myself in here. Start on Jamie's papers. Ross reckons the whole clear-out should take me a few days. Oh, and by the way, I imagine there'll be river association material that you want to have back.'

He'd leant out of the window to smile down at

her. For a moment, she thought he was going to touch her face.

'Eh . . . anything that you think relates to the association, just leave to one side. I can pick it up whenever. But, are you sure you're up to the job? I mean, it might be a bit difficult. Upsetting. Ross should have asked me to go through it. I can come over again tonight, no matter how late . . . '

He leant further down to her, his hand dangling. Should she take it?

'And I'd like to apologize. Properly. I shocked myself by lashing out at Sutherland. I've been thinking about little else since it happened. I used to be a bit of a hard nut, a real scrapper in my youth. But violence is so far from my life now. I guess I have a lot of underlying resentment and frustration towards him. The whole lot of them, in fact. One way or another they'd made my life, and Jamie's, hell. Anyway, if you want me tonight, I'm here.'

She shook her head. 'Thank you. Really. But not tonight. Ross will be here soon. He's coming round to show me exactly what's to be done.' Then she'd remembered. 'And . . . speaking of Ross . . . he told me that you knew each other. When you were kids? You didn't mention it.'

He moved back into the driver's cab and for a second she couldn't see his face. Then she heard his laugh as he leant forward, smiling. 'What? Oh, that. Well, we hardly knew each other. We inhabited rather different worlds, Ross and I, socially speaking. Me and my lot were, not quite from the wrong side of the tracks, but . . . eh, we thought everyone who lived round Ross's part of the river were the posh lot. I guess they were, actually. I remember we had a fight once, me and Ross. But I was only staying nearby for a very short time. My parents rented a cottage for a while. Funnily enough, the one Bonnie Campbell lived in. It was a kind of stopgap when my dad was between jobs. Then we moved away.'

He leant backwards into the Land Rover again and started the engine, talking over its noise. 'That was one of the main reasons I wanted this job. To be near the river I remembered from my childhood. Look, I'll let you get on. Take care. I'll miss you.'

Kirstin raised her hand in farewell and wandered back through the house into the study. She sipped at her wine, surveying the endless piles of paper and notebooks on the desk and floor, alongside various cardboard boxes marked in Ross's scrawl, 'Dad's river work'. She readied herself for work, but Glen's visit stayed in her mind. He had been too good to be true after all. Now she knew at least one of his faults. *Please let that be the worst.*

But, as she bent over Jamie's desk, ready for her task, the niggling doubts refused to melt away.

28

She'd *still* not made a start on Jamie's study. Instead, for the last hour, she'd allowed herself to be waylaid by some photos of Jamie, taken early last summer before the awful events at the Cauldron. Glen had given them to her, along with Jamie's baseball cap, during their first evening together. The memory of that recent generosity lifted her doubtful mood, and she felt more optimistic about him again.

She heard a car door slam. Ross.

'Kirstin!'

She scrabbled to hide the photos under a pile of papers. *Shit*. She should keep them in the car, away from Ross's prying eyes. The last thing she wanted was him asking any questions. Where are they from? Who gave them to you? She certainly wasn't up for anything tonight. Just a quick guide through Jamie's study and what had to be done.

Ten minutes later, they were sitting looking out at the darkened garden and river. Ross had picked up on her downcast mood and they'd abandoned the work in the study to open a welcome second bottle of wine.

He was being genuinely sympathetic. 'The thing is, Kirsty, I'm sorry to hear Morag Ramsay's taken an overdose, but she's clearly a very troubled woman. Leave her to the professionals. There's nothing you can do.'

She shook her head at him. 'I don't agree. I'm going to be her voluntary helper, carer, if you like, for the next week or two. Until her therapist gets back from the States. I'm also going to ask my friends on the Devon coast if they can help her out with work. She's going to relocate somewhere. Why not the south-west? It's beautiful, and far enough away from here.' She paused before making her final point hit home. 'Your dad would have approved.'

Without warning, he stood up. The action was abrupt, unexpected. She stared up at him. 'Ross?'

He walked the length of the room in silence and then returned to sit down again, his hand raised in appeasement. 'I want you to hear me out on something. Please.'

He looked at her for consent. She gave an almost imperceptible nod and began to feel the tug of anxiety.

Ross seemed relieved. 'Good. Okay.' He took a deep breath before going on. 'When Dad began to get what I considered to be over-involved with Morag Ramsay, her case and all that, I wanted to do something. I was worried about him for a number of reasons that we both know about. But this murder, or rather manslaughter, thing was just about the limit.'

He broke off to refill their wine glasses. Kirstin sensed he was reluctant to go on. 'To be frank, I didn't trust this woman. Look, I'm no naïve fool. I know the police get things wrong and their investigation of the Cauldron killings was a joke, by all accounts. On the other hand, they'd

231

looked at all the victims' contacts and eventually locked on to her. It wasn't some arbitrary decision on their part. I'm sure they thought they had the right person. I gave all this careful thought as I witnessed Dad being sucked further into it. And, I was suspicious. In short, I thought Morag Ramsay might be using Dad. So I began my own investigation into her.'

Kirstin felt her stomach muscles tighten. Where the hell was this conversation going? 'What d'you mean, 'investigation'?'

'I *mean*, I wanted to know a bit more about the woman whom my elderly father was going out on a limb for. As it happens, I didn't get very far. He died soon after visiting her on remand and . . . I had other things to think about then.'

Kirstin saw the hint of tears in his eyes. 'But what did you do, what did you find out, before that?'

He brushed a hand down his face, as if tired, trying to hide his real emotion. 'I went to see someone you should meet. I have an old law school acquaintance. Harry Kinnaird. He's a corporate lawyer at the pharmaceutical firm that Craig Irvine worked for. Harry and Craig became friends. Saw a lot of each other socially. Until Morag Ramsay put a stop to that.' Ross paused. He was finding it difficult to go on.

Kirstin prompted him. 'Meaning?'

'I mean, Harry tells a tale of an excessively jealous, unstable woman, who would fly off the handle at Craig with disturbing regularity. Break stuff up in the house and she certainly hit him on more than one occasion. In short, she was a bit of a bunny-boiler.' Ross held up both hands. 'Yes, you can say this was maybe just lads' pub talk, slagging off women. But Harry's not like that. I know he spoke to the police, he was so concerned after the killings. I would have got Dad to go and see him. Maybe that would have changed his mind. But . . . but he died before I could arrange that. I think you should go and see Harry, though. Please. I don't want you . . . to be . . . adversely affected through being too kind to this woman. Yes, she may be innocent. Who knows? But I think you should find out more about her before you offer too much of yourself to her cause. I'm serious, Kirstin.'

He held out a pleading hand. 'Let me put it another way. As a favour to me, will you please go and see him? Tomorrow.'

29

The east end of Princes Street gardens, down the slope from the Scott monument, was surprisingly quiet. The main throngs of tourists were elsewhere and it was still too early for the gangs of office workers, desperate to catch some lunchtime sunshine. Kirstin sat on a shaded bench, staring blankly at a couple of feuding pigeons ten feet away.

Harry Kinnaird had sounded surprisingly personable on the phone. She'd wanted to dislike him. Giving her prejudices free rein, she had him down as insufferable and arrogant, like all overpaid corporate lawyers. But he'd seemed far from that. Rather, he'd been quietly spoken with a warmth to his voice.

Nevertheless, she still felt guilty about being here. Later today, or certainly tomorrow, she'd have to face Morag. Pop in and see her, pretend that she hadn't met up with someone who quite possibly thought her guilty as sin. And why was she here to see this person? As a sop to Ross, who was obviously genuinely worried about her? Yes, but that wasn't reason enough. There was something nagging away in the back of her mind about Morag, however much she wanted to ignore it. Two things, in fact.

First, there was Morag's frantic phone call after she was attacked by Alistair Sutherland. Her first words. '*Kirstin! Kirstin! I've killed him.*

It's happened. Again!' Again. What did she mean by that? Was it merely a panicky reference to her fear that she was going to be unjustly arrested for killing *again*? Or, did the reference have another meaning?

Secondly, Dr Lockhart at the hospital. Although apparently confident of Morag's mental resilience, Kirstin had picked up on . . . what? A hesitation? A doubt? Something the doctor couldn't discuss with a lay person?

Kirstin was ninety-nine per cent sure that Morag was a wronged victim. Yet still, she was here . . .

'The woman in red. That was a good idea of yours. Hi, I'm Harry.'

She twisted round in her seat to see a tall, slim man in shirtsleeves smiling at her. 'Oh? Hello. Yes. Just as well I'm the only one in the vicinity wearing red.' She stood up and took his outstretched hand. 'Shall we just sit here?'

He smiled, hanging his sunglasses from his shirt pocket. 'Yeah, why not.'

He sat down with his body turned towards her, the suit jacket slung casually over his knees. 'I had another chat with Ross this morning. He told me about you . . . you knowing Morag Ramsay . . . and *helping* her?'

'Yes. Look, I'm sure Ross will have told you that I have a *very* different perspective on Morag than either of you. Just because I'm here doesn't mean that I in any way seriously doubt her. However, as I used to say to myself when I worked in criminal law, if you're going to take the side of the angels, you'd better be sure that they really are angels you're fighting for.'

Harry Kinnaird looked amused and glanced away from her, down the slope to a group of teenagers cavorting on the grass. 'And if you discover they're not?'

She followed the direction of his gaze, and gave an involuntary smile at the joyful group. 'Then you have to live with that. And, hopefully, learn from it. You obviously think Morag's no angel. I'd like to know why.'

Harry Kinnaird's open features closed, leaving his expression serious, almost stern. 'I was, I *am* still very upset at Craig's death. The shock of it. The way it happened. I didn't immediately jump to the conclusion that Morag had done it. Whatever I thought of her, I couldn't imagine her doing something like that. No, at first I thought it was just incredibly bad luck. That some nutcase had come upon them.'

He shifted in his seat, trying to get comfortable. 'And that *may* still be the case. One must always keep some part of one's mind open. But what made me become suspicious of Morag was when Ross got in touch with me. I'd only met Jamie a few times at Law Society do's and suchlike. He was a great old guy. So when Ross told me he was worried about his father becoming involved in her case, I was prepared to help.'

He looked directly at her, his voice low but firm. 'And from what I could gather, the Morag that Jamie knew seemed a million miles away from what I'd heard via Craig, and seen with my own eyes.'

236

Kirstin glanced over his shoulder, not wanting to meet his penetrating gaze. The story was beginning to sound familiar. As with Jamie, was there another version of Morag?

She met his eyes. 'Who was the Morag that you knew?'

He bent his head to the ground and began toeing a loose tuft of grass. 'Let me start at the beginning. This part I know only through Craig. We didn't become friends until he moved to Edinburgh. A job Morag headhunted him for. Craig was a bit blown away by her then. Granted, headhunters aren't shrinking violets, but she'd oozed determination, delivered with charm, and she showed a real knowledge of what his work was about. She's a science graduate herself, so they could speak the language, as it were. In a flash she bagged him for the job and, ultimately, for herself. Though her . . . her . . . *possession* of him took a while. It was a slow-burn process, you see. And all the more chilling for it, in my view.' He moved his jacket to the back of the bench before continuing. 'Let me explain. The first year saw each of them being a bit cautious. Both admitted to a string of unsuccessful relationships. He *did* have some long-term relationship history. But that was in his early twenties when he was fast-tracking on his PhD. He'd welcomed stability then. And, for a while with Morag, he thought he might again.'

Kirstin nodded. 'So at one time he *was* serious about her? After all, they were together . . . what? Two and a half, three years?'

'Yes. But after a while, he began to crave

237

change. Like many men, afraid of emotion and commitment. It coincided with Morag buying the house near the river and hooking up with that lot. Craig was a big hit with them, and it went to his head. Morag hated that.' He gave a hopeless shrug. 'It was a mess. He'd thrown himself into the relationship with Morag while it suited. But he was far from happy by this stage. She wasn't happy either. That was obvious. If only she'd made the first move to end it. The thing was, Craig told me that Morag had never been the kind of woman whose neediness was immediately obvious. She'd fooled him. As soon as she got wind that he was restless, the trouble began.'

Kirstin frowned. 'So far it's a pretty everyday story of love going wrong. What exactly was this trouble?'

Harry Kinnaird stretched out his long legs and peeled his sticky shirt from his back. The day was now sweltering. 'Craig made a big mistake. Two mistakes. Although they spent most of their time at her house — not surprising, really, it's beautiful — Craig still refused to move in with her. Secondly, and I witnessed this after a boozy dinner party, Craig raised the subject of open relationships. I don't know what possessed him. Maybe it was a coward's way of saying 'I want out'. But it created a state of near hysteria in Morag. He'd known her insecurities were there under the surface, but this seemed to push her almost over the edge, leaving him wishing he'd never raised the subject.'

He loosened his tie and unbuttoned the neck

of his shirt. 'Morag walked out of the dinner party . . . Craig batted it all off as 'unimportant', just 'a topic of discussion', but you could see he was upset at her behaviour.'

Kirstin half smiled. 'Well, she's got a point, don't you think? I'm sorry, Harry, all that you've told me seems iffy second-hand gossip from Craig, and he had his own motives for demonizing her. He wanted rid of her, after all. Her reactions seem perfectly reasonable.'

He scowled, shaking his head in disagreement. 'What's *not* reasonable is what she did to him outside that dinner party. I was there. He went after her, and she smashed him in the face with a heavy umbrella. He needed stitches. She then went round to his flat, drowned his new laptop in the bath, and smashed a couple of picture frames with photos of them together. That wasn't the last time episodes like that occurred. She also had an obsession, a deep insecurity about her age.'

'Her age?'

'Oh, yes. Morag lied about her age to everybody. She was actually something like ten years older than Craig. But hid it well. Spent a fortune on keeping young. That particular insecurity surfaced regularly. And ended inevitably in another violent scene. Granted, these episodes were often committed under the influence of drink, or something she'd shoved up her nose or down her throat. But they were hardly 'reasonable' behaviour.'

The sun was too much for him, and he plucked the sunglasses from his shirt pocket.

'Look, I'm not sure if she lost it that day. Knew about an affair that had been taking place under her nose for ages. I simply don't know. What I *do* know is that the version of herself she sold to Jamie, and may be selling to you and others, is not the full story. At the time of his death, Craig had had enough.'

'What, you mean he was going to leave her?'

'That was the plan. By the end of the summer, Craig wanted to have made a fresh start. Preferably with Iona. He knew he'd have to get his timing right, but he was definitely going to tell Morag. I remember the last time I saw him. He said that one thing was certain. Morag's reaction would be a big problem. I still recall the words he used. '*Heaven help me when I break the news. I'll need a suit of armour to face her.*''

30

Kirstin threw the keys on to the hall table and headed straight for the garden, grabbing an ice-cold bottle of mineral water from the fridge en route. She made her way across the lawn to the river's edge, and dropped down on to the grass, exhausted. All the way back from town she'd gone over what Harry had said. Just as had happened with Jamie, a completely different person was now being described to her. And, coupled with the nagging queries that had lain in her mind for the past few days . . .

'Hello! Where are you?'

The shout jolted her into life. She twisted round, ready to jump up. Ross was wandering down the garden, smiling. Uninvited, he plonked himself down beside her. 'Harry said he enjoyed meeting you but reckons he lost his case. Did he?'

She was beginning to tire of him popping in to see her whenever he liked. They weren't married now. It wasn't her house, but she had to be allowed her privacy. She managed a forced smile. 'Hi, Ross. His case against Morag is weak and circumstantial, I'm afraid. And sexist. At least he had the good sense not to call her a bunny-boiler in my company, unlike you. She's got problems, yes. But I knew that anyway.'

'Wow!' He held up both hands in mock surrender. 'Play the gender card if you like, but I

241

think you're missing the point with Morag Ramsay. You bloody softie! That woman'll run rings round you. But let's leave that for now ... I've come to pick up those boxes for the recycling centre *and* to invite you to have some fun.'

She needed to be alone. Company, any company, was the last thing she wanted and, to make matters worse, Ross was in one of his jolly moods. She knew what that meant. 'You win *your* case this morning, Ross?'

He laughed. 'Hah! I did indeed. But instead of running off straightaway to wallow in champagne with the rest of the team, I thought I'd try and tempt you to an all-afternoon lunch with us. I think you need cheering up. There'll be some familiar faces.'

She kept staring ahead. The slow-flowing river and its quiet gurgling had an almost hypnotic effect. Ross would never change. When he was happy and upbeat like this, it was infectious. In the last few minutes, he had lifted her tired spirits a few notches. But the thought of having to face his colleagues — people she'd never particularly liked anyway — had her groaning inwardly.

'Kirsty? What's up? You'd be very welcome. And ... Annelise won't be there. She's on a girls' shopping weekend in London.' He sighed and shifted his body away from her, at last picking up her message: *I need space.* 'I'm sorry that you seem so ... so low, sad. Maybe you should leave off going through Dad's stuff. Take a break, rest up. You're very welcome to stay here

242

for as long as you need. At least, until I can organize getting the place cleared properly. It's all been a bit piecemeal to date. I must speak to Glen. I need more time.'

'I'm seeing him.' She blurted it out with no attempt at control.

Ross shifted round to look more clearly at her. 'Oh, right. When?'

She stood up and moved a few feet along the riverbank, keeping her back to him. 'No, I mean I'm seeing, *seeing* Glen. He's a nice guy.'

Silence. And then she turned. Ross was staring down at the dry grass. His face blank. What she'd done, or rather the way she'd done it, had been cruel. He lifted his head to look at her. She avoided his gaze and scuffed a foot across the lawn, waiting for him to speak. Christ, she hated herself at this moment. She knew she was getting back at him. For not telling her about Jamie's death. For being such a sod at times during their marriage. For finding happiness with someone else. For making a baby. And maybe, just maybe, for trying to sabotage her belief in an underdog.

She moved towards him, hands outstretched. Ross was standing up now. 'Look, Ross. I'm sorry. I sh — '

But he was holding his own hands out as he stood up and stepped forward to take her gently by the shoulders. 'Listen, *listen*. It's okay, it's fine. I'm glad for you. Truly. My . . . my only slight surprise is that it's Glen. But, yes he is, I'm sure, a nice guy. Dad liked him very much. It's fine. Really. Look, maybe we could all go out one night. In a foursome?'

She clasped one of his hands and smiled. That was pushing it a bit. But she was relieved. There had been no scene. And there was an obvious reason for that. He didn't love her any more. He was happy. If she had been trying to hurt him, she'd failed. *Let that be a lesson. Let the past lie.*

31

The call from Morag had come just as she was saying goodbye to Ross and assuring him that she'd make a start on Jamie's study. It had been disconcerting. *'Hi, where are you? Doing anything nice? I wondered if you'd do me a favour and collect some more stuff from my house?'*

Kirstin now stood in Morag's hallway, bulging holdall in hand. She was hovering at the front door when the phone rang. Morag again, with more orders?

'Hello.'

'Is that Morag Ramsay?'

It was a young, male voice. Strong, Glaswegian accent.

'Eh . . . it's Kirstin. I'm sort of looking after Morag. Who's calling?'

'I'm Jules Moncrieff. A friend of Bonnie's. She said you were looking after Morag. Bonnie talked to me the day she died. After she saw you. Gave me Morag's number. I . . . wondered if she'd like to see me?'

Kirstin couldn't answer immediately. This was a surprise. Given all that had happened, she had quite forgotten about Jules. 'Oh . . . eh, yes. I'm sure Morag would like to see you.' Kirstin felt wrong-footed. 'I . . . I'm very, very sorry about Bonnie. Where, when would you like to see us? I'd probably have to come too. Morag's not in a great state right now.'

'That's okay. I know it's short notice but I thought Morag would want to know. The police have released Bonnie's body. Her funeral's going to be on Monday. Maybe we could meet there.'

★ ★ ★

'I don't think I'm up to it, Kirstin. Really, I don't. Dr Mackeson's recommended some new medication and it's making me very tired. And the funeral's in Fife? I can't travel all that way. I'm sorry.'

Kirstin glanced round the sitting room of the clinic's inpatient wing. Not surprisingly on such a lovely day, everyone else was outdoors. Not Morag, though. She was looking pale and drawn. Far worse than the last time Kirstin had seen her. Her condition made Kirstin feel even more guilty at having met with Harry Kinnaird.

'Okay, Morag. That's fine. Why don't I just go on my own? You can meet Jules another time.'

Morag nodded slowly, seeming uncertain. 'Yes . . . you go, by all means. God, I had no idea. Ally and Jules Moncrieff. That day, it was Iona who trotted up and told me about Jules. I thought he was one of *her* latest conquests. Huh! Little did I know, Craig was fulfilling that role only too well. Iona would have been livid if she'd known that Ally was seeing this Jules. They'd had big rows about that sort of thing before. She forbade him to see her gallery people.' Morag nodded again, more firmly this time. 'Well, well. How very interesting. Yes, you go. See what he's got to say.'

246

32

Kirstin weaved her way through unusually heavy traffic but that didn't trouble her. She felt better today. Since receiving Jules's invitation to meet, she'd spent the weekend taking Ross's advice. He'd recognized her need for rest, and so she had spent most of the time sleeping or enjoying the garden. There was plenty of time to get back to her task of clearing Jamie's study. Perhaps later in the day, after seeing Jules.

Being the holiday season, this corner of east Fife, with its coast of picturesque fishing villages, was as popular as ever. She knew the church Jules had directed her to. In happier times, she, Ross, Jamie and Jean would have days out visiting the prettiest spots within easy driving distance of Edinburgh. She parked away from the handful of other cars; she wasn't a mourner and wanted to keep back until Jules made an appearance. He'd given her a physical description of himself and she'd told him what car she'd be driving. The open vista in front of her lifted her mood. The Fife coast was a few hundred yards ahead of her, down a gentle slope of farmland. The view over to East Lothian was clear, the Firth of Forth blue and calm. Strangely, although the river and the Cauldron were beautiful spots, the entire area, including Jamie's house, was beginning to set off familiar feelings of claustrophobia in her. She lifted her head to the fresh, sea-scented air. It was mercifully cooler here than in town, and she welcomed the gentle breeze coming up from the coast. To her left, on the far side of the churchyard, she could see a sparse grouping of mourners. It was an appalling day for Bonnie's loved ones. But, at least they had the chance to say their farewells.

She moved forward to lean on the wall of the car park, enjoying the blowy day and thinking back to that tense encounter with Ross at Jamie's graveside, such a short time ago. She: angry, outraged, determined. Ross: defensive, infuriating. And how did she feel now? The answer was simple. Confused and tired. She'd been caught up in an emotional storm of her own feelings, about Jamie and about Ross. And then she'd allowed herself to become involved in another person's emotional storm. She'd made a rod for her own back these past days. It would be time to call it quits very soon. Once Morag was back on her feet, and after she'd sorted out Jamie's study, that would be it. Where it left her in her feelings about Jamie, who could say. *Just remember the good Jamie*. And Glen? *Just take it easy.*

'Are you Kirstin?'

She broke off from gazing at the sea, and turned to find him standing behind her.

'I'm Jules.'

He was dressed in mourning, but with a difference. The three-quarter-length tunic with Nehru collar was of expensive black linen, and the matching baggy trousers, billowing out in the breeze, exposed tanned calves. Slim, brown feet were shod in soft leather sandals. Finally, his dark hair was loosely tied back in a ponytail to reveal fine, almost girlish features with a full sensuous mouth and striking but sad grey eyes. He was, quite simply, a beautiful young man. Kirstin thought he could be no older than twenty-four.

She stepped forward. 'Yes, I'm Kirstin.'

He began darting quick glances at the approaching gaggle of mourners. 'Do you mind if we take a wander down to the sea? Get away from that lot?'

Kirstin held out her hand in invitation. 'Please, lead on.'

She followed him in silence down a dusty path at the side of a field, and then he turned sharply to his left. He obviously knew where he was going and, within a minute, they were sitting on a secluded bench overlooking a small inlet. Despite the calm conditions, the current was strong, forcing the waves to break heavily on the black rocks a few yards away.

Slowly, he slid a battered tobacco tin from his tunic pocket, smoothing his long fingers over a scratched representation of an ornate bridge. He moved his hand and she could make out the words, *Venezia, Ponte di Rialto*, written in gold underneath.

'Ally took me to Venice when we first got together. Bought this for me in a second-hand shop. It's tacky, but I like it.'

He pulled out a ready-made roll-up, cupped a hand as he held his lighter to it, and then inhaled deeply. 'So, Bonnie told me your father-in-law had something to do with the river?'

'That's right. My ex-father-in-law. Jamie Munro. He's dead now. He was a river warden and guide. He and Ally's group, particularly Iona, didn't get on. They must've talked about him.'

He shrugged. 'Oh, I vaguely remember something about all that. But, you know, Iona was always moaning and being irate about so much, I kind of switched off. I don't like conflict.'

He took two more slow puffs. He seemed reluctant to start talking about why they were meeting up, so she decided to take the initiative.

'Was Ally there today? I just wondered . . . you wanted to move away from up there.'

He brushed a flake of ash from his thigh and gazed out at the sea. 'I didn't think he'd have the nerve. Fraser Coulter was there, though. He looked terrible, slugging away at a hip flask. He seemed pissed. Another one who's gone off the rails. We had a brief chat. There certainly seems to be no love lost between him and Ally now. In fact, I think he hates him.' He held up a hand, the hint of a smile playing around his full mouth. 'Listen. Isn't the sea such a fantastic sound? Comforting.'

She smiled her agreement and they sat for a moment, listening. Then he shifted his eyes from the sea, and back to his tobacco tin. 'I've been thinking about what happened last year at the river. Thinking a lot. More so since Ally and I split up. And . . . and the shock of what's happened to Bonnie. It's made me see things a lot more clearly.'

She noticed a mild, nervous tremble as he raised the cigarette to his lips. 'Jules? Are you okay?'

He was still looking wistfully at the turbulent waves. There was a preparatory clearing of the throat before he began. 'I've not been to many funerals. It was nice, in a strange way. Sad and nice. Odd combination. I don't know if Bonnie would have approved of a conventional Christian burial, but I suppose it helped her folks. I liked Bonnie. Only got to know her recently. But she was an interesting person. Authentic. Despite what others might think. Ally used to call her hippy-dippy, stuff like that. But he made enough money out of her, and out of Fraser Coulter. Though he messed up with Craig and lost a fair bit then. But Ally knew how to make money, he was good at that. Using people. They both were. He and Iona. They could suck you in, as if they had an invisible magnet. Looking back on it, I was playing way out of my league when I hooked up with them. Funny you can't see things like that at the time, isn't it? That's not to say I didn't have a good time. Iona helped my career . . . and with Ally, I . . . I thought that I was in love with him. Maybe I was . . . or maybe I was just flattered.'

Kirstin spoke gently. 'And Ally? Bonnie said that he cared very much for you.'

He ground the tiny roll-up stub under the heel of his sandal and let his eyes wander back to the waves. 'He did. He *was* in love with me. And I think that's why I've been loyal . . . quiet about last summer for all this time. But I know how much he's changed . . . '

At last he broke free from staring at the sea and looked at her. His eyes were even sadder than when she'd first greeted him. Kirstin watched as he fumbled with the tobacco tin. He seemed about to speak. Then he hesitated, clearly trying to choose the right words. 'This is difficult for me. I feel guilty and disloyal. Even being here feels . . . sort of wrong.'

Kirstin let the silence lie for a moment before gently prompting him. 'Guilty and disloyal?'

Jules shifted in his seat and then began in a low, even voice. 'Iona and Ally were big, flamboyant characters. Especially Iona. She appeared . . . more one-dimensional than Ally. There was probably a lot more going on inside than she'd ever let you see. She was no fool. But, essentially, Iona was a flatterer, a flirt. But, and I mean this, she was great fun *and* she did a lot for me. Launched my career. I will be eternally grateful to her for that. And for meeting Ally through her. We all had good times together. That I'll never regret.'

'How did you and Ally meet?'

'We met through the gallery. At a private view. When we got together, Ally said Iona mustn't know about us. Not for a while. I should have guessed from that, that there was going to be trouble.'

Kirstin shrugged. 'But why wasn't he allowed to see who he wanted? I don't get it.'

He lit up and took a slow satisfying drag, his

eyes again fixed on the breaking waves below. 'Ally explained that Iona had a habit of pouncing on guys he liked. Seeing if she could pull or 'turn' them. She positively revelled in that game. And . . . well, he'd let her get away with it. I once asked him why. He just shrugged and said that she could do what she liked. He *had* to let her. I dropped the subject then, but I thought it was a bit weird, to put it mildly. What Ally *did* say, though, was that if there was someone he *really* liked, he kept it to himself. And he said straightaway that he really liked me. And he caught my attention too. You see, like his sister, Ally could be the life and soul of the party, but he had depth . . . and something else. A melancholy air. I knew he'd been hurt in the past. You can tell these things, even though it was a long time before I knew what had happened to him. The thing that had made him who he is.'

Kirstin thought back to the sobbing figure, collapsed over his snooker table. 'You mean he'd had painful relationships?'

'It was more than that.' Jules offered her a sad smile. 'Let me tell you a story about Ally. The one I was going to tell Morag. I don't think another living soul knows about this.'

He stopped again to enjoy his cigarette, as if trying to put off the inevitable. After a few moments, he sat up straighter and seemed ready to go on. Kirstin began to feel the early, premonitory pangs of anxiety and knew what they meant; she was going to hear something awful.

33

'Ally was sent to public school in Edinburgh at an early age. As a boarder. His parents had a big country house and estate up in Perthshire at the time. Iona was a day pupil at a local girls' school. Needless to say, Ally felt rejected and abandoned. Iona, meanwhile, got all the attention during their childhood and adolescent years. Ally hated, absolutely *hated* school. He was variously ridiculed and bullied for being clever and for being a weakling, a skinny beanpole. He was beaten up a few times. Of course, given the culture of these brutal and brutalizing places, he kept quiet about everything. Both to his teachers and his parents. He confided in Iona, though. Despite her preferential treatment by their parents, and his feelings of resentment about her being their favourite, they were close. Or rather, Ally saw her as his only friend. It was his parents whom he hated, not her. So, every holiday he'd rush back home and spend the summer with her, dreading his return to school for the following term. On and on this went. Ally the needy, Ally the weakling. Until the worm eventually turned.'

He looked at Kirstin and she nodded for him to go on. 'Once Ally hit adolescence, he came into his own. He shot up in height, put on weight and muscle, and became a solid rugby player. At last, he could look after himself. He had brains, *and* brawn, to protect himself. And then he gained something else. He'd just turned seventeen and he fell in love. With another rugby-team member.' Jules smiled to himself. 'The way Ally told it, it sounded as if it had come straight out of a homoerotic, alternative *Boys' Own* story. Miraculously, they managed to keep the affair secret. And during the holidays, they had the best cover. They would visit both sets of parents. Two best buddies — stars of the rugby pitch, and swots with top marks into the bargain. No one knew, no one suspected the truth. Until Iona.'

'Iona?'

'Ally had confided in her ages before about his 'special friend'. Anyway, he and his lover had been invited to spend the summer in Perthshire. And that's when it happened.'

Kirstin was having trouble controlling her impatience. 'What did?'

'They and Iona had spent a long, sleepy day down at the lake, larking about, skinny-dipping and generally having a laugh. They'd also had a bit to drink. Ally had sneaked back up to the house to plunder his father's wine cellar yet again. As he reached the top of the stairs, he saw Iona. She had just turned fourteen. A physically and temperamentally precocious fourteen, mind you.' Jules dropped his head and began smoothing out a wrinkle in his trousers. 'She was weeping, looked dishevelled, had scratched and bruised thighs. And worse. Ally's lover had raped her.'

'*My God!*'

Jules gave a single, knowing nod. 'Oh, yes.

Heavy stuff. Ally raced down to the lake to confront the boy. He, for his part, denied everything. But Ally stood by his sister. Iona promised to say nothing if the boy left that evening. He did. On some pretext or another, citing illness I think, and his parents came to collect him. Before that, Iona also made Ally promise never to talk to his lover again once they were back at school. He agreed. But, in the event, the promise wasn't needed.'

Kirstin frowned. 'What do you mean?'

'The boy killed himself two weeks later.'

'*Jesus!* Did Ally tell anyone about what had happened?'

Jules shook his head, 'Oh, no. It was just put down as another overachieving, depressed adolescent who had turned to suicide.'

'And Iona never told anyone?'

'Nope. Not a word about the rape. Not a word about the gay affair. Ally was in her debt. He owed her.'

Kirstin raised her face to the wind and stretched her legs. She was beginning to feel drained. It had been a dreadful story, but it at least gave some insight into the character of Ally. A man who could, it seemed, be both threatening and, at the same time, deeply sad inside.

Jules was stretching his legs too, and then suddenly he got to his feet, the wind picking at his trousers. 'But that's not the end of the story.'

'No?'

'Oh, no.' He took a step forward and faced the sea. The wind was gaining in strength and tugged intermittently at his ponytail as he inhaled the salt-tanged air. 'I sometimes wonder about timing in life, synchronicity, all of that. I don't know what possessed Iona to tell me this. Maybe it was that she . . . well, she said as much . . . she had discovered in me her greatest artistic 'find', as it were. And . . . and I think she may have had other plans for me. Sexually, I mean. Her sexual radar didn't pick up on anything other than heterosexuality. Iona was very blind about all that unless it was absolutely obvious. Another example of her one-dimensional nature. And she was drunk when she told me, showing off a bit, I think. Trying to shock, test my boundaries. That's what made her tell me.'

'Tell you what?'

He turned around, moved slowly back to the bench and sat down. His face was troubled. 'Iona had made up the whole rape claim. She'd been attracted to Ally's friend for ages and had been jealous. That day, as Ally trotted back up to the house in search of wine, she tried to seduce the boy. But he rebuffed her. And so she tore her clothes, roughed herself up, and ran to tell her lies. It was pure envious spite.'

Despite the beauty of the view before her, Kirstin was beginning to feel hemmed in. The sea now sounded unnaturally loud, and the wind seemed deafening as it whistled past her ears. Had she heard right? 'Iona made it up? All these years she'd been carrying that with her? The boy's death? *No!*'

Jules shrugged. 'I know. People's lives. But . . . the reason I told you this . . . and why I feel

257

guilty, *responsible* even, is . . . well, I told Ally. When we got together, when I knew we were serious, and he was telling me this awful story . . . I *had* to tell him.'

'And how did he take it?'

'He went very quiet. For days. No big confrontation with Iona, no histrionics. Nothing. The . . . pain, the betrayal ran so deep I don't think he could take it in at first. And then, again, the worm turned.'

Kirstin nodded for him to go on.

'Yes. He'd obviously spent those unnervingly quiet few days hatching his revenge and . . . to be truthful . . . I thought it a bit mad. Almost childish. But then, that was what was going on. He *had* reverted to adolescence in a way. Hell-bent on getting his revenge on his little sister, in a suitably puerile way.' He stopped for a moment, lost in memory.

Kirstin prompted him. 'What was he going to do?'

'He was going to produce me at the river party as his lover, the love of his life. One she couldn't destroy. We'd been together for a while by this time and had managed to keep it a secret. From everybody. We both believed that this was the big one and wanted to keep it to ourselves until we were sure. Anyway, we had big plans. We were going to go away together. I know it sounds dramatic, and it was. Ally was going to liquidate the business, and we were going to settle somewhere. A place where I could paint and where he could change his life. Do something completely different, maybe run a bar or a restaurant, somewhere hot. But I wanted him to be straight with Iona. Tell her, so she could make plans. I was working as her paid assistant at the gallery, *and* she was planning a big show for me. We couldn't just leave her in the lurch like that. But no. He had other ideas. He was going to present me, present us, as a fait accompli at the river party. Announce our intentions to Iona in front of everyone.'

Kirstin shook her head, wondering at the nastiness of it all. 'And her reaction?'

He laughed. 'There would have been hell to pay.' Suddenly, his eyes flickered, as if he were in pain. 'And, by God, there was. But not in the way I expected. No one could have predicted the hell of that day.'

He flicked the second roll-up away, watching it arc its way towards the waves. Then, head bowed, he turned his attention back to the tobacco tin, clicking and unclicking the lid. 'Look, I know I'm being slow in coming to the point, but it's complicated. It's not been easy working out what to do for the best. Ally and I were to meet up at a prearranged rendezvous that Sunday. It was going to be late afternoon. Ally was in charge of the arrangements, the plan. I was just going along with it. So I was waiting at the meeting-point, opposite the hotel that's up from Bell's Mills. You know it?'

Kirstin nodded. 'Yes, I know where you're talking about.'

'The thing is, Ally was late. When he did turn up, he seemed drunk, which I'd have expected given what sort of day it was, but he was also overexcited and agitated. I thought he might be having second thoughts about confronting Iona. But no, we just kept walking up towards the Cauldron area. And then his mobile went. It was Fraser. All Ally said after that was, 'Something's happened. Go home. I'll call you later.' He was very, very firm about it. Shouted at me. I think I told him to fuck off. It was only later that night, when he called, that I found out about Iona and Craig.'

She was straining to hear his low voice above the crashing of the waves. 'But you never went to the police? They asked everyone, and they meant *everyone*, who had been in the vicinity that day, to come forward.'

Jules shrugged. 'It was Ally who asked me not to. Said it would be lots of hassle, and there was nothing I could do to help. He said it might be bad for my career if I was seen to be involved in a murder investigation. So, I just left it like that. Until now.'

'And what's made you change your mind?'

He looked back up the hill towards the church. 'Bonnie, mainly. And Ally, how he's been behaving lately. You know, I didn't see him for days after Iona died. We just talked on the phone. He said he didn't want to see anyone. I accepted that. Bereavement and shock take people in different ways. But when we did start seeing each other again, slowly he became very strange. I mean ... grief you would expect, anger too. Though he became increasingly aggressive and furious. Furious with the world and, it has to be said, with himself. He would often say he was the world's biggest fool.'

'What did he mean by that?'

Jules shook his head hopelessly. 'I don't actually know. All he would say was, 'I should have seen all this coming.' And then, after a while, he just disappeared inside himself. I begged, *pleaded* with him to get help. See a therapist or something. But he refused. Eventually there was nothing left to have a relationship with. Well . . . nothing I wanted. He took my leaving very badly. Hounding me, hassling, ringing me at all hours.' He turned to look at her. 'I don't know what happened that Sunday . . . and I may be wrong . . . but I think it's *possible* that he had some part in it.'

Kirstin turned to face him full on. 'Really? I mean, granted, what she did to him and his adolescent love was unforgivable. But it's a long, long way to travel from that to what happened to Iona. No one's ever said Ally was violent or aggressive *before* the killings. In fact, I saw him break down and cry recently. He seems to me to be a man more consumed with grief and anger at his loss than anything else. He's obviously troubled.'

Jules drew a long, almost weary, breath. 'Listen. I think Ally was, is, deeply conflicted. He loved his sister. He hated his sister. It was Craig's bad luck to be caught in the middle. Be in the wrong place at the wrong time. Maybe there was a row between Ally and Iona that got out of hand. Maybe he decided to confront her about the rape story and forget about the pantomime of using me. I don't know.'

'But he's been telling anyone who'll listen that it was Morag.' Kirstin shook her head in puzzlement. 'I mean, he even came blundering round to hers to accuse her of killing Bonnie. If he's pretending, it's quite an act. In any event, he certainly seems to have it in for Morag.'

He sighed. 'Yes, and that's almost the worst part of it. If I'm right, he's done a really wicked thing in bringing suspicion on her. But he always disliked Morag. It's easy to see why.'

Kirstin couldn't agree. 'Really? I think she's a bit tricky. A complicated person, but not disagreeable. What did Ally have against her?'

'Going by what I've heard about her from Bonnie, I agree with you. She wasn't that bad. But it's not that straightforward. I know for a fact that Ally fancied Craig like mad before he met me. He knew he didn't stand an earthly with the very heterosexual Craig, but he thought Morag wasn't right for the guy. Yes, it was naughty of Ally and yes, it was none of his business. But there you go. And, remember, before I told him about Iona's rape claim, he was always on her side. Sure, when Iona got her hands on Craig, he felt a bit jealous. But he also made it plain that Craig would be better off by far having a fling with Iona than some dreary terminal relationship with Morag. Though what he didn't tell Craig was that he was no big deal to Iona. He'd do, for the time being. She saw other men. She always had a few on the go. As I say, it was naughty and interfering of Ally to meddle with Craig and Morag. Let's just say . . . he could be like that at times. Not the greatest quality. I thought I could wean him off it.'

'And what about spiking Morag's drinks. Did he know or take part in it?'

Jules lifted a hand. 'Oh, that was so out of order. Really nasty. Ally didn't do it. Iona and Craig did, but Ally found out about it eventually. Iona told him to keep quiet and so, of course, he did. I noticed what was going on one night at a gallery do and challenged Ally. He was sheepish but said Iona was a law unto herself. Iona went down in my estimation that day. And it wasn't long after that that she told me the rape story. And actually, thinking about it now, she knew she'd blown it with me when she told me that story. How she could ever have thought I'd find it amusing. She was way out of touch with what I'm about. Still, she did well by me and no one should have to die that way. But . . . she was an easy victim, although not the easiest.'

Kirstin shook her head, puzzled. 'What do you mean?'

He nodded his head towards the churchyard.

'Perhaps Ally's easiest victim is lying up there.'

★　★　★

They stopped by the wall of the car park, and took a last look at the sea. Jules smiled at her.

'I don't know what I'm going to do about all this, if anything. I've no proof. Just feelings. Maybe I'm the one who's losing it and I'm just being paranoid. In the meantime, though, tell your friend Morag that I'm sorry for all her

263

trouble. I'm sure it's been hell. And tell her to keep away from Ally. Just in case I'm right. Whatever he might, or might not, have done, I know one thing. Ally is teetering on the edge. Who knows what he's capable of? So, tell Morag to steer clear of him.'

Kirstin smiled back at him. 'Believe me, she's been trying to avoid him. But . . . do you really think he could be a danger to her?'

'One way or another, Ally is against her. Either he genuinely thinks she killed his sister and now Bonnie, and will do anything to have her punished for it. Or, he has carefully implicated her to hide his own guilt. Either way isn't pretty. I feel sorry for her.' He opened the driver's door for Kirstin. 'Thanks for the talk. You're a good listener.' She slid past him, settling herself before starting the engine. He was about to close the door on her when something on the back seat caught his eye.

'Who's that?' He had his head cocked and was squinting over her shoulder.

Kirstin cut the engine and turned to see what he was looking at. 'What's what? Oh, those are photos of Jamie. Why?'

He raised one eyebrow. 'Right. It's just that I saw him that day. After I left Ally. I was cutting up one of the side paths and I saw him rush by on the main one, completely oblivious to my presence.'

'*What?*'

'Yeah, he was running past me. In a hurry. He must have been off to get help.'

Sunday, 13 August 2006

Jamie lowered his binoculars. It was hopeless now. His hands were shaking too much to hold any image in focus. The female screams were echoing across the Cauldron, male shouts and curses intermingling with the women's hysteria.

He had to leave here. Immediately. He picked his way across the splash of vomit now almost washed away by the river's flow. He'd been unable to stop his stomach turning. But, forget that, he had to get to the path quickly.

On arrival he'd been cock-a-hoop. He could never have wished for a better vantage point. Over by the old sluice gate on the far side of the weir. But he hadn't banked on the pain in his hip coming back. He winced. The anaesthetic effects of the pills were wearing off. Could he last out until he got back to the car? He was perfectly mobile when the pain was dulled, but now was another matter.

Please, please, please, let me get away from this, from them.

Blocking the sounds that pursued him down the path, he secured the backpack on his shoulders and began to gain pace, thrusting his hiking stick into the ground with heavy stabs. The car was near the hotel. The

265

crossing to the other side wasn't far. He hobbled on, thankful that the light was fading. There wasn't a soul about. Suddenly, he pulled up. He felt the acid tug of nausea again and retched over the wall, down to where the current was running fast. He touched a shaking hand to his mouth, looking round and back again. Still no one.

The final push to the car just about killed him. The keys fell to the ground twice. And then he was in. With trembling fingers, he unscrewed the flask top, hurling it to the car floor and draining the whisky-infused tea in one welcome gulp. He half thought his stomach would reject it, sending the liquid straight back up again. But, instead, it burnt down his throat and chest, leaving a comforting warmth in his empty belly.

He fumbled with the ignition key, revved the engine three times, and then switched it off again. Tentatively, he reached for the backpack on the passenger seat, slowly unzipping the main pocket. The camera felt cold to the touch. He pushed the 'on' button. And then pushed it off again. Not here. He had to get away. Drive normally. Even too slowly. You're an old codger. People will expect it.

As he swung round into his drive, he knew he'd been lucky. No police car had flagged him down. The only other worry was if he'd been caught by a speed camera. Unlikely. He'd come by the back roads. Christ, let me get inside. I need a drink, need something!

'Damn!'

He stabbed the key into the front-door lock. Once. Twice. Got it! He was in and heading straight for the kitchen, tearing off his uniform jacket and cap, suddenly feeling overheated. The whisky, the whisky! Where had he put it after filling the flask? Over there! He dragged the bottle noisily across the worktop, sloshing the first nip into the tumbler. Then another. He found the nearest chair and slumped down, lowering his head into his hands. He needed his heart to slow down, his breathing to ease. He'd forgotten the pain in his hip. In fact, it seemed to have disappeared. Or was it the explosive effect of the drink as it hit his brain, eclipsing what should now have been agony? He welcomed the fuzzy sensation in his head, the burning heat coursing through his innards.

He snapped his head up. What was that? Something at the window? He peered intently. But only his reflection gazed back. It was dark now. He must have been sitting here, trance-like, for ages. Easing himself to his feet, he wandered over to the back door and stared out through the glass towards the river, now in darkness. He turned his head to the left, imagining he had the long-range, X-ray vision of a superman. All hell would have broken loose a mile downstream an hour or two ago. He could imagine what the scene had looked like. The emergency services converging on that most inaccessible of areas. The shattered group of friends huddled nearby, the men with their arms round the women. The bloodied mass at their feet . . . no more! He closed his eyes, hoping against hope to regain composure.

He'd be fine here now. Where he'd been all evening. In his own home. Minding his own business. With his sore hip. Indisposed. No patrols.

Verdicts

34

Sitting at Jamie's desk, Kirstin rested her head in her hands, the possibilities swimming around her mind from the morning's encounter with Jules. He'd had no idea of the bombshell he'd dropped about Jamie, let alone his suspicions about Ally. Jules had seemed to think an old man rushing by after a brutal murder had every right to be there, particularly if he worked on the river. He'd not thought to mention it to Ally at the time, or to anyone else. Jules had been adamant; he just wanted to forget about the whole wretched day. Somehow, Kirstin had succeeded in hiding her shock and surprise from Jules at his news, but it was devastating. The simple fact was that Jamie had denied being anywhere near the river on the Sunday. Yes, Glen had shown her evidence from Jamie's notebook that he had *planned* to go there that day. But his transcripts confirmed that he didn't make it. She had been relieved to read that. *No patrols*. But Jules's story told another tale. Jamie had lied. Why? What did it mean? Should she tell Ross? Speak to Glen? Donald?

So much was conflicting now. Ross and his friend Harry had Morag as the guilty party. Jules had Ally — not very convincingly in her view — filling that role, though she gave his theory considerably more credence than Ross and Harry's. And what of Jamie? Playing devil's advocate, *if* Jules was right, and it was a big 'if', then could Jamie have seen Ally? Over there, in the wooded area? But he would have told the police. Or did he see *something*, but didn't know what he was seeing . . . until later, much later perhaps? Was that why he was so convinced of Morag's innocence? Because he saw who *was* there? But still, he'd have gone to the police. And what if someone else knew Jamie was there? Knew what he saw . . . and six months later, he was gone. *Jamie, Jamie. What were you doing there? What did you see? Why did you die?*

★   ★   ★

The light had long gone and it was only now that she was aware of the silence. Even through the open window, she could pick up only the faintest of murmurs from the river. She'd shut herself off in this room, ignoring messages from Ross, Glen and Morag, who'd left the inpatient unit and was now resting at home. The past few hours had been strangely therapeutic for Kirstin as she skim-read and sifted through ream after ream of river-related material: internet printouts, flyers, ideas for new walks, proposals for the volunteer programme. The clear-out was almost complete, but had left her pitifully short of answers.

Only the drawers were left, two on either side. She began pulling them open. Jamie didn't seem to have much use for drawers. The upper ones had a selection of pens and pencils. Tucked away at the back of one was a spare river association baseball cap. She pulled it out. It made her think of Glen. She needed to talk to him. The truth was, she'd missed him. The third drawer was stuck . . . no, locked. Definitely locked. Perhaps there was money in there, or some other valuable item? The last drawer opened freely, revealing a half-empty bottle of single malt rocking to and fro.

Maybe it was time to call it a day. She'd finish the job in the morning. As she leant forward to replace the baseball cap in the drawer, she felt something hard round the seam. The tiny pocket had been custom-made with a Velcro seal. Gently, she pulled. And out it fell. The key to the third drawer. Her heart rate picked up as she turned the stiff lock.

She slid out the thick hardbacked A5 notebook, involuntarily stroking a palm across the front cover. The handwritten label was still pristine white: *Alternative/Backup Logbook. Year 2006*.

The book fell open at a well-creased page.

12/8/06

ALISTAIR SUTHERLAND: he is alone. He shares many traits with his sister or, at least, those that have led him to keep a busy but lonely life. I have seen what he does and who he does it with. He is a sad man. A weak man. VERDICT: NOT PROVEN (YET)

FRASER COULTER: he is largely an unknown quantity to me, although I know he can be rough and boorish. He is often away from his rather grand house up there on the hillside. When he is in residence, he drinks to excess on his own. I am told (by Morag) that Coulter has some creative talents. Hard to believe. I suspect Fraser Coulter is also essentially alone. VERDICT: NOT PROVEN (YET)

BONNIE CAMPBELL: seems unknowable. I have not felt it proper to watch her. It would be intrusion rather than surveillance. I think she is a genuine if rather strange person. I hope she will be able to help Morag when she needs it, as she undoubtedly will soon, I fear. VERDICT: NOT GUILTY

CRAIG IRVINE: I care little about this specimen. I know what Mr (he's not fit to own the title 'Dr'!) Irvine is doing and he is an abomination. I care not if he is alone. I do care, however, that he will leave Morag a lonely and sad person. Swine! Swine! Swine! VERDICT: GUILTY

IONA SUTHERLAND: she is alone. I know. I've seen how she lives. A busy but empty life. A people-using, exploitative, self-serving life. She, like me, abhors her own company. I'm sure of it. I've seen her. Watched her. She is a restless and devious being. But she is alone, alone to her core. VERDICT: GUILTY

Alone. Alone. They are all alone, I am all alone. In that, and only that, we are together.

I will keep my eye on them all. Some to protect. Others to CONVICT.

Sentence should be SEVERE.

She shoved the notebook away from her, as if its very proximity would contaminate her. But as she did so, a page fell out. A sketch. In pencil. No colour. Thankfully. The representation was unmistakable. The two bodies intertwined. In sex. In death. Around them, details of trees and foliage, those in the foreground picked out with extreme, detailed accuracy.

And then there was the third figure. Pointed hiking stick raised. Ready to deliver another, unnecessary blow. A tall figure. In uniform. Complete with baseball cap, and emblazoned on it the familiar logo: WLRA.

A self-portrait.

35

A shaft of pain pierced behind her right eye. Kirstin pushed her seat back, out of the glare of the lamp and away from what lay on the desk.

How long she had been here, she had no idea. A deep chill had taken hold of her and what had started as a dull pain had turned into a full-blown headache. She moved stiffly and painfully to shut the windows despite the balmy night. She hugged herself, trying to get warm, and began wandering aimlessly through the house, eventually stopping to pour herself a drink. The smell of alcohol immediately turned her stomach, and she threw the nauseating liquid down the kitchen sink before switching on the kettle. Tea. Strong, sweet tea. She moved robotically around the kitchen, revisiting the sketch in her mind as she drank.

She'd lost track of time. Then, throwing what she could scrabble together of her belongings into two plastic carrier bags — to hell with the rest of her things — she checked for the keys to her flat. Safe in a side pocket. All she wanted was to get away from this place. Except, she had nowhere to go now that her flat had been rented out.

She slumped down on to the bottom of the stairs. *I need time, a place to think!* Moments later, she jumped up, grabbed her bags and headed out to the car. She breathed deeply

. . . and then again . . . trying, willing herself to find some composure. The night air was warm with a hint of welcome humidity. She tumbled her bags into the back seat and moved behind the wheel. As she lifted her hand towards the ignition key, she noticed the shaking, and she struggled to insert the key. Now what? Where in God's name was she going to go? Ross was out of the question. *God, Ross! How am I going to tell you? How?*

She fumbled with her phone and, falteringly, her trembling fingers found Glen's number. Surely she could go round to his place tonight? She was a fraction away from pressing the call button, when she let the phone drop into her lap. No, not Glen. He wasn't the right person to discuss this with first. He must have hidden the other logs from the police for good reason. To protect the association, and to protect Jamie. Now what was she going to tell him? That Jamie had duped him, had duped them all.

She leant forward, head pressed against the steering wheel, and closed her eyes as if that very action could negate the last hour. Numbness. A cold, anaesthetizing numbness. To her core. No tears. No cries of unimaginable pain, shock, horror. Just shaking. Trembling. And a feeling of nothingness. She was aware of her own laboured breathing, the one sign that her body was responding to trauma.

The rat-a-tat on the driver's window was thunderous.

'Kirstin? *Kirstin!* What are you doing?'

Morag's scowling face was inches away from

her own, separated only by the glass. Kirstin stared back, making no immediate attempt to open either window or door. Morag took the initiative and wrenched at the door handle.

★　★　★

Kirstin sipped greedily at the warm tea. Sitting in front of her, Morag was turning the notebook over and over in her hands. Eventually she dropped it on to the coffee table and reached for her drink. She ignored her own tea and grasped the brandy, throwing a mouthful down and grimacing.

'I cannot understand this, Kirstin. I can't believe . . . '

Kirstin nodded as Morag trailed off into incredulous silence. 'I know, I know. But look at the sketch. Why? Why would he do that if . . . ? I mean, it's a sick thing to draw under any circumstances. If he drew that and he . . . well, and he wasn't *involved*, that would be unforgivable in itself. But . . . the whole *tone* of the log. There's no other explanation. *Jesus.* I need to speak to Ross. And the police.'

Matching Morag, she swapped the tea mug for her brandy glass. 'You've been vilified all this time. It's been so wrong. *So wrong!*'

'Indeed.' Morag was nodding her head, surprisingly unflustered. 'It also offers a clearer idea of why Jamie died. It must be looked at as suicide, surely?' She sipped slowly at her drink. 'I find it baffling. Jamie wanted to help me. So he said. Why? Why do that?'

278

Kirstin offered a sad smile. 'Because he didn't want you, of all people, to get into trouble for what he'd done. Remember, he must have believed, given what was probably going through his mind at the time, that he was ridding you of a menace. Craig.' She paused, feeling surprisingly refreshed, lucid and composed. She couldn't afford to lose control just yet. For Morag's sake, even though she seemed to be holding up well. Of all the people to turn up at that moment, she'd been the one to come over, frustrated at her phone messages being ignored. And what had she found? A practically catatonic Kirstin, unable to function. Morag had taken the wheel and driven them back to her house, provided tea, booze, and eventually extracted the truth from her, remaining remarkably calm throughout.

Kirstin leant forward. 'Look. This is all too new to take in. I don't think we're ever going to know exactly how it happened. But I'm convinced now — and I think Ross was right on this — that Jamie was ill. Mentally ill. I tried to deny that before, when Glen showed me some of the logbook entries. But, it was like another Jamie. Full of bitterness, fury, hate. And one who could unleash terrifying violence. I suppose . . . well, they say we're all capable of doing that, given the appropriate circumstances.'

She caught Morag's frown — of disagreement? Disapproval? And quickly she held up a hand.

'I'm not, and please be clear on this, Morag, I am *not* excusing the inexcusable. I'm just casting around for some sort of explanation. I can't

279

begin to know what this news must feel like, what you've suffered. Losing Craig, losing your freedom, the persecution, everything.' She paused for a second time. 'I think that whatever Jamie did was done on the spur of the moment. He lashed out. I don't know why. Maybe there was a row. Perhaps he was . . . well, appalled at finding them there, in that position, and it all escalated. I don't know and . . . frankly, I can't believe I'm sitting here trying to justify bloody murder.'

The tears came at last. She felt Morag stir but make no attempt to physically comfort her. Instead, Morag was staring past her, the face stony, unreadable. Had she offended Morag by trying to defend him? Why wasn't she jumping up in fury and outrage at the misery Jamie had caused her?

Kirstin heard her give out a short, almost nervous cough.

'At least we have some answers now.'

36

'Here. I should have . . . I *meant* to destroy them.'

Kirstin accepted the bundle of photographs from Ross's cold, trembling hand and held his fingers, just for a moment. He nodded his gratitude, eyes still reddened. She'd seen him cry before, but it was still heartbreaking to witness. She'd called him just as dawn broke and, though she'd been cautious in her wording, he'd picked up on her tone immediately and was instantly awake. He knew something was very wrong. By the time she'd arrived, he was showered, shaved and on to his second coffee. And waiting. Anxious. She handed over the notebook and the sketch. Minutes later, his life had been changed forever.

Now Kirstin shuffled through the sheaf of photographs Ross had handed her. Various security cameras had tracked Jamie's stealthy progress through Iona Sutherland's extensive garden, culminating in a shot of him at the side of her house, peering through an open window. Kirstin shook her head in disbelief.

Ross sat down opposite her. 'She gave me an ultimatum. Confront him with these. Stop him, or she'd make 'big trouble', as she put it.'

'But . . . after she died? Didn't these come out?'

Ross shook his head. 'No. Last year, when

281

these were taken, she was getting a new system put in. They're the only copies. I promised to have him reined in. And if it didn't work, she could have the photos back and do what she had to. I . . . I didn't have the guts to show them to Dad then. Only after, when . . . when everything happened at the Cauldron.'

His eye was drawn again to the bundle of photographs. 'I should have taken these more seriously. I mean, Iona Sutherland had had to come to me before. Over some letters that Dad had fired off to her and her group. I felt defensive towards Dad then. I mean, most of them were a bunch of shits really. Overgrown spoilt brats. Anyway, Glen called me too and, for God's sake, we both should've sat up and paid more attention. And yes, I know. You've told me often enough. I'm rotten at paying attention to the important things. But anyway, both Glen and I had to cover Dad's back with the police. In truth, they weren't interested in the river feud. And from what I could gather from the police, the likes of Alistair Sutherland and the rest of them weren't interested in that either. They'd all just had the biggest, most traumatic shock of their lives. A petty feud with a seventy-year-old bore wasn't uppermost in their minds.'

She looked at him. 'But it must have been in your mind? Just a bit?'

He shrugged and rubbed at his reddened eyes. 'No matter what I felt about him as a father, I could *never* have believed him capable of such violence. Of course I trusted him. I wanted to. I *had* to. He assured me he knew nothing that

282

would help the police and so, a bit like Glen with the logs, I colluded with Dad. And that was that, I didn't think any more about it. I got kind of distracted by all his other behaviour. His interfering with Morag's case. And then . . . he died. *Jesus, God!* Why the hell didn't he leave a note or something?'

She saw the tears well up again, and gently touched his arm. Laying down the photos and picking up the logbook, she nodded. 'He did. He left this. But, you know, I don't think he planned it, his suicide. Not for that night in February specifically. If he had, I think he *would* have left some other explanation.' She paused, thinking about how best to go on. 'Tell me, I don't suppose you've seen the letter Jamie left for Glen?'

Ross shook his head.

'Right. Well, I'm sure Glen will let you have a look. It's about Mill House, the bequest. But, the thing is, I think the letter reads like a suicide note.'

Ross looked as if she'd struck him. But she knew she had no choice. Ross had to know everything that she knew.

She tried a reassuring smile. 'So you see, your instincts were right when you described Jamie's bequest as a suicide note. I mean, how could anyone go on living after doing what he'd done? I want to believe that Jamie didn't mean to do what he did. But he did it, and then he panicked. And then things got worse with Morag's arrest, and then . . . he was his own judge and jury, finally delivering the only verdict and punishment possible on himself. But the truth is, we

283

don't know what happened. Though maybe, in some mad way, he was hoping to make amends with this bequest.'

Ross shrugged again, a single tear rolling down towards his quivering lip. Gently, she wiped the tear away with her finger. He'd covered his face with both hands, and she moved closer as he rocked to and fro, the sobs silent but powerful as they wracked his body.

'Look, Ross, come on. Come on now. We've got to decide what to do. See the police. All that. There are people grieving for Craig Irvine and Iona Sutherland. Their loved ones. We owe it to them to get things sorted out. It'll be horrible. As soon as you can, I think you should go away. I've told Morag to. She thinks that, luckily, Alistair Sutherland has already gone away. Bonnie said as much before she died. Just as well. I don't know about Fraser Coulter, but Alistair Sutherland *will* come back as soon as he hears. He's completely unbalanced. You'll need to protect yourself. I mean it.'

She caught the flicker of concern as it crossed his face. Ross was no physical fighter. 'Right. Okay. If you think that's best. But . . . when d'you want to talk to the police, then? I suppose we need to do it straight away. Should someone come over here, or to Mill House? Or shall we go in and see them, or what?'

Normally so cool in a crisis, he was now utterly impotent, disempowered. She gave his arm another reassuring squeeze.

'It doesn't really matter about that. Whatever we decide, we can do it together. But, first, there are two people I must go and see.'

'Glen?'

She nodded. 'Yes. And Donald. It's only fair. What we know will wait until after I've seen them. Both deserve some warning. I fear Glen'll be heading for some trouble over the logs. And the publicity will be disastrous. And Donald, *Christ!* It doesn't bear thinking about.'

Ross sat up. 'But . . . I'm not sure about that. I mean . . . shouldn't we go to the police *now?*'

She stood up. 'No, I think we owe it to Glen and Donald. They both put themselves out for your father. Let me deal with them. After that, we'll do what needs to be done. And we'll do it together. You'll get through it, Ross. We both will.'

37

As she approached Donald Ferguson's house,
Kirstin felt the humid air claw at her skin,
heightening the anxiety that had been growing as
she envisaged the encounter ahead. Unlike Ross,
Donald failed to pick up on her tone of voice
over the phone. Just as well. In fact, the old man
seemed excessively jolly, insisting that she come
for afternoon tea.

For twenty minutes she half listened to his
news while trying to swallow cake that tasted like
sawdust. Finally, she could take no more.

'Please, *please*, Donald. I have to talk to you.'

★　★　★

The notebook lay open at the sketch, the bundle
of Iona's security photographs beside it, both
nestling incongruously among the detritus of
afternoon tea. Donald was very pale now. And
still. His voice had been kept to a low whisper.

'But he told me he had been at home all day.
With his hip. I don't, I just don't understand it.
How . . . tell me, how can you know someone for
so long, know him so well, like a brother. And
then . . . *this*? How can that happen? He was a
good man. I thought Jamie was a good man.' He
wouldn't look at her. Just kept his glazed eyes
fixed on the sketch.

'Donald? *Donald?*'

At last he jerked his head up to make eye contact. He seemed to be having trouble focusing on her, blinking repeatedly as she talked.

'Donald, you're right. Jamie *was* a good man. Once. I'm sure of that.' *God, how long can you keep going on saying that?* 'But something happened to him. I don't begin to understand what. You'd need to be a psychiatrist to analyse that. And Jamie's gone. Any attempt at understanding him is redundant.'

'That's not what those poor people's families might think. They'll demand to know why their loved ones had to die.' Donald's simple observation held an accusatory tone.

Rightly so, Kirstin thought. 'That's true, very true. And I didn't mean to seem so callous about the victims. They *are* the most important thing in all this. Maybe I, maybe Morag and I, should have gone straight to the police last night. But first I wanted to tell Ross, tell you, and Glen.'

Now it was Donald's turn to apologize. He sat forward, hands held out. 'No, no, no. I didn't mean to criticize. It was a kind thing to do, coming here. Frankly, I don't know what I'd have done if the police had just turned up here with *that* sort of news about Jamie. It was bad enough when he died. But *this*? It would have just about killed me.'

Kirstin gave Donald's hand a final squeeze and stood up. 'I must go now. I'm going to see Glen and then, after that, well, it'll be time to talk with the police.'

As he escorted her to the door, one hand

lightly on her shoulder, Donald slowed his pace and then stopped. They were standing in the hallway. He moved back from her, a look of worry on his face. 'I should have thought more about this at the time, and especially after his death. But I put it to the back of my mind. I was actually going to tell you about it when you first came to visit a couple of weeks ago.'

Kirstin frowned. 'Tell me about what?'

In answer, Donald moved to a small wedge-shaped door positioned under the stairs. He opened it and disappeared down some concrete steps. Two minutes later he emerged, clutching a slightly battered cardboard box, sealed with brown packing tape.

'See this? Jamie left it with me. Under strict instructions never to give it to anybody unless he said so. He was very firm, very secretive, very obsessive, almost hysterical about it. It was when he was acting at his oddest. When he died, I felt very strange about having this. But a promise is a promise. He didn't give me permission to look inside. Nor have I. I was going to destroy it. Chuck the whole damn thing on a bonfire come the winter.' He paused, shaking his head at the box. 'Now I'm going to break my vow. Here. Have it.'

Reluctantly he held out the box. Kirstin took it, feeling faintly bewildered. He moved swiftly to open the door for her.

'Goodbye, Kirstin dear. We'll meet again. But please, unless you have to, don't ever tell me what's in that box.'

38

Kirstin was relieved to be sitting in the quiet lay-by off the A70. The rain had, at last, arrived. Its steady hammering, as the deluging stair rods hit the roof of the car, was strangely soothing. The break in the oppressive weather seemed, uncannily, to match her mood. A cathartic outpouring, but also the sort of dull grey light you could hide in. A cocoon.

Donald's farewell words had remained stubbornly with her as she'd driven out towards Glen's offices. Once she'd placed the box on the back seat she'd decided she wasn't going to open it here, alone. She put the car into gear and prepared to pull away, taking a final glance at the notebook and the bundle of photographs lying beside her. Glen was the last person she had to show them to before the police saw them. Then she could relinquish all responsibility for them. God, how she looked forward to that moment. There would unquestionably be some raised eyebrows when it emerged that she'd withheld evidence for a day. But she'd face that one when it came to it.

The reception desk was deserted. No Rory, struggling with the switchboard. She stood stranded in the middle of the floor, casting around for any sign of life. But along the corridor all the office doors were firmly shut. Then she heard the click of one opening.

'Hi.'

He was strolling towards her, smiling.

The next moment she had collapsed into his arms, the sobs that had been held in for so long at last finding their voice.

★ ★ ★

She'd awoken to the smell of cooking. She could hear the reassuring sounds of Glen moving about his kitchen as he prepared dinner. From the bed she could see the rain, still in stair-rod formation, sheeting down outside, the battering on the iron balcony rising and falling as the downpour periodically lessened and strengthened again. And underneath, the whoosh of a now swollen Water of Leith as it swirled by. A flash of what the Cauldron must be like at this moment — perilous, as on the night of Jamie's death — passed through her mind. She pushed the image away.

Resting back on the pillows, she thought over the last hours. Following her collapse at Glen's office, he'd given her a drink that had been, temporarily, restorative, allowing her to unfold the story, complete with notebook and photographs. Oddly, she couldn't recall much of his reaction. This fourth retelling had just poured out of her between uncontrollable sobbing. He'd looked stricken, for sure. But he'd been gentle and calm. Driving her back to his home, he'd held her hand constantly, cooing reassurances at her. '*It'll be all right, Kirsty. It'll be all right.*'

Padding through to the kitchen, she caught

him unawares, humming along to the delicate strains of Vaughan Williams's *The Lark Ascending*. His choice of music left her with mixed feelings. It had been one of Jamie's favourites.

Hearing her, Glen swung round, wooden spoon in hand, a look of surprise and joy on his face. 'Well, well. You look a billion times brighter.'

She moved forward to hug him. 'I am. I feel a bit . . . wobbly. But I'm fine. I think I'll take a shower. Oh, but before that, I need to go down to the car. Where are my keys?'

He frowned. 'They're on the hall table. You going for the box?'

She nodded.

'You sure?'

She smiled. 'Yes, I'm sure.'

★　★　★

She sat cross-legged on Glen's bed, the unopened box before her. Glen had understood and left her alone. He'd switched on a bedside lamp for her and shut the door gently behind him as he returned to his kitchen duties.

The tape peeled away easily. She noticed the trembling in her hands as she pulled back the flaps. Part of her had an almost irresistibly powerful urge to package the thing back up again. Hide it. Have someone else do the dirty work. But no. Now was the time.

Her first reaction was disappointment. Stuffed on top was the familiar blue-and-green fabric of one of Jamie's uniforms. She pulled it out, the

291

faint scent of Old Spice floating upwards, catapulting her back to countless hugs and embraces over the years. For some reason, the memory of an exceptionally happy Christmas six years before stayed with her for a moment. Jamie, smart and spruce as ever, with a silly tinsel scarf swirled round his neck, beaming at her as he plied her with more champagne. *'You're the best thing that ever happened to Ross. You're a bit of a miracle.'*

She peered down into the box. A couple of buff cardboard document wallets lay flat at the bottom. But it was the small black zipped bag that caught her eye. As she lifted it out she saw the word and knew immediately what she was holding.

Nikon.

39

The camera wouldn't work. She'd tried all the buttons, and then she realized. The battery. Fumbling with the case, she unzipped a side pocket and found a spare one. The particular model of camera was unfamiliar to her, but in a couple of minutes she'd worked it out. The rectangular viewing screen came to life.

Nothing.

There were no images. The camera's memory card was blank.

She shrugged and sat back, staring at the box. A moment later, she leant forward and delved into it. Running her hand over the top of one of the document wallets, she felt a bump — or was it two? Her fingers latched on to something. Pulling it out, she nodded. Another memory card. She found herself fumbling again with the unfamiliar equipment. But this time, when she brought the screen to life, there was something there.

Thumbing through the initial images, she recognized the terrain. There was the viaduct. After that, long shots of the path leading to the Cauldron. And then the weir. The next ones were unfamiliar. At least, in their camera angles. She squinted at them. It was the weir all right. But . . . What angle? . . . Yes! They were taken from the other side. There was the wall by the weir, and the Cauldron as seen from the opposite side.

The next photographs offered a flurry of images. She caught her breath as she recognized the subjects. He'd caught them all. In groups and individually. The attractive woman in the bikini had to be Iona Sutherland, leaning on her brother. Bonnie Campbell was next, throwing stones into the Cauldron. And . . . yes, that was Craig Irvine. She'd seen photographs of him at Morag's house. He was swigging from a large beer bottle with . . . Fraser Coulter, presumably.

Kirstin paused. What were these photos? How often did Jamie try to film the group? And why? To catch them out? Tentatively, she thumbed forward. At last, there were some images of Morag. At the wall, looking blank. On her own. Then she was leaning against it. Finally, she had her eyes covered with some kind of blindfold, her lips open, mouthing something.

Numbers.

One to a hundred. The hide-and-seek game. So that meant . . . Kirstin flicked back through the images. She'd not been paying attention. But now it jumped out at her. The burnt-in time code was there. As was the date:

13.08.2006

Kirstin dropped the camera on to the bed, suddenly aware again of the rattling from the kitchen, the battering of the rain on the balcony, the rush of the river below. She shut her eyes tight, predicting what was to come. Preparing herself for the next images. Not a pencil sketch. No. Rather, the fleshed-out, technicolour-bright

294

depiction of ghastly reality. Still with eyes closed, she felt for the camera and found the button, pressing it to bring up the next image. Painfully slowly, she opened her eyes and found the rectangle of light.

Her breathing stopped. What? What the hell was that? Frantically, she flicked forward a couple of frames and then back again. The vantage point still the far side of the weir. But the lens was looking away from the Cauldron and the picnicking area, up towards the hill behind. A figure. That was it. There was a figure. She flicked forward again. Each frame brought the shape closer and closer. Binoculars. Holding binoculars to their eyes. Looking down at the Cauldron. Next: male, the figure was definitely male. Next: bare arms and red clothing. A T-shirt, the wording on it indistinct. Next: arms lowered, binoculars in hands. Next: each piece of visual data assaulted her simultaneously. The red T-shirt. Abercrombie. The sun-bleached hair. There he was in close-up.

'Kirstin?'

She yelped as the door opened. The camera dropped from her hands, bouncing off the bed to land on the carpet at his feet.

Face up.

40

Head tilted, Glen peered at the object on the floor. Then, as if in slow-motion, he lowered his body to a squat. One strong hand reached out to grasp the camera and hold the viewing screen in front of his eyes. He seemed to take forever, scrutinizing and studying the image, an expression of puzzled interest creasing his features. And then she saw a look of recognition flutter across his features. He knew exactly what he was seeing. And what it meant.

Kirstin shifted. The bed gave out a complaining creak, and Glen snapped his head up. Unhurriedly, he stood to his full height and approached her. Immediately, she leapt off the bed but found herself marooned. It was like the Alistair Sutherland episode all over again. Glen was between her and the door. The bed lay between them. The balcony, and a sickening drop into the tumult of the river, was her only means of escape.

He stopped and took a step back, holding the camera out in front of him. 'Look, this is not what you think. I . . . I had no idea . . . is this . . . this from the box? Jamie's box? Is it?'

She nodded, and her eyes began scanning around the room, searching hopelessly for another way out.

He was staying put. 'Please, Kirstin. I didn't know Jamie had this. I can explain, please.' He was inching forward again.

'Keep away from me!' She was aware of something sticking out from under the bed. With her eyes fixed on him, she allowed herself to bend slightly at the knees. She sneaked a quick glance, reached out, and grasped her weapon: a canoe oar.

Raising both hands in submission, he backed off. She used the breathing space to pounce forward and snatch her mobile phone from the bed.

'What the hell are you doing, Kirstin?'

Her immediate panic had subsided. She had a lifeline. Two. The oar and the phone. 'I'm doing what I should have done last night. Calling the police.'

At that, he let the camera fall, and moving with breathtaking speed, leapt across the bed to imprison her in a bear hug. 'No, please don't do that. Don't! Let me explain.'

Her scream ripped through the rain's incessant hammering on the iron balcony, drowning out the rush of the river below. The mobile and the oar fell from her hands as she began lashing out, kicking and scratching. For a moment, she thought his grip was going to snap her spine and then, without warning, he released her.

Quickly, he backed off to resume his place by the door. '*Please, wait.* I admit, I was there that day. Like Jamie was. He raised the issue with me a few days later. He'd seen me. I think he thought I'd seen him. I hadn't. He told me he'd been determined to catch them out. And that Sunday was going to be his best, probably his only chance for the rest of the summer. They were all going away after that. I laughed when he told me. Because that's exactly why *I* was there. I deliberately never told him what I was going to do. I didn't want him there that day, perhaps losing his rag, spoiling my chance to sort those . . . little shits out. I believed him when he called me to say he wasn't going to be able to go out, because of his hip. Thinking back, I wonder if he was just checking to see who else might be about.

'The truth is, Kirstin, I left before anything happened. I'd seen what I needed to. With my own eyes. The booze, the drugs, the littering, the whole bloody shooting match.' He let out a half laugh. 'I was even going to call Jamie when I got back that Sunday to tell him what I'd done. I knew he'd be pleased as punch. But I changed my mind. I'd had enough of work for a Sunday. I just wanted to chill out. You can believe it or not. But it's true. *It's true!*'

The oar was back in her hands, but the mobile was out of reach somewhere under the bed. 'Why didn't you tell anyone? You should have gone to the police.'

He bent down to pick up the camera, one hand raised in a gesture of surrender, and moved forward to perch on the far end of the bed. She had the advantage of height over him now. He let out a long sigh. 'With hindsight there are so many things that I should have gone to the police about. The logs, for one. I should never have hidden them. But I didn't want Jamie getting into trouble. And yes, before you say it, I was worried about my job and the association. Of course that was a consideration. But that was nothing compared to being there that day. Me and him. *Shit!* It was enough, me deciding not to tell the police I was there. But when Jamie came to me, I knew what had to be done. The two of us would have to lie. Yes, I admit again, I did wrong. I lied. But I felt I had nothing to tell. I didn't see anything. Jamie claimed the same thing. I believed him. I had no reason not to.'

He paused to wipe a finger across his face. He was sweating heavily now. 'So, yes, we made a sort of pact. To protect each other. And what a fool he made of me.'

He shifted further along the edge of the bed. She was tracking his every move with suspicious eyes.

Her grip tightened on the oar. '*Pact.* That's a funny word to use. It implies conspiracy. Were you accomplices? Is that what was going on? You and Jamie. All cosy together. And is that what the bequest was all about? He gives you Mill House in some perverted quid pro quo arrangement? And, you know what else? Maybe that . . . that *wretched* sketch wasn't a self-portrait of Jamie after all. *Maybe . . . maybe it was of you!*'

He jumped to his feet, shaking his head. '*No! No, no, no!* For fuck's sake, Kirstin. Listen to yourself. That's . . . *delusional nonsense!* I did *nothing* to anybody. No harm. I swear it!'

He tossed the camera towards her and retreated to the door. With a firm tug, he opened it. 'There's nothing else I can say or do. You either believe me or you don't. I'm sorry, I should have told you I was there that day. I'll obviously tell the police everything. It's the least I can do. Oh, and by the way, I've never worn a river association uniform in my life. So why the hell would Jamie sketch me in one, tell me that?'

He disappeared through the doorway. Her body was still trembling and she collapsed on to the bed, the oar falling at her feet. She looked around the room. Suddenly she was aware of the hammering rain outside, the gushing river below. But everything was crowding in. Trapping her. Hurriedly, she stuffed the camera back into the box and folded down the flaps. In the hallway, she found her shoes and bag. For a moment she stood listening. Where was he? Not a sound. No music. No television. No signs of life. But he was somewhere. Heaving the box under her arm, she turned to go, clicking the front door gently behind her. As she tip-toed down the steps, she heard it. The sound of a mobile ringing. Her mobile. She cursed as the memory hit her. Her second lifeline was lying out of reach under Glen's bed.

Pray she wouldn't need it.

41

Morag was grateful, happy even, for the rain. She sat in her darkened kitchen with the patio doors open, allowing the spatters of spray to shower her bare legs and feet. The heatwave had broken. The thunder had started its rumbling overhead and she could just about make out faint lightning flickers far into the distance. She sighed and sipped at her champagne. She had known one day there'd be a use for that last bottle, hidden at the back of the fridge.

The remnants of a solitary but satisfying dinner lay at her elbow. It was a good sign that she was eating. That she had actually cooked. And there were other signs of improvement. She'd had her hair done. Actually walked boldly into a top salon in town and paid for a makeover. And then splashed out on new make-up. She felt like a lottery winner.

Her spirits had lifted into the stratosphere. But — and she had to be careful in admitting these feelings of exultation, especially to Kirstin — the bombshell about Jamie was a blessed relief to her. All day she'd fought the urge to run outside, jubilant, proclaiming her news. *'I'm innocent! I'm innocent! To hell with you all!'* And then she'd fallen back to earth. Her salvation would come too late. She had to be resigned to losing her home. That was imminent, unstoppable, though bitterly unfair. The thought drove her to

301

near fury. But exoneration would be hers eventually, if not fast enough. She could sell her story, seek compensation perhaps? And then use the spoils to bury herself in anonymity. Starting a new life, making a fresh start, would still be the only answer. She should be cheered by the thought. Either that, or she could sink back into her recent despair.

She stood up to close the patio doors against the rain and approaching thunder. The lock secured, she stood gazing out at the blackness. The unseen river. The Cauldron would be living up to its name tonight. A seething whirlpool. Grasping her glass and the champagne bucket, she wandered through to the front of the house. The rain was flowing freely through the living room's open windows. So what if it soaked a wall? She needed to let go of this house. Starting tonight. Leaving the lights off, and curtains open, she lay back on the settee.

She saw the flickering of headlights first, followed by the roar of an engine as the car skidded round the driveway. Jumping up, she peered through the curtains. Kirstin! Damn! Hurriedly, she drained the remnants of her glass and tucked the half-drunk bottle of champagne behind the settee.

She raced to the front door to release the lock, just as Kirstin, wielding a cardboard box, almost fell through the door, her face an ashen mask.

★   ★   ★

Kirstin stared down at her hands. They were still trembling. Even though she'd been settled in Morag's comfortable kitchen for some time, the effects of her encounter with Glen had left her badly shaken. She looked towards the window. The rain was relentless, its steady downpour set for the night, for days maybe. A summer monsoon. At last the thunder and lightning had arrived. Directly overhead, the noisy rumbles and flashes were making themselves known above the house. Kirstin was relieved. The oppressive humidity, which so closely matched the claustrophobia of her anxiety, worry and fears, had been broken. She glanced back at Morag, sitting straight-backed at the kitchen table. Only now did she take in the change. Morag seemed like a different woman; physically altered. Though still slightly wan and tired, she was well groomed and . . . yes, there was a hint of radiance. That was it, the inner strength and confidence were beginning to shine through. Thank God, at least one of them was improving.

Morag was still nursing the camera in her hands, a look of doubt on her face.

'For your sake, I don't want to believe that Glen's involved in any way. I understand your worries. But let's look on the optimistic side. Or the least worst-case scenario, if you like.'

Kirstin gave a slow shrug. 'Please do. I . . . I just can't go there. I can't afford to believe that he's involved.' She wiped away a tear and watched Morag continue fiddling with the camera as she spoke.

'It's true that Glen has lied to you about so

much. Or kept so much from you, which in my book's just about the same thing. He kept quiet about being there that day, about Jamie being there, the logbooks, even knowing Ross when they were kids. It all adds up. A mindset of deceit. And the violence. Laying into Ally. That's bad. But not all-incriminating. And the sketch issue. We have only his word for it that he never wore an association uniform, but it would be easy enough to check up on. So, whoever Jamie was drawing it wasn't Glen. It was . . . and I'm sorry . . . it had to be himself.' Morag looked from the camera to Kirstin, her face stern. 'Tell me, truthfully, before *this*, this camera episode, you were having some doubts about Glen *but* only about his . . . how can I put it . . . his *macho* side coming out. It was a bit of a surprise, yes? But you didn't really believe Glen *wanted* to kill Ally in that horrible fight?'

Kirstin turned back to look at Morag. 'No. I've been over that again and again in my mind. Glen just lost it. But I didn't think then that he had any *real* murderous intentions. He *did* admit to going over the top. And that made me feel odd for a while. But I'd more or less got over it. We were getting on okay, and then . . . the camera and his being there . . . the pact with Jamie. It was, *is* such a shock. What do you think? Really think?'

Morag sighed. 'All right, if you want my true opinion, it's this. I don't think you should worry about Glen being a raging psychopath. Nor do I think you should worry about any conspiracy theory. It sounds much simpler than that.' She laid the camera down on the table. 'Glen's been a bloody fool. Protecting Jamie is one thing. Not telling the police he was there that day is another matter. And quite simply idiotic.'

Suddenly restless, Kirstin stood up and walked over to the patio doors to watch the sheeting rain. 'I've no idea what to make of it. But I'm sure of one thing. I certainly made a *very* bad error of judgement about Glen. I'll never be able to trust him again. *I've* been the idiot.'

Morag let out a harsh laugh. 'Yes. But he *is* a pretty face, so I wouldn't be so hard on yourself. Anyway, whatever the truth, Glen's going to be in for it from the police. They'll grill him good and proper. And I suppose he'll lose his job?'

'I'd think so. It'll be a blow. But . . . well, I get the impression that Glen's a survivor. I'm sure he's been in scrapes before. He'll probably land on his feet, *if . . .* '

The unsaid words lay between them as they sat listening to the thunder move away at last. Kirstin finished the sentence off in silence: *if he's not involved.* She wanted to believe his explanation, that he was protecting Jamie and his own job. But Jamie was now dead. And the association would be looking for a new head of conservation. A short while ago, she could have felt sorry for Glen, but not now. If Morag was correct, the overriding truth was that he had brought the situation on himself. And there was one final aspect of his behaviour that had stuck with her. Tonight, when she'd been so terrified that she'd armed herself with a weapon, his response had been to physically restrain her.

305

Those were not the actions of a man who could understand a woman's fear. He shouldn't have laid a finger on her. And *that* insensitivity gnawed away at her. Even if he was guilty of only lying, being foolishly protective of his job and Jamie, that act of physical insensitivity alone was enough to have driven her away for good. It was clear that Glen didn't understand physical boundaries. She prayed his lack of control was limited to just that. But despite Morag's upbeat assertions about Glen, Kirstin still felt the dull ache of doubt.

Still restless, she moved towards the kitchen door. 'You know what? I'm going to drive over to Mill House and collect the rest of my things. Want to come?'

Morag nodded towards the window. 'In this rain? No, thanks.'

Kirstin shrugged. 'I want something to do. I'm a bit jittery.'

Morag followed her through to the hall. 'Here, take my waterproof jacket or d'you want the sou'wester and oilskin? That big yellow bugger over there?' She raised her eyes to look upwards. 'You might need it. Sounds like the thunder's going to be following you. It's heading east. Here, take my mobile. Hang on, I'll just . . . okay . . . done it. I've put the landline number here in the phone book under 'my house'. If you're having any problems, or feel scared or anything, call me. Okay?'

Kirstin nodded her thanks and chose the lightweight jacket, placing the phone in a side pocket. It was like the blind leading the blind.

Kirstin sighed as she readied herself for the outdoors. Tomorrow was another day. She would have her power back. Especially once she and Ross had gone to the police. With a quick wave of farewell to Morag, the door was closed behind her.

Morag listened to the sound of Kirstin's car fading into the distance before moving slowly back to the living room. She retrieved the champagne bottle from its ice-filled bucket, and topped up her glass as she wandered back to the kitchen. She set the bottle and bucket down on the worktop, her hand hovering over a drawer handle. Why not? Slowly, she slid out a packet of cigarettes, ashtray and disposable lighter. Then she took her seat at the table and stared at the camera, frowning. She pressed the 'on' button and began reviewing the images. Those of her blindfolded and counting to one hundred made her jaw muscles tighten. She turned it off and slid the camera away, spinning it round and round on the scrubbed wooden table. Mentally she replayed the images, her mind's eye stopping at one in particular: Iona, bikini-clad, tanned, fit, flirtatious. A good imitation of a sex goddess. Any straight male would look more than once. And try to touch? Suddenly, she slammed a hand down on to the spinning camera. A fresh thought occurred to her, one that apparently hadn't occurred to Kirstin. Would Glen have taken a second look at Iona? Iona would have had a pleasing pair of studs in Craig *and* Glen. *The bitch!*

Morag took a long sip of her champagne and

dragged the box that was on the floor towards her. She pulled open the flaps and placed the camera inside the box. Tilting her head, she paused. Kirstin hadn't said what else was in here. Had she even been through it all once the panic of finding the camera had taken over? Probably not. Morag's hand hesitated over the flaps. Lifting the box on to her lap, she emptied the contents carefully on to the table, spreading them out evenly with her hands.

'Hell!'

Something had fallen on the floor. She scraped back her chair and craned her neck under the table. With stretched fingers she slid it towards her. *Got it!* She frowned. The memory card had been marked with an orange fluorescent dot. Odd. She retrieved the camera and began swapping the cards over. She thumbed the 'on' switch and the tiny screen lit up. She flicked through a sequence of badly composed images, and then stopped.

It took several seconds for her to understand what she was seeing. What it meant. Then realization hit.

'*No. Oh, God. No!*'

42

Sprinting from the car to Jamie's front door, Kirstin began scrabbling for the house keys. As the latch gave way, she shook the rain from her hair and sucked in one long deep breath. *Be calm. It's just a quick in and out. Pack the bags and then go. No hanging around.* The familiar smell of Jamie's house brought memories rushing back. As she hit the hall switch, the spotlights lining the walls came to life, illuminating the photo gallery. Head down, she made for the stairs and the spare room she'd been using, determined to avoid eye contact with anything that reminded her of Jamie. She bundled various items of clothing into one holdall and moved into the en suite bathroom to scoop her toiletries into another.

She dumped her luggage at the bottom of the stairs, then went down to the study. The lightning flashes were playing blue and silver across the carpet. She jumped as a bolt earthed somewhere out in the garden, and the trees outside the window danced eerie shadows over the desk. Flicking on the overhead light eased her anxiety. She scanned the room. Only one thing of hers: a light summer shirt hanging over Jamie's chair. Quickly she stepped over to grab it, flicking the light off again as she left. The temptation to hold both hands to her ears was hard to resist. She could almost hear Jamie's voice calling out to her from his desk. '*C'mon, Kirstin, my dear. Come in here and keep an old man company. How about a wee dram before you go?*'

She slammed the study door shut, and ran down the hallway. Tugging open the front door, she gathered up her luggage. Then she heard it. The mobile's shrill tones jolted her to a halt. Dropping a bag, she fumbled in the roomy pocket of Morag's waterproof. The mobile's glowing screen cut through the darkness, letting her know who was calling. *My house.*

'Morag. Hi. I'm on my way ba — '

Weird. It had sounded like a hang-up. Or maybe it was the mobile cutting out. She dumped the other bag by her feet and began fiddling with the unfamiliar phone to call Morag back.

Four rings. Then straight to the answering machine.

'Morag? You there? You just tried to call me. Hello? Hello?'

Damn! Kirstin hung up and rang again. Four rings. The same thing happened. She hung up and redialled immediately, trying to override the answering machine before it reset. Maybe Morag had gone to have a bath or something. If the phone kept ringing, she'd have to answer it eventually.

After two more attempts, Kirstin gave up. It was time to go. With a final glance down the darkened corridor, she grabbed her bags and stepped out into the rain.

'Hi! I'm back. It didn't take me that long, did it?
I tried calling you back.'

Odd. It felt like no one was home.

'Morag? Morag!'

The answering machine's digital readout told
the story of her repeated attempts to call back.
Plus one. Kirstin hit the replay button. Again
and again she heard the strains of her own voice
and fast forwarded. Then, the tones changed.

'Hello, eh . . . Morag. It's Glen Laidlaw here.
I wondered if, eh . . . if Kirstin was back at yours
yet. She's left her mobile here and . . . I . . . I
wanted to organize getting it back to her. I could
drop it off. It would be no problem an — '

She stabbed a finger at the 'off' button to stop
the machine. Glen could wait for his answer.
And no, he couldn't drop by. The kitchen was in
darkness. It was much as she had left it. Except,
on the table there was an empty glass and an
ashtray with a single cigarette stub. The acrid
stench of cigarette smoke still lingered in the air.
Funny? She was sure Morag didn't smoke. But
. . . wait! Where was the camera? And Jamie's
box? Both had gone. Maybe Morag had tidied
them away to another room, or . . . ? Kirstin
turned on her heels and jogged towards the
stairs, taking them two at a time. The anxiety was
back now. What if Morag had . . . no, she
mustn't think like that. Morag's troubles, or the
worst part of them, were over. She had no need
to harm herself, did she? *Did she?*

'Morag, you upstairs? Morag!'

She could hear the quiver of stress in her voice as she kicked each door on the landing open. Nothing. She raced up to the top floor. Nothing. Christ, where the hell had she gone? And with no bloody mobile. Was her car in the garage?

Within seconds she was back down on the first-floor landing. As she turned towards the last flight of stairs, her peripheral vision caught sight of a flickering light. But the lightning had moved east, hadn't it? She stepped towards the full-length window that housed the telescope. Cupping her eyes with her hands, she peered out through the glass. Impossible. Nothing but sheeting rain. She'd imagined it. And then she saw it again. Flickering light coming from the river! She manoeuvred herself round behind the telescope and bent her head to the eyepiece. *Damn!* It was too dark. Inch by inch she swivelled the long barrel to her right. There! The beam from a torch! Held by an invisible figure. But in front of the beam she could clearly make out the second figure.

Dressed head to foot in a yellow oilskin and sou'wester.

The Dead Pool

43

As Kirstin hurtled the car through sheeting rain towards the river, she replayed the scene in Morag's house. The cigarette, the smell of smoke. *Ally!* Jules had been right in one thing. All his feelings, intuitions about Ally being dangerous, about teetering on the edge, had been right. She shouldn't have dismissed them so easily and stuck by her belief that Ally was sad rather than bad or mad. Now Ally had gone over the edge and was taking Morag with him.

The options were racing through her mind as she skidded to a halt under the viaduct. Her trembling fingers struggled with the phone. Quickly, she tapped in Ross's number. *C'mon, c'mon!* Straight to his answering machine. *Another damn answering machine!* And then she remembered the state he'd been in when they had talked about Jamie's guilt. If he was hell-bent on getting pissed tonight, by now he'd be out for the count and have switched off the phone in the bedroom. But ... maybe, just maybe, he'd forgotten about his mobile. Ross was umbilically tied to it. She waited, heart racing, as Ross's mobile rang out. *Please answer. Please.*

Voicemail. No! She beat the palm of her hand against the steering wheel, willing the outgoing message to end ... *at last!* The hysteria was building up in her and, with a split second to

315

spare, she pulled back from screaming uncontrollably down the phone.

'Listen, Ross. It's me. Morag's in trouble. Ally Sutherland's taken her from her house. They're heading for the Cauldron. He won't believe a word she has to say about your dad. He's out of control now, Ross. He'll think she's making it up. She's in danger! We need to help her. I'm at the river. Under the viaduct. I'm going to try and cross on foot. Save time. Can you come? I don't want to call the police. If Ally sees them, it'll just make him do God knows what. *But we need to help Morag!*'

She stopped to take a badly needed breath, and released the central locking system.

The wind tore the car door from her grip as soon as she opened it. Body bent at the waist, she staggered round to the back of the car and unlocked the tailgate. She had no idea if the wellington boots from Morag's would fit. They looked as if they would. At least the chunky waterproof camping torch worked, its strong yellow beam cutting through the rain with ease to bounce off her intended destination, so near yet so far. The other side of the river glistened back at her a tantalizing few yards away. At least it wasn't cold. Just an unseasonal summer storm. Thankfully, the wind brought no deep chill. Otherwise she'd have had to rethink her strategy.

Securing the torch to her wrist by its carrying cord, she headed for the gap in the fence that had been there for years. Would it still be there? Yes! Once through, she immediately lost her footing in the wet foliage and mud at the top of the riverbank. Slithering at frightening speed, she managed to stop herself by tugging on a tuft of strong grass, the jolt to her shoulder socket sending agonizing waves of pain down her left side. She lay back, trying to let the agony wash away, and shone the torch down to her crossing point. *Fucking hell!* The sight caught her breath. The water was running almost as deep as any winter deluge, and the rapids at this point, usually much slower in summer, seemed just as deadly. She'd have to go back to the proper entrance at Roseburn Cliff. But that would waste time. Time that might be critical. Time that Morag might not have.

Kirstin stood, stranded on the bank, feeling her heart rate speeding up to panic levels. Her options were narrowing by the second. If Ross got her message, he'd move heaven and earth to get to the Cauldron in super-quick time. Despite his self-centredness, after hearing such an urgent message from her, he would never leave her to face this alone. But it might still take him fifteen, twenty minutes. It was too long. She could save precious time by crossing here. But she needed one other prop: a long, stout stick. It would help her keep balanced as the rapids tried to dislodge her footing. The rocks underneath would be slippery, and invisible under the murky silt-churned waters. The rubber soles of her wellingtons wouldn't hold her. And once she lost her footing . . . well, her next stop would be down at the weir. Probably drowned.

As she hunted frantically along the bank, among broken boughs and branches, the guilt began to take hold. Ross had been right. If they'd gone to the police straightaway, as he'd wanted, then this wouldn't be happening. Morag quite possibly might have been in with the police for much of the day, as would Ally Sutherland. At the very least, the police would surely have contacted him to tell him new evidence had come to light. Now, because of her delay, Morag was in danger.

Kirstin almost shouted with glee as her eyes lighted on a thick stick half buried under foliage. Right, it was time to get going.

Halfway into her journey, her right hand was having trouble keeping hold of the stick. It was stout enough, but a fraction too short. Too bad. Turning back now was out of the question. She was teetering midstream, the torch beam wavering manically as she tried to hold the flashlight more firmly in her left hand. But that side of her body was hurting more than ever.

The sound of the rapids gushing round her was deafening, the walls and arches of the viaduct above acting as an echo chamber. At least she was sheltered from the wind here. But the final discomfort had just hit her. The waters, running almost winter-deep, had invaded her boots. Although the shock/cold sensation gripping her legs and feet was strangely energizing, she'd have extra weight to carry each time she picked up a foot to step forward.

Gingerly, she inched ahead. Just three steps more. One . . . two . . . three! She reached forward to grab an overhanging branch, to hoist herself on to dry land. Immediately she knew she'd misjudged its thickness. With a sickening snap the branch came away in her hand. *Keep your balance, keep your balance. If you go in, the river will sweep you away. Bob down. Lower your centre of gravity.* Her right knee took the weight of her fall. The kneecap had hit a hidden rock underneath. Tears of pain welled up, blurring her vision. *Keep scrambling forward. Not far now.* A fierce tug on her right hand told her that the current had stolen her stick. But her left wrist still had the torch swinging by its cord. Thank God. She couldn't operate blind in these conditions. Gritting her teeth, she prepared for the final heave. *One jump and you'll be home.*

Go!

She'd landed in the mud and gravel. Drenched from the waist down, she lay on her belly, gasping huge lungfuls of air. That had been close. But she was across. Now, only a wall and railing to negotiate. With a final, aching effort she was up on the raised walkway, one hand leaning on the viaduct wall as she emptied her boots, ignoring the discomfort of wet feet. She peered ahead. The ground was soaked. She'd have to watch her footing. Holding the torch well out in front, she began a cautious jog along the path. Her right knee was stiffening. It wouldn't support her full weight and her left shoulder socket was emitting low-level, constant pain. But she had to keep going. How long had it taken her to find the wretched stick and get across here? Six, seven minutes? She risked quickening her pace. The rumble of thunder was returning and she could make out faint flickers of lightning far in the distance. Other than that, all was dark and quiet. Apart from the rushing waters.

Kirstin winced. Any further pressure on her knee was going to be impossible. A limping jog was all she could manage. The footbridge was first to come into view. Momentarily, she allowed the torch beam to bounce off the wooden struts before pointing it again at the footpath ahead. If she slipped now, that would be it. She wiped at her eyes, cursing the persistent wind that whipped the rain horizontally into her face. Where were they? *Oh, God. Let me be in time.*

'Morag? *Morag!*'

She continued her painful jog towards the Cauldron.

'Moraaag! It's Kirstin!'

Nothing.

She could hear the weir now, the frothing waters sounding perilously fast. Again she cast her beam ahead and then, in the distance, she spotted it. Approaching through the sheeting rain. A lone figure. Clad head to foot in yellow.

'*Morag! Morag! Thank God!* I saw you through the telescope. He's here, isn't he? Isn't he?'

She limped forward just in time to catch the staggering figure. Carefully, she pushed the sou'wester back off the face. Morag was sickeningly pale and her cheek and temple were bruised and bleeding.

'Come on, come on now, Morag. I'm here. You're all right.'

But clearly, she wasn't. Gently, Kirstin half dragged Morag to the shelter of a clump of trees, while scanning anxiously in front and behind for any signs of Ally Sutherland. Once safe in their shelter, she switched off the torch.

Morag twisted and let out a long moan. 'Ahhh . . . I . . . '

The voice, already tremulous and weak, faded away. Slowly, she slumped to the ground, melting into a swoon. Kirstin watched as a semi-conscious Morag struggled to move a hand towards her pocket. And then the arm dropped, limp and lifeless.

'*No, Morag! No!*'

Kirstin wrenched off her jacket and, fashioning a crude pillow from it, manoeuvred the inert body into the recovery position, before placing her ear close to Morag's mouth. *It's okay, it's okay. She's still breathing.* Kirstin edged away to the fringes of their tree shelter. Keeping the torch switched off, she peered left and right along the pathway. A sudden noise from behind made her jump through one hundred and eighty degrees. Only darkness. So where was Ally Sutherland? She turned back and squatted down, feeling Morag's pulse and checking her body position.

There was nothing for it. She had to face him. Immediately the wind attacked her and, within seconds, the thin T-shirt, her only protection, was soaking. The jeans, already drenched from the river crossing, flapped against her legs once and then stuck fast. Her boots felt unnervingly slippery underfoot. The pain in her knee had eased, but she'd still have to be careful. Step by slow step she approached the open ground near the Cauldron, the torch clutched tightly in her hand, acting as a weapon.

She'd reached the wall. How strange poor light and bad weather made the landscape look. It was like a different place. A threatening place with a bogeyman in every shadow. The sudden flash and deafening crack of thunder directly overhead made her jump. That was it. Should she call Ross again? As she looked across the rushing waters of the weir, a new worry presented itself. Was Ross okay? What if Ally Sutherland had somehow got past her, was thundering towards the exit, and met Ross coming the other way? Ross wouldn't stand a chance against him. She should call him. No. The mobile was in the jacket under Morag's head. Breathless, she spun round ready to make her way back.

'*God, no!*'

Her scream of shock rang out over the Cauldron, its echo ricocheting back as she tripped and fell into darkness.

44

Why couldn't she move? Where was the wall? She felt something warm on her forehead trickle down the left side of her face. And then the taste of blood. She shook her head, glancing frantically around. She knew where she was. He'd propped her up against the wall by the weir. She tried to get up but the pain in her right knee had gone beyond agony. The leg felt useless.

'I'm sorry. I didn't mean to frighten you. You knocked your head and your leg as you fell.'

The voice? The face? Realization hit with the rush of relief.

'Ross! Thank God! I thought you were Al — '

'Ssh. I know, I know.'

Uncannily, he seemed, on first sight, like Ally Sutherland at his worst. Dishevelled. Exhausted. He wiped a soaking strand of hair from her face, darting quick, nervous looks behind him.

'You got my message! Thank God! Ross? Please tell m — '

'Message? Look, we must get to shelter but I need to look at that cut first. Come on, sit down by the bridge.'

He guided her the short distance, before setting her down on a broad wooden strut, and offered a reassuring smile. Carefully, using the light from the torch, he began scrutinizing her head wound, dabbing at it gently with paper tissues.

He crouched over her, trying to see what he was doing. 'I tried to ring you this evening. On your mobile. Glen Laidlaw answered. He said you must have gone to Morag's, since you weren't with me. He explained about the camera and the box. He said he was worried about you. So was I. I decided to go round to Morag's. And that's when I found her. Poring over everything in the box. She was very, *very* upset.'

Kirstin tried to lift her head. 'Upset?' She flinched. The pain was worsening by the second.

Ross nodded, his voice rising to compete with the waters rushing towards the weir. 'Yes. Frantic. She was getting ready to leave the house with the box when I arrived. Said she was going to the Cauldron. I don't know why. She just mumbled about something having jogged her memory. I thought she seemed strange, maybe meant herself some harm, and then she ran out. Left me there. But I ran after her. It was madness to go down there in this weather, but I offered to take her in my car. She seemed reluctant, and by the time we got on to the path I was feeling . . . I don't know . . . wary. I had every reason to be. Look.'

Kirstin gasped as he pulled open his jacket. His shirt was torn and the gash in his torso was glistening with blood. He moved position, obviously trying to ease his discomfort.

'Once we reached the Cauldron, she tried to push me in. I . . . I had to fight her. I saw you with her just now. It looks like I've hurt her badly. I . . . I had to defend myself. I suppose I should go and see to her but . . . '

324

He paused to glance over his shoulder again, and then turned back to her. He looked terrified. 'I don't know what happened here last summer. Please God, it didn't involve them both. Her and Dad. But . . . if it did . . . I wonder if . . . somehow she lured Dad here, or had him chasing after her the night he died.'

Stunned, Kirstin watched as, painfully, Ross got to his feet, one hand outstretched to help her. 'Look, we need to get away from here. Get the police. I've no phone, though. I lost mine when she tried to pu — '

'*Bastard! Bastard!*' The stumbling, yellow-clad figure staggered into the torch beam.

Kirstin found her voice. '*Morag! Keep back!*' She looked helplessly at Ross as a shambling Morag approached. Kirstin tried to raise herself, but her leg failed and her head felt woozy. She caught her breath as Morag came racing into full view, her twisted, bloodied face looming palely through the darkness, both trembling hands brandishing a thick tree bough above her head. Ross moved to meet her, but staggered back as the branch caught him a blow to the shoulder and then to his bleeding side.

Kirstin struggled to get up, but the pain in her leg was too much. '*No, Morag! No! Leave him!*' She grappled with the handrail of the bridge. *Forget the pain. Get up! Get up!* Ignoring the agony in her leg, and the blood still flowing freely from her forehead, she limped forward. But she was too late. Morag and Ross were locked in an embrace. He had disarmed her of the branch, but she was dragging him by the hood of his waterproof, over to the swollen edge of the Cauldron. The elements were with her. A fierce gust of wind and vicious sheet of rain momentarily unbalanced him. Suddenly his footing was gone. Morag stood aside as he clawed futilely at the air, before falling backwards into the racing waters. Within moments the current had turned his body over, dragging it towards the weir.

Kirstin felt the yell tear from her throat. 'Noooooo! *Help him. Get to the weir!*'

But Morag was standing, rooted to the flooded riverbank, her eyes following the progress of Ross's body, his arms flailing uselessly against the current. Kirstin dragged her leg, cursing at her snail's pace, reaching the wall just in time to see the lifeless body slither over the weir and disappear into the darkness.

Kirstin stumbled back against the wall, a prisoner of her injured leg. '*What have you done? What have you done? Stay away from me!*'

She had no way to protect herself now. With unnerving casualness, Morag wandered over to collect the torch and then, wordlessly, returned to place it back on the wall. Its strong yellow beam shone across Kirstin's lap, and disappeared into a vanishing point far ahead in the undergrowth.

The wind had dropped, and the rain was down to a fine mist, leaving a patina of damp on her face and hands. All would have been silent. But the weir continued its endless shushing as the swollen waters made their way downstream, the freshwater scent more pungent than ever.

This is my final memory. The last sound. The final smell. The last sensation.

Morag coughed and wiped a hand across her bleeding face before reaching into her pocket. 'I have something for you.' The voice was strangely calm, confident, resigned.

Kirstin shut her eyes as Morag moved slowly towards her.

45

Kirstin inched backwards across the wall. Not again. Surely this was the final time she would find herself trapped. Behind her, the raging Cauldron and weir. Before her, Morag with legs astride, trying to keep her balance, a bedraggled vision of insanity. Kirstin reached for the torch. If this was to be her only weapon, then so be it.

Morag took a step forward. 'I want you to stay where you are. You're injured. So am I. And you're not in control of yourself.' The voice was surprisingly steady. 'Just stay.'

Morag's look nailed Kirstin in place. *Okay, just wait, bide your time. She's unbalanced. She's dangerous, gone over the edge. But she is injured. Maybe she's weaker than you.*

The steady voice wavered as Morag took a painful inhalation of breath. 'Iona Sutherland was the cause of her own death bec — ' She stopped abruptly, another wave of pain taking over. Then she began coughing, wincing at each splutter. 'Because she played with people. There must . . . be countless men out there who raised a silent cheer when they heard of Iona's death.' Another pause. Kirstin saw Morag's eyes flicker and wondered if she was going to lose consciousness and collapse. She tensed herself, ready to escape. But, within a second, Morag had rallied. 'Iona's lovers had all been used and discarded by her. Craig would have suffered the same fate. He'd have deserved it. *The bastard!*'

She pulled the object from her pocket. Kirstin recoiled and raised the torch. And then she gasped. It was the camera! Jamie's camera. As Morag manipulated the various buttons, suddenly her face was transformed by the screen's glow into an eerie, uplit gargoyle.

She thrust the camera towards Kirstin. 'I found another memory card. Here.'

Still wary, Kirstin reached out her trembling arm. And then her focus shifted. Over Morag's shoulder she saw him. Ross! He'd come back from the dead! He looked like a feral creature, barely human. His torso was bare and peppered with bleeding scrapes and cuts. His clothes must have been ripped off by the powerful currents. Morag realized too late what was happening. He caught her in a bear hug from behind, and the camera fell from her grasp, its tiny screen still beaconing out through the soggy grass below.

He was holding Morag in a tight stranglehold, speech and movement beyond her. 'I've got her, Kirstin! Are you okay?'

Slowly, Kirstin slid her painful body down from the wall. 'Yes . . . yes, I'm okay. We need to call the police. The phone. There's a phone back there. Where I left her.'

'Okay, you go on. I'll hold her here.'

Kirstin called back, ready to get on her way. 'All right. But try not to hurt her any more. She's ill. She needs help.'

The shriek was ear-piercing, reminding Kirstin of the animal wail Morag had let out on hearing the news of Bonnie's death. Despite the obvious agony it had caused her, Morag had managed to free herself. Ross had been too injured to hold her, and he fell to the ground as she kneed him in the groin and then began kicking him repeatedly in the stomach.

'No, Morag! Wait. We'll help you, whatever happened. We'll help!'

Kirstin watched, helpless, as Morag foraged on the ground. *The camera! She's after the camera.* But Kirstin was wrong. In her hands shone a large rock, gleaming black from rain and river water. Ross, now on his knees, was struggling to get to his feet.

'Morag! Don't, please don't!'

Kirstin watched in terror as Morag raised the rock above her head. The single blow felled him, leaving his inert body prostrate on the mud-soaked ground. Kirstin felt her control snap and, ignoring the agony screaming from her right leg, she threw herself at Morag.

'No more! Haven't you done enough? I wanted to help you!'

Morag dodged out of her way and Kirstin felt her right leg collapse under her as she fell, face first, into a flooded dip in the ground. Her mouth was filling quickly with rainwater and mud. *Get up! Get up, or you'll drown!* She spat the filth from her mouth, gasping frantically for air. And then she sensed it. Turning over on to her side, she saw Morag towering over her, one hand raised. *This is it. Be quick. Please, be quick.*

Then, to her surprise, Morag was on the ground with her, the camera thrust inches from her face. Roughly, Morag tugged painfully at Kirstin's sodden hair, pulling her head back so she could focus on the tiny screen.

'*Look! Look at this. And the next one, and the next one, and the next one! Then back again, back again, back again! Look! Understand!*'

Kirstin blinked as myriad images flashed in front of her eyes, and Morag's manic mantra screamed in her ears.

And then the data went in. The brain processed, analysed.

The static images came alive in her imagination.

Iona, writhing in orgasmic pleasure. Underneath a grinning, jubilant Ross.

46

'This way, Ms Rutherford.'

She followed the police officer down the silent hospital corridor. Her progress was slow as she hobbled along, the walking stick taking as much of her weight as possible. The officer stopped and invited her to go ahead of him. The room was darkened, but she could make out what she needed to. Morag, flanked by a plain-clothes officer on one side and by Dr Lockhart on the other, was sitting facing a window that gave out on to another room. As Kirstin took her seat, Dr Lockhart whispered a soft, 'I'm so sorry.'

The senior officer spoke quietly but firmly. 'We have all the necessary consents in place. He is asking, pleading, for you to go in. Be with him?'

Kirstin felt all eyes on her, and shifted her weight further on to the stick. She glanced from them to the small hospital room, containing one bed, with half a dozen people clustered around it, clearly visible through the glass.

'No. Absolutely not.' With that she took the offered seat and waited. A disembodied voice sounded out behind her.

'The following is being recorded in the presence of a representative from the procurator fiscal's office and is at the request of the accused, Ross James Munro.'

Above her a television monitor flickered into life. The camera zoomed in and refocused. Ross was unrecognizable. His head was swathed in a white skullcap. Thin plastic tubing was laced into his nose and the side of his mouth. A variety of sensors were attached to his body and the tip of a finger, as the life-preserving machines emitted their steady chorus of bleeps. But he was conscious and lucid. His eyes, remarkably alert, gazed directly into the camera lens. *Looking at her?*

An indistinct figure by Ross's bed nodded at him. Kirstin breathed deeply and sneaked a glance at the TV monitor as he began.

'I first met Iona Sutherland because of my father. She came to my office to complain about his behaviour towards her and her friends. And to show me some photographs of him trespassing on her property. That's how it began.' He paused to swallow. Kirstin was amazed at how strong his voice sounded, his delivery hurried, almost garrulous. Had they given him drugs to get through this?

'I thought we had something special, really special. I was going to give up my fiancée, Annelise. I would have had to leave the firm because of it. So I was giving up everything for her. I wanted Iona. And then, early last summer, she dropped me like a stone. 'Too serious.' That was what she said. She didn't want to be tied down. I kept trying to get her to see me, but she got angry. Threatened to tell Annelise. And then I found out about Craig Irvine and about the river party.'

A neutral voice interjected. 'How did you find out about that?'

He didn't answer immediately and, once again, Kirstin darted a quick glance up at the monitor. He had his eyes shut, the pale lids trembling with uncontrolled spasms. Then suddenly, the eyelids opened and he was staring down at her again, the multiple bleeps of the machines fading into the background as he spoke.

'Through my father. His surveillance logs, and photographs he had taken of the two of them. I used to go through his study to find out what he had been up to. I decided to go and watch her that Sunday. Have it out with her.'

The neutral voice was back. 'Describe what happened.'

Ross's voice was weaker now. 'I went to the art gallery that day. Hung around, and then I used the back steps down to the river and cut through to the wooded area. From there I could see what was going on. Sure enough, it looked like she was with Craig. I could tell from her behaviour. I watched for a while, wondering what to do, and then they started this game. Hide and seek. Suddenly, the two of them were skipping over the bridge towards me. I hid and before I knew it they were . . . they were having sex. Right in front of me.'

There was another pause. Kirstin couldn't help herself. Sure enough, the eyes were closed again. *Is he seeing it? Reliving it? Re-enacting it!* The rhythmic bleeps of the machines were beginning to tear at her nerves now.

The questioner's voice broke in. 'What happened next?'

'I *was* going to talk to her . . . I mean, before they started . . . but once they'd started . . . I came out from where I was hiding to confront them. And . . . '

'Please, go on.'

'And she opened her eyes from underneath him and smiled. *She saw me and smiled! A wicked, wicked smile!*'

Kirstin gave in. She shifted her position to look directly at the monitor. His face was contorted now, his voice a near whisper.

'There was an old metal oar lying very near, so near. I think it might have been one of my father's. He lost one around there a long time ago. I used that. It didn't take long. And after . . . afterwards . . . when I saw what I'd done, I could hear people coming my way. I saw my father approaching from one direction and Morag Ramsay from another. I scrabbled higher up the slope. My father actually saw the bodies. He had his camera raised. I think he thought they were having sex and he was going to catch them. And then he realized what he was really looking at and ran away. But he must have seen Morag about to arrive. At the time he probably thought he'd be suspected. After all, he had been in a bitter row with the group, Iona in particular. All of that would have been swirling round his mind. But there is one other thing. My father had spent time in the army as a very young man. He'd seen violent death at close quarters. He knew the two of them were beyond help. I think if there had been any chance of them surviving, things would have been very different for him. And for me. But no, he fled, panicked and began lying. Once he started lying, he had to keep going. And that must have torn him apart. He hated lies.'

Kirstin looked back into the room. For the first time she could see the questioner. Medical staff had been blocking the view before. A middle-aged police officer with his head bent over a file. 'What did you do with the weapon?'

'I drove to St Andrews, played golf, and threw it and my clothes into the sea.'

The questioner shifted slightly in his seat. 'What do you know about the death of your father?'

Kirstin shut her eyes this time. *No. Please no.*

Ross gave a dry cough. 'My father had no idea of what I had done until, by accident, we swapped cameras. I bought him the same model as mine as a gift, since he'd been admiring it for ages. He took mine home after lunch one weekend. When he brought it back, I just knew. It had had a selection of photographs that Iona and I had taken of ourselves. Having sex. He confronted me. I admitted the affair. But denied being there that Sunday. I knew he didn't believe me. He kept the memory card. He told me he'd been there that day and when Morag was arrested, he was an inch away from telling the police that. I tried to convince him that she'd done the deed, and that what he had seen was her returning to make sure that they were dead. He didn't believe it, but I know this planted a seed of doubt about him coming forward. What if the police, hell-bent on getting Morag, threw this theory back at him? He would be in deep trouble for lying. Maybe he'd be accused of colluding with her. Why was he taking such a close interest in her case?

'I know he thought of little else during those weeks after the arrest. And then he'd obviously made his judgement. He gave me an ultimatum. Prove that I wasn't at the river that day and he wouldn't go to the police. Of course, I couldn't. That night, he called me and said . . . he had a heavy heart. He was g — ' The dry cough was back.

A doctor looked sharply at the interrogating officer. 'He can't take much more of this.'

The officer gave a curt nod in reply. 'What happened to your father?'

'He said that he was going to do th — ' The voice was faltering badly now. 'He was going to do the right thing. I begged, pleaded. And then hung up on him. I . . . I had another idea.' A nurse moved forward to check the tubing in his nose and then melted away into the background. 'I called him an hour later. Said I was on my way to the Cauldron. I was going to end it my way. I couldn't, wouldn't, go to prison. Then it was his turn to beg. He pleaded with me to come with him to the police, admit what I'd done, have my day in court and take whatever punishment I was given. I rejected everything, and eventually he said he was coming down to the Cauldron to see me. *That* is what I wanted.'

The neutral voice again. 'What happened there?'

'Conditions were appalling. He nearly *did* fall accidentally, but . . . '

'But?'

'I helped the elements. *My own father! Going to turn in his own son! What else*, what else *could I do? Damn it all!*'

The last outburst had taken its toll. He coughed again. A nurse bent over him for a moment, and then he was in shot again. 'I thought . . . I thought I could get over it all then. Everything would be all right, until . . . '

'Until what?'

Kirstin, now chilled to the bone, knew what was coming. She leant back, eyes tight shut.

'Until my ex-wife, Kirstin, returned and wanted to know why my father died. I did all I could to dissuade her, but she was determined. Utterly determined to find out the truth. *Now she has what she wanted.*'

Eyes still shut, Kirstin lowered her head into her hands. *I don't want to hear this. I don't.*

'Eventually, in desperation, I was forced to falsify one of my father's logs. The one with the 'guilty' verdicts and that incriminating sketch. Ever since childhood I have been able to copy my father's handwriting. And I also share his ability to draw. It seemed . . . easy, simple. My father had always been secretive about his logs, and he kept the key to the desk drawer hidden in a baseball cap. I left it for Kirstin to find. And then the bombshell dropped. I had searched high and low in Mill House for that memory card. It wasn't there, so I hoped he might have destroyed it. I called Kirstin on her mobile, but Glen answered. He said she'd left the phone at his flat. He told me about the box she'd been given by Donald. Then I knew.'

'Knew what?'

'I knew . . . the card must be in the box. My father would have turned me in to the police. I know that. But, I also know that part of him would have been conflicted. He'd have kept the evidence, but he'd have wanted it away from him. It would have been a contaminant to him. His shame and hurt about me overwhelmed him. And he knew that if I could destroy what he had, I would. So, he hid it. When I heard about Donald — his most trusted friend — having a box of my father's, I was sure. I thought it a miracle Kirstin hadn't found the memory card. Prayed I was wrong, and that it wasn't there. But I had to be sure. Glen said something about them having had a row and that he thought Kirstin must have gone to Morag Ramsay's house. She had nowhere else to go. So I raced over there. Kirstin was gone. But I saw Morag had found it. She was trying to call Kirstin as I arrived. I stopped her. I took Morag to the Cauldron, never expecting Kirstin to know where she was.'

'Why did you take Ms Ramsay there?'

'I . . . I was going to dispose of her in an 'accident'. But she managed to steal the camera and run away from me. By then, I thought I had probably critically injured her. I'd get the camera back. And then Kirstin arrived.'

She kept her head down, hands over her ears now. *And were you going to dispose of me too? In an 'accident'?*

It was clear he was a spent force now. His pallor was grey and the drug-induced energy of earlier had leached out of him.

The neutral voice sounded louder than ever. 'There is one matter you have not covered, Mr Ross. Bonnie Campbell.'

She couldn't stand it any more. Flinging her chair back, Kirstin struggled to her feet and hobbled towards the door. Dr Lockhart grabbed her arm and Morag stood up, putting a hand on her shoulder. 'You need to hear this.'

Kirstin nodded weakly and leant against the door frame.

He had his eyes shut, the spasmodic, REM-like effect more erratic than before. His voice had reduced to a hoarse wheeze.

'Bonnie . . . Campbell had been wandering around up at the art gallery that Sunday. I . . . didn't remember seeing her until she and my . . . she and my ex-wife met outside my office recently.'

He paused to swallow, giving out another dry cough. 'I thought she'd recognized me. You see, one morning, Iona and I were leaving her house and . . . and Bonnie had driven by and waved to her. Iona said Bonnie hadn't seen me and I thought no more of it. Until I saw her outside my office. I could see the look of puzzled recognition. She would work it out. I couldn't let her. I didn't.'

Without warning, he sat bolt upright.

340

Somehow, he found the strength to wrest the plastic tubing from his nose and mouth, followed by the sensors from his chest and finger. The low-level background rhythm of bleeps turned into a cacophony of alarms. Medical staff swarmed around the bed. And just for a second, as the wave of people parted, the camera picked it up. He opened his eyes once and looked straight at her, his voice finding a last gasp of volume.

'I only wanted Iona because I'd lost you, Kirsty!'

As she fled the room, she heard one final sound screaming out above all others.

'No! No! No!'

The sound of her own horror.

47

Three weeks later, August 2007

The Water of Leith

It had to be the hottest day so far. Kirstin kicked off her sandals and sat astride the wall, relieved to have the full use of both legs once more. Eyes closed, she raised her face to meet the welcome heat of the midday sun and listened. A mere gentle background hiss. The Cauldron was a silent millpond and the weir was running low. Far in the distance she could hear fragments of laughter intermingled with high-spirited banter. For a moment, she could almost imagine Jamie, stick in hand, striding along the river path, issuing his 'welcome's and 'good afternoon's.

Jamie.

No. Don't be sad. Don't. He's gone. But he's still here.

Slowly, she opened her eyes and stood up, padding over to the bench, its fresh new wood shining brightly as the sun's rays bounced off the thick varnish. She sat side-on, fingering the metal nameplate.

In memory of JAMES ROSS MUNRO
Born 24 March 1936
Died 11 February 2007
Peerless river guide and father-in-law
From Kirstin and Donald
With love always

'It looks wonderful.'

Kirstin swung round. Morag was standing smiling, looking cool in a pale-coloured linen dress, sunglasses in hand.

'When did they bring it?'

Kirstin shrugged. 'Oh, just this morning, I think. They gave me a call. You look . . . dare I say it? Happy?'

Morag stepped forward and sat down. 'I think you could say that. Something I should get used to being, maybe? And in shock. Good shock. You'll never guess who visited me last night. Ally Sutherland, would you believe? Quite a changed man. Genuine, very genuine apologies pouring out of him.'

'Really?' Kirstin frowned. 'You sure?'

Morag laughed. 'Oh, yes. And I'll tell you how I know. He offered to pay off the arrears on my house. I was astonished. He rang this morning. It's done. The bank has backed off. I'm in the clear. All I need to do now is get a job.'

Kirstin leant forward to embrace her. 'That's fantastic! Don't suppose you fancy a job in Devon still?'

'Maybe. But what about you? You going back there?'

Kirstin looked away, across to the Cauldron and beyond to the wooded area. 'I honestly don't know. Too soon to say. This is all going to take a very long time to get over. But I'm determined to do so. It's funny. Deep down, I'm all right. I feel free. Yes. Free.'

'And Glen?'

Kirstin shrugged. 'I've talked to him on the

phone. About the bench, among other things . . . but . . . too much has gone on. It can't work for me. It's broken. Can't be fixed.' She met Morag's eyes again and half smiled. 'It's the trust thing. You know what I mean?'

'Oh, yes. I know. Look, I can't stay. Just wanted to see you in the flesh. Check that you were okay.' Morag opened her bag and handed her the newspaper. 'It's all over the news. So weird. But fitting. It's probably not sunk in yet but, if you need me, just call. I'll be there.' She stood up. 'Oh, and here. Have these.' Kirstin held out a hand as Morag offered her the sunglasses. 'I don't need them any more. See you!'

She answered Morag's playful wave with one of her own and, sunglasses on, bent her head to read.

FINAL TWIST IN THE CASE OF THE REAL 'CAULDRON KILLER'

Wrongly accused: 'I have seen justice at last.'

Ross Munro, the man charged with the notorious murders known as the 'Cauldron Killings', has been found dead in his prison cell.

Munro, 41, was arrested and charged three weeks ago. Although critically injured, Munro managed to stagger towards the river. After a dramatic night-time manhunt, he was found unconscious on the banks of the Water of Leith, near to the spot where Dr Craig Irvine and Iona Sutherland were found dead in August last year.

Munro was captured downstream from the Cauldron. He was near to death after falling into the river and made a full confession while in hospital. Against all expectations he recovered and was remanded in prison. However, yesterday morning Munro was found strangled in his prison cell, having put together a makeshift garrotte from clothing.

Ironically, this is the method attempted by Morag Ramsay earlier this year, when she was on remand for the same murders. Speaking through her solicitors, Ms Ramsay issued the following statement: 'I am thankful beyond words that I have seen justice at last. But, more important than my exoneration is the fact that the victims of this horrific crime have received justice. However, for all concerned, it would have been preferable if Ross Munro had spent a long life in prison paying for what he has done. But he has robbed us of that opportunity. Finally, I would like to extend a heartfelt thanks to all who believed in me during my darkest hours and to convey my deepest condolences to the families of Craig and Iona.'

Kirstin lifted her head and sighed. The gaggle of excited voices was nearer now. She saw them, over to her left. A loose grouping of young men and women in shorts and bikinis, weighted down with beer, wine, food and picnic rugs. Gathering her sandals, she got to her feet smiling.

And why not? Let the place live again. Picnics, laughter, loving.

Barefoot, she passed by the happy crowd and

smiled at one of them. 'Have a great day!'

'Yeah! And you too!'

Raising a hand in a valedictory wave, she took a final look at the glassy, inviting waters of the Cauldron.

Oh, I will. I will.

We do hope that you have enjoyed reading
this large print book.

Did you know that all of our titles
are available for purchase?

We publish a wide range of high quality
large print books including:
Romances, Mysteries, Classics
General Fiction
Non Fiction and Westerns

Special interest titles available in
large print are:
The Little Oxford Dictionary
Music Book
Song Book
Hymn Book
Service Book

Also available from us courtesy of Oxford
University Press:
Young Readers' Dictionary
(large print edition)
Young Readers' Thesaurus
(large print edition)

For further information or a free
brochure, please contact us at:
Ulverscroft Large Print Books Ltd.,
The Green, Bradgate Road, Anstey,
Leicester, LE7 7FU, England.
Tel: (00 44) 0116 236 4325
Fax: (00 44) 0116 234 0205

Other titles published by
The House of Ulverscroft:

THE RECKONING

Sue Walker

In June 1973 the bodies of three missing teenagers were found on the tiny Scottish island of Fidra. And when his father was arrested for the murders, eleven-year-old Miller McAllister's life fell apart . . . Thirty-two years later, Douglas McAllister has died in prison and Miller returns home after decades of self-imposed exile. Because, though the rest of his family protested Douglas's innocence, Miller always maintained his guilt . . . But when Miller is given the legal archive and a letter his father wrote to him just days before his death, suddenly everything looks less clear. Could Douglas have been innocent after all?

THE REUNION

Sue Walker

Hearing Isabella Velasco's name on her answermachine makes Innes Haldane's blood run cold. It's a name from her past — a past she has tried hard to forget. For in 1977, a fifteen-year-old Innes spent a year in Edinburgh at the Unit, an experimental home for highly intelligent but dysfunctional teenagers. There her fellow patients had included shy Simon Calder, aggressive Alex Baxendale, rapist Danny Rintoul and the beautiful Isabella Velasco. Now, nearly three decades later, Isabella is trying to make contact again. But Innes never finds out why. For only days later she reads a newspaper account of Isabella's suicide. Innes's shock quickly turns to fear when she hears that Danny, too, recently committed suicide. Has some dark event, buried deep in 1977, come back to haunt them all?

STILL SUMMER

Jacquelyn Mitchard

Back in high school, Tracy, Olivia, and Holly were known as The Godmothers, the girls everyone wanted to be and know. Unlike many friendships, their bond survived the years. But twenty years later, their glamorous leader, Olivia, whose wealthy Italian husband has died, suggests they reunite on her return to the United States with a luxury sailboat crossing in the Caribbean. With Tracy's college-aged daughter and an attentive two-man crew, they sail into paradise. But then, the smallest mistake triggers a series of devastating events. Suddenly in a desperate fight for survival, they battle with the elements, dwindling food and water, the threat of modern-day piracy, and their own frailties.